I0764579

RED ONYX

RED ONYX

Mike Trial

Compass Flower Press
Columbia, Missouri

This is a work of fiction. Characters, places, and events are the product of the author's imagination. Any resemblance to real people, companies, institutions, or incidents is entirely coincidental.

Published by Compass Flower Press
Columbia, Missouri
compassflowerpress.com

Cover painting by John Harris. Used with permission.

ISBN: 978-1-951960-70-4 Trade Paper

For Dane Thorson and Derek Calver, who led the way.

Chapter 1

From the control room in the Tiran orbital satellite, Kapil Sheer ordered the lighting level reduced in the high bay. The bay was in vacuum, the doors at the opposite end open to deep space. The artifact hung weightless, a dull white cylinder twenty meters long. He changed a view on one screen and inspected the artifact's makeshift cockpit. His technicians had built a modified medbox into the one opening in the otherwise featureless skin of the artifact. The volunteer pilot, in a full-armored spacesuit, was inside and ready to start the test.

"Launch," Sheer said softly, and the cylinder accelerated slowly out into space.

"Controls aren't smooth," came the muffled voice of the test pilot. The medbox had been fitted with quadruple redundant buffers rated to ten gees. "Even the slightest movement of controls seems to switch the power on or off. Can't make smooth transitions." But he made it through the test regimen. The final run was to come in at a slight angle and decelerate at half a gee. The artifact began curving on the display screen, then it departed the green line of the planned flight path and began rapidly accelerating.

"Emergency stop!" the controller shouted to the pilot, but the artifact continued to accelerate.

"Past eight gees, sir," someone said.

"Energize the tug's energy fields; capture it and slow it down," the lead controller said. Two fans of purple light appeared on the display, indicating fields of energy radiating from two deep-space tugs. A white speck brushed the edge of one purple fan, and the tug was upended and pulled along into the energy vortex behind the artifact.

Soon the artifact and one tug had disappeared out of range of the display.

"Track it on the commercial datanet," Sheer snapped.

One of the controllers scrabbled at his board. "One eight five, sir. Toward Xbalc space. A full 10X acceleration even dragging a tug. We've tried to contact the pilot, and the tug, but there's…nothing."

"No surprise," Sheer said. "Get the remaining tug into the carrier and launch immediately toward the artifact's projected course."

"That's Xbalc space, sir."

"I know!" Sheer hissed. "Go!"

Sheer stalked out of the control room, went to his comfortable office, and called up a display of nearspace. "Has the carrier departed yet?" he queried the AI. A stubby red line showed the ship accelerating at maximum speed toward the transition gate. Sheer slumped in his chair. The great Naru, Prime Minister of the Tiran revolutionary government, second only to Leader Devir, would arrive here tomorrow. With the artifact apparently uncontrollable and who knows how far away by now, the conversation would be painful.

Sheer called up his mantra and calmed himself.

• • •

On board the Talus Company ship *Tawli*, in lightspace en route to Tiran, alarms began whooping. Econ Officer Basil Ajami dashed to the control room and slid into his jump seat behind the nav station. Captain Arin was at the command console, looking unperturbed. The big board showed *Tawli* converging with another ship. The display bar above the board indicated guns were activated and defensive screens extended.

"Varil Company ship *Ivo*, sir," the weapons officer reported. "Transponder is not lit, but the datanet shows she is en route from Nokendai to Tiran and two days overdue. She's drifting; her drive emissions are at idle."

The captain turned to the weapons officer. "What was that other signal a few minutes ago?"

Demaris touched controls and the big board displayed lavender fans of light making a full sweep of the lightspace miniverse around *Tawli*. "I don't know, sir. Nothing inside our event horizon." She pushed the gunsight up for a moment and studied the board. "No explanation."

"Speculation on what that pulse was?" Arin persisted.

"We're near the dark matter lattice that surrounds the Tiran emergence gate," the nav officer volunteered. "Could have been reflectance."

"Too fast, sir," Demaris said.

"But back projection is straight…"

"But not from the gate." Demaris shot him a cold look. "Exactly the way a transient pulse off the lip of the gate would look. Anyway, the *Ivo* looks like an easy target of opportunity."

Captain Arin scrutinized the board. He ran a replay of the past hundred hours, which showed no activity, then told Demaris, "Well, it's a target anyway. Anybody else around?"

Basil watched the board display Demaris's long-range scans around the Tiran outer marker. Raiders often waited near the gates, but the scan lines indicated no ship activity aside from the drifting *Ivo* and the unexplained pulse they'd received.

"Just us and the *Ivo*, sir," Demaris said.

Arin put the home office general orders up on the board. "I want all of you to see this." It took Basil a few moments to realize Talus Shipping Company had authorized raiding actions against Varil Company ships.

"I know many of you have spent time in Varil ships; most of us feel a great nostalgia for Varil Company as it was." The document faded and Arin's face filled the screen. "But Varil has changed, and we are hungry for income."

Basil had been querying the AI while the captain had been speaking. "Sir! AI was able to open the *Ivo*'s manifest…"

Demaris chimed in. "We can get scans into her, sir. Her defenses are not activated. Looks like there's been fighting aboard. No one in the control room." A quick series of views of the ship interior, ragged burn marks from Saris gunfire. The control station was unmanned.

Basil put the *Ivo* manifest up on the board.

"Ora," Basil said. Then a view of the cargo deck. "Mass indicators show only two boxes on board. Far less than half a full load."

"Is that significant?"

"Don't know, sir. Could signify a hurried departure," Basil said. "The price of ora at Tiran Station has been increasing recently…"

"Or could signify she's already been raided," the nav officer interrupted.

"Why would they leave two…?"

"Alright," Arin interrupted. "Slow us down, merge our fields, and let's take her, but I want it done fast. I want us back on our scheduled flight plan before we reach Tiran Gate's outer marker." His expression hardened.

The bar over the big board turned red and Basil could hear the attack alarm sounding belowdecks. Engine power came up, and the plot line to the target adjusted itself to the new speed. The first officer disengaged his buffers and went below.

Captain Arin turned to Basil. "Ajami, you'll be in the boarding party. Check those boxes to make sure there's nothing wrong with them."

Basil clicked off his buffers and hurried to the ready room where he opened a suit locker, tabbed up his shipsuit, and backed into the padded armor. It closed around him, morphing to his size.

When he'd finished his checklist, the first officer, Cereclo Dathe, stood in the center of the crowded chamber and addressed them over suit com. "Two teams. The number one team goes with me, in through cargo and up to control to secure the ship. Ajami, you'll lead team two. Stay in the cargo hold and immediately start moving cargo."

"I'll have to extend rollaways," Basil said.

"Understood."

Ready lights changed, the room decompressed, and they stepped out into vacuum and zero gee. Basil concentrated on following Cereclo's armored figure with the Dathe family emblem on the back of his helmet. The *Ivo* was a hazy white sphere in the glow from the miniverse field. Basil gritted his teeth to stop his jaw from shivering.

Suit propulsion took them quickly to *Ivo*. Up close, the skin of the ship was a mottled light blue, gray, and dull white, textured with thousands of points and dimples. He knew not to touch it. His suit decelerated him into the grab bars at a personnel lock beside one of the cargo hold doors.

Basil and his teammate followed Cereclo and his teammate into a dimly lit radial passageway. Suddenly clumsy in armor as they crossed into the ship's gravity field, Basil energized his Saris pistol and waved his teammate forward.

No one in sight. They moved down the companionway toward the cargo deck.

In Basil's helmet com Cereclo said, "Top deck corridor, three dead crew members, all in Varil utility uniforms." There was a pause. "Killed by Saris fire."

The round room at the center of six radial passageways felt horribly vulnerable.

Basil reached the cargo management station, set his com scan over the control panel, and activated the AI code breaker to open one cargo hold door. “Here goes,” Basil said tightly. “I’m engaging the hold-opens.” Although safety rules strictly forbade any explosives near ships’ doors, Basil had seen confidential message traffic indicating some ships were booby-trapping cargo doors to discourage pirates. His scan showed nothing, but scans could be fooled. He activated the final sequence.

“Number four is opening now,” his teammate said.

“AI, have you got the distancing synced?” Basil asked.

“Confirmed.”

The lower hemisphere of the virtual yellow sphere above the desk where Basil stood showed the number four hold open. Basil overrode *Ivo*’s gravitic tie-downs on the container nearest the open door. Basil had already had *Tawli*’s rollaways extended almost to the *Ivo*’s surface. Basil ran a quick scan over the two boxes in the hold. Nothing out of the ordinary. Manifest said they were ora. Basil’s teammate expertly clipped a maneuver unit to the box and edged it onto the rollaway, which immediately trundled it toward the open hold door on *Tawli*.”

In a moment, the first box was safely inside *Tawli*’s hold. As the second box began to move, Basil keyed his com and said, “Cereclo, cargo is moving. Estimate…”

A shout crashed over Basil’s suit com, then silence. Basil crept up the companionway one level past the air barrier and into atmosphere. The corridor was dark. Basil ducked behind a control console, opened his suit helmet, and listened. The air was cold and scented with something he couldn’t identify.

• • •

"Cereclo?" Basil whispered into his com. There was the soft sound of quick movement around the curve of the corridor. He switched on his Saris pistol.

The sounds got closer. Two figures, women, in dark-blue Varil shipsuits piped with silver, came around the curve and started for the companionway to the cargo deck. Both had Saris pistols in hand.

Basil shouted, "Stop! Drop your weapons!"

One woman fired twice at him and Basil returned fire, four blasts in quick succession, then snapped his helmet closed and rushed out. Both women lay on the deck. One lay face up, her uniform scorched from the Saris blasts, a pool of blood seeping out from under her. The other woman rolled over and fired straight at him. His helmet visor went white and his com blared, but his armor held. Basil pivoted awkwardly and fired two shots as his visor began to clear. He overbalanced and fell. When he got to his feet, both figures lay still. He opened his helmet and stared at the dead, burned and swollen from the internal rupturing of Saris pulses. He kicked a pistol away from a dead hand, then he closed his suit and went back down to the cargo deck.

Cereclo came down the companionway. "How much longer?"

Basil glanced at the cargomaster display on his suit screen. "One box aboard *Tawli*. Another minute to get the second box aboard."

"Let's go." Cereclo pushed out into vacuum, pivoting to align his suit tracking system to the open cargo hold on *Tawli*.

Basil paused until the second box was halfway down the rollaway, then pushed out into zero gee. Out of habit Basil moved to close *Ivo*'s cargo doors, then stopped. What did it matter if the cargo hold doors were closed? Only the dead rode in this ship.

The *Tawli* emergency action alarm blared over his suit com. "Emergency warning! Unidentified object approaching. Secure for unsymmetrical gee loads in one minute."

Out of the *Ivo*'s gravity, Basil turned toward the *Tawli* and waited for his suit to get a lock on the airlock targeting trefoil, then he pushed off and dialed up the maneuvering speed to 100 percent.

"Cargo tied down?" he called to his teammate.

He heard grunting on the com. "Almost. This box is warped; it will take a couple of minutes…"

"Throw a temporary tie-down on it!" Basil said.

The alarm blared again in Basil's helmet. "Unsymmetrical gee forces in thirty seconds! All personnel into buffers immediately. Close all external doors immediately. Repeat, close all external doors immediately."

Basil hit the landing pad hard, scrambled to his feet, and pushed the emergency retract on the rollaway controls. The rollaway quickly slid back into the receiver on *Tawli*, leaving the second box drifting in zero gee.

"Get into buffers!" he yelled at his crewmate still fumbling with a temporary tie-down on the first box. Basil hit the emergency close button on the cargo hold door. The door slammed shut, and atmosphere began blasting into the hold as Basil and his crewmate thrust themselves into the row of buffers. A monstrous hand seemed to push the ship sideways. The buffers screamed, pushed to their limits. Dazed, Basil heard the screech of stressed structural ceramic. But tie-downs were holding. The condensing moisture turned everything white as air howled into the hold. His teammate muttered a prayer to obscure gods; Basil sagged against his suit, held upright in the buffer.

"The tie-downs held," Basil breathed. "And that box outside didn't come back to hit us."

Chapter 2

Captain Arin was on the annunciator, asking for status reports. Basil responded in turn, and a few minutes later control announced, "Ship secure. Officers to the wardroom."

"Check cargo box tie-downs," Basil told his crewman, Barit, a sullen-looking guy but a good worker.

"Look at this," Barit said. He had the structural sensors for the entire cargo hold displayed. "Yellow along the door seal. It looks like it is slightly warped. I think the emergency rollaway retraction damaged the hold door and banged up that box we took aboard."

"Get AI to run a hull integrity analysis around that door. I just told the captain everything was fine down here. I'll look at the damaged box when I get back. Is it leaking content?"

"No."

Basil sped up to the wardroom where the captain and the other officers were waiting.

Arin paused for a moment, then said. "You all know I like concise reporting, so each of you tell me, in one minute, your actions and your assessment of the situation."

Cereclo led off. "There'd been fighting aboard the Varil ship. No crew survivors that I saw. I counted four dead and Ajami killed two more. No casualties on our part, no booby traps, no accidents. The ship appeared to be intact. I did not take the time to analyze its course, but assuming the AI autopilot is still functioning correctly, it will exit the Tiran Gate at fairly high speed. Its AI should have emergency programming to direct it into a parking orbit somewhere, but we may want to alert Tiran..."

"No. We will not alert Tiran," Arin said mildly. "I want no discussion of our activities. I am confident the *Ivo*'s AI will shunt the ship into a safe parking orbit."

Arin turned to Basil. "Ajami?"

"Sir, we retrieved two boxes, both marked as being ora. One box is in our hold, the other was lost when whatever that was passed us."

"Your assessment of the situation on the *Ivo*?"

"There had been fighting. In self-defense I shot and killed two *Ivo* crew. The ship had only two boxes in cargo. I don't know why."

Arin paused. "For your information I received a coded message from Talus HQ. It is believed there was a mutiny aboard the *Ivo*. It departed Sigma without a full cargo load. There was probably fighting en route. Tiran authorities can sort that out."

No one said anything.

"Varil is falling apart," Arin said. "Which is a shame. It used to be one of the best shipping companies in the Curve. Many of us older hands have served tours of duty on Varil ships." He tilted his head. "Well, that is the past."

Arin turned to Demaris. "What passed us back there? A ship? Or was it some other phenomenon?"

"One other thing, sir," Basil interjected. "One of our hold door seals was slightly damaged as we took the box aboard and retracted rollaways. AI is running a hull integrity check now."

"Let me know the results as soon as you have them," Arin said. "Now back to you, Demaris. What passed us? A ship? And why would a ship be on such a course at such a speed?"

Demaris nodded, "It was almost certainly a ship. Mass and shape match what we would expect for a translight ship. However, there were no emissions typical of Istan drive. But our scans were fragmentary. We might have missed an emission profile."

"Any speculation as to why it was on a course that brought it so close to us that our lightspace fields merged?"

"No speculation, sir. By the time its field began to interact with ours, we could see it was something coming almost directly at us. Scans couldn't read its velocity correctly."

There was silence for a moment, then Arin added, "If anyone has more thoughts about this incident, let me know next staff meeting. On another topic, the political situation on Tiran is deteriorating. I want nothing said about our raid on a Varil ship or the incident involving a high-speed pass by something we can't identify. I want everything to appear normal. Cargo load and unload at a normal pace, but I want a departure request filed as soon as we dock." Cereclo nodded.

He turned to Cereclo. "Organize shift schedules to allow everyone to take leave if they want." Eyebrows rose. "I want everything to appear normal. But, I want everyone in uniform anytime you leave the ship, no matter for how short a period. And I want everyone in parties of at least two, got that?" There were nods.

"Now, I want to take a look at that damaged door seal, Ajami. Accompany me to cargo."

When they got to cargo level, they found Barit standing with a gray box in his hand. Inside it were six Saris pistols in factory wrapping.

"Found this inside the box with the torn seal. There are more boxes like it in there. It's hard to see…"

Captain Arin looked thoughtful. "Weapons intended for one of the counter-revolutionary factions on Tiran that Devir says don't exist." Arin thought for a moment, then said, "Repack the contraband exactly as you found it, and close up the torn seam best you can."

After Arin left, Basil helped Barit replace the box of pistols as far back in the container as they could reach.

"Wrap this torn end with a tie-down…no, that is too obvious. Just put some packing inside the box so nothing will fall out, and leave the tear as-is."

Regulations call for notifying Talus HQ and local authorities if contraband is found in cargo—I guess Arin will take care of that. Basil hesitated for a moment before logging himself off-duty. *I should make a log entry, but I guess I won't. Arin's entry in the master log will cover it.*

Basil went up to control to report that all was in order for docking. Arin was in the command seat, Demaris in nav. The big board showed only a handful of ships, everybody in the right lanes, transponders lit. Nothing out of the ordinary. Captain Arin had the command override activated. Nothing on com. In the big board inset, Basil noticed Talus Ops had withdrawn authority for any Talus ship to raid Tiran-based shipping, effective immediately.

"That directive was fast," Basil whispered to Demaris. "Othman must really be nervous about the situation."

"A bunch of fearful bureaucrats back at the home office," Demaris muttered. "Why'd Arin pull you off cargo handling duty?" she said.

"Captain's going to have the freight forwarder to do it all this time." Basil decided not to mention contraband.

Basil went to his cabin, intending to get a few hours' sleep before docking. But first he pulled up the ship's recording of the event in lightspace. The drifting *Ivo* emerged from lightspace fog. Figures crossed to it from *Tawli*, cargo holds opened, and one box emerged and was transferred to *Tawli*. A second box emerged, then a clear wave seemed to pass through the lightspace fog around *Tawli* and the viewpoint canted as *Tawli* was shoved aside. One rectangular red cargo container drifting free of *Tawli* suddenly deformed, then exploded as differential forces rippled across it. Debris fountained into darkness, then disappeared as it passed the lightspace event horizon. Basil slowed the video down and watched the container tear open and spray its contents into gray lightspace—all in three seconds. A thought occurred to him; someone could be refurbishing the mass drivers the Kogon used for their sunkillers. Firing something at high velocity through lightspace, targeting a ship's lightspace envelope—it could be a major weapon development, if a ship's lightspace envelope could be tracked and targeted, which was currently not possible.

While Basil slept, *Tawli* docked at the Tiran elevator head.

Two hours later, Basil woke and went to get coffee and a protein bar.

"What do you think passed us?" Cereclo said from behind him.

Basil gulped his coffee. "I have no idea."

Cereclo got coffee. "You're a hero. Salvaged one box."

Basil ducked his head. "We'll all benefit from an increased profit margin on this trip."

Cereclo smiled a little too broadly. "By the way, Arin put you in for a citation."

"I assume Arin has notified Talus HQ and Sigma management about the, whatever it was, that passed us?" Basil asked.

"He sent a coded message to somebody," Cereclo said nonchalantly. "Demaris and I are going exploring. Why don't you join us?"

Basil hesitated. "Sure, let me check cargo, and I'll meet you at the exit port."

In the cargo bay, Basil checked that the boxes from *Ivo* were aligned for unloading along with the Talus cargo. "Hope Arin's thought of some way to get rid of this stuff," Basil muttered.

"Beautiful," Cereclo said. Demaris looked gorgeous in her dress uniform.

"I was referring to the view of the great Tiran city," which was on the wall video. The glow of the biggest city in the Curve misted the continent below. Three elevator towers glowed red and black and white, the colors of the revolution. Basil stared at the black tower standing astride the world it claimed to have freed from tyranny.

"It is beautiful," Demaris said.

"Because it's big?" Basil said.

"No, because it is orderly. An orderly society."

"Dictatorships are orderly," Basil said. "Read some of the writings of Piaro, the political scientist who designed Devir's government."

"Which is a dictatorship," Cereclo said.

"Naru has made it one. It didn't start out that way."

Demaris flashed a smile at Basil, linked arms with Basil and Cereclo, and pulled them away from the view. "Come on, you two, let's spend some of that increased profit we're going to get. I hear they have beautiful red onyx jewelry here."

Later they stopped in a tiny café for tea.

"You should have gotten a citation too," Basil told Demaris, "for interpreting that compression wave for what it was."

"Something coming straight at us." Cereclo restated the obvious. "Scanners weren't measuring the approach velocity correctly."

Demaris turned her striking eyes on Basil. "You were lucky to get back aboard in time."

Cereclo continued his lecture. "Translight fields can't easily be merged because the fields diminish at their edges. The closer you get to the edge, the weaker the effect, so theoretically two ships could pass and their fields would not even detect each other. There's a whole chapter of symbolics that describes the translight universe edges in the advanced course that everyone pretends to understand and nobody does."

Pontificating to impress Demaris. He barely passed his continuum physics courses at Colresh. "Except Mera Reigel," Basil interjected. "But whatever passed us had so much momentum it pushed the fields together briefly."

"That ghost ship entered our field and almost blasted us out of existence," Demaris said.

"Ghost ship?" Basil said with a smile. "That was a pretty substantial ghost."

The three of them sat staring out across the vast expanse of city.

"It's time to get back to the ship," Cereclo said.

Chapter 3

At the top of the black tower that was the Tiran government center, Naru sat across a bare table from Kapil Sheer. The vast city around them was lost in the haze of morning light.

Naru's black eyes were expressionless.

"Political leaders can never be seen to change their minds," Naru said. "Followers perceive it as indecisiveness, a trait evolved into our species to keep the hunter-killer genetics pure, I suppose. I am clearly backing you and your project to weaponize the artifact you found on Karaghia. But your first test with it was not successful, and my staff is aware of that failure."

Sheer said nothing.

Naru leaned toward Sheer and dropped his voice slightly. "I gave you my support. I arranged for your expedition to Karaghia. I provided you lavish facilities in Tiran orbit with staff, equipment, funding. All this to turn this artifact of yours into something usable. But what happens in your first real test? You lose control of it, high-gee forces kill your test pilot, and I had to accept risk and divert resources to recover it from Xbalc space. Those resources could have been used elsewhere. Several of my staff are recommending the experiment be terminated."

"Testing new devices involves failures. The artifact is back at the orbital lab," Sheer said, his yellow eyes unreadable. "Testing is proceeding."

"Why did it go where it went?" Naru asked pleasantly.

"We don't know yet. It apparently has internal programming that returns it to an uninhabited planet near, not in, Xbalc space."

"I realize that," Naru said. "Your report said you believed it would have descended to the surface of this planet, number 985. Why it did not, and why it has been quiescent, you don't know."

"That is correct. The recovery team caught it in orbit and returned it to our orbital facilities. The team encountered no Xbalc forces while they were operating near 985."

Naru sat silent for a moment. "I want you to learn to control the artifact enough so it can be installed in a ship giving it the speed the artifact has demonstrated. And I need that done soon."

Sheer said nothing.

"To improve your efficiency, you and all of your researchers and engineers are moving to a new home." Naru touched the desktop controls and a visual of a mountain valley replaced the Tiran cityscape. All around the two men were green meadows and snow-capped peaks. A small campus-like complex was visible in a valley near a tiny sapphire lake. "That is Hendai Valley," Naru said. "There is a complex of buildings there, a small campus. It was once a merit retreat on The Way." Naru smiled. "Lord Enthebi, its former owner, prided himself on his support of The Way. Now that the revolution has eliminated wealth and privilege, I control it. You and your colleagues will live and work there." He gave Sheer an opaque glance. "Your families will remain on Tiran, for safety, of course."

Sheer rose and walked to the invisible wall, studied the mountains and the lake. "No one else is more qualified than me to decipher this…this artifact. It is the single greatest technological puzzle of our age…"

"How long will it take to do as I've asked?" Naru interrupted. "Your chief researcher, Zarian, estimates six months."

Sheer suppressed his anger, kept his stare on the mountain scenery. *That spying bastard, Zarian.* "I will need more AI capacity."

"Zarian has already ordered ten more. You will get what you need," Naru said affably. "I remind you that all the resources I am providing you could be used elsewhere. For something that has a defined development schedule, such as the gamma-burst sunkillers…"

Zarian's pet project. "Refurbished Kogon weapons from the distant past," Sheer said calmly. "It will take a hundred years for the hydrogen–iron reaction to collapse the star's outer shells. Too slow to be anything but a doomsday weapon."

Naru stood. "I'll not debate this with you. When we meet next, I will expect a schedule from you indicating when that artifact will be installed in a warship."

• • •

Basil activated the cargo door on hold one and watched it roll up and back—fully functional. The scent of the Tiran docks came into the ship. His com chimed, and Captain Arin's face appeared. "The freight forwarding company is going to do the cargo handling, from dockside."

Basil was a bit offended. *Arin doesn't trust me?*

"I want you to personally get the documentation done. All of it, import/export duties, cargo manifests, weight and balance, all of it."

A short woman in Ajisai uniform bustled up to Basil. "Hold two door is inoperative?"

"Yes."

"You'll withdraw the hold separation bulkhead…" she continued, "…after we've got hold one empty." Basil didn't much like her brusqueness.

She had port-side rollaways in place already, and as he watched, two cargo handlers operated by recons rolled up them, anchored down at ship hardpoints, and began to quickly move boxes out of the ship's hold. The Ajisai woman positioned herself at a portable control panel and attached and disconnected inertial cancelers as boxes were positioned. Basil's display tracked the boxes leaving the ship, each with an Ajisai flower icon on its electronic image. None displayed the Varil icon.

Counterfeit box-tracking logos? A dangerous business in a dictatorship.

Basil reviewed the consignment and authorized payment, including an increased freight-handling fee.

She's a risk-taker and a profit-maker.

Basil inset another window into the display and went to work on his cargo manifest and layout for the departure. It took a couple of tries to get it optimized for load balance and efficiency of loading and unloading. The break-even point was twenty boxes of the machine tools they were taking back to Sigma. His display told him the export boxes were ready now. He calculated the export duty and authorized AI to make payment, while the Ajisai supervisor waited. Up close she was attractive in an elfin way. She held out her com. "Your receipt for cargo delivered."

Basil touched his com and received it. She nodded and grinned at him. *She looks better smiling.* "Thank you," he said, slipping his com back in its holster. "Customs on their way?"

"Any minute." She looked around at the four box handlers and the recons in their control buckets.

"You got our request to load our export cargo? The port net shows it's ready to go."

"Let customs check things over first."

A squad of Tiranian port security soldiers was approaching dressed in pale-green uniforms. "Don't forget that Ajisai now owns those boxes you just unloaded," Basil said softly.

She grinned at him. "Quit worrying." She went over and exchanged a few words with the squad leader. To Basil's horror, she opened one of the boxes they'd just unloaded. But the trooper gave it only a cursory glance, consulted his instruments for a moment, then moved down the line to another box. She opened that one for him. He departed soon after.

"Ready to accept cargo?" she told Basil with a cocky grin.

She'd be attractive if she'd slow down a little.

Basil checked his flex, but there was no approval to load cargo from Captain Arin.

"Captain Arin indicated we could load cargo now," the woman said.

"Just a minute," Basil snapped. "I'm…"

"Want to check with your captain again?"

Basil's com bleeped— it was Arin. "Customs clearance received. You are authorized to load cargo. Notify me when complete." Arin signed off.

Basil turned to the woman. "Proceed."

"Ajisai. The name of the company," the woman said, already moving toward the first box handler. "But we use the old Tiranian symbol, not text, under the logo. Devir's revolution, you know." She put her com pad against the connective surface of the first squat machine, then went to the next. "We can take it from here," she said.

"I'll take a receipt," Basil said.

She nodded amiably, touched her com, and Basil's com lit with the document. Basil took a perverse pleasure in reading it slowly. The box handlers were already moving boxes into the ship's hold.

The woman shot a winning smile at him. "Don't let this security stuff get you down. It's a way of life in Devir's revolution." She put away her com and hurried away down the loading dock.

A jovial Cereclo strolled up to Basil. "Get into your dress uniform. We've got four hours' leave authorized…"

"Can't. I've got to go pay the export duty in person."

"We'll do that first; I'll go with you." Cereclo clapped Basil on the back. "Afterward, we can sightsee."

Ten minutes later, dressed in red and gray Talus Company uniforms, Basil and Cereclo marched off the ship. At the main concourse, they paused to admire Tiran City spreading out to the horizon in all directions. "Amazing!" Basil said.

"Yes," Cereclo said off-hand, but he lingered, absorbed by the view.

Basil pulled Cereclo away from the view. "We need to get to the customs office. Afterward we can sightsee." They stepped onto a slideway and rode in silence. The slideway was not crowded, nor were the arcades that branched off the main concourse.

"Surprisingly little activity here," Basil offered.

"Embargo, privateering, increased security," Cereclo said. "And not many ships in, either—I'm sure you noticed." Cereclo dropped his voice. "The revolution is now a dictatorship. That's the usual sequence. Humankind never seems to realize that getting rid of one government doesn't mean you are automatically substituting a better one…"

"Here's our stop." Basil led Cereclo off the slideway at the entrance to a stylish facade with a sign in multiple languages indicating the import/export control office.

They stepped through an ionized air zone that indicated a security field.

After ID check, they were directed up two levels to the customs office at Tiran Port Authority. A Tiranian woman in a pale-blue uniform was standing just inside the door. "May I help you?" she asked in beautifully accented Basic.

"We're here to pay the export duty." Basil showed her the flexcom. "Talus Company ship *Tawli.*"

"Station five."

At station five, a young woman dressed in a neat gray uniform bowed to Basil. Her eyes shifted to a display just out of Basil's line of sight.

Basil brought his com within her desk's field.

"Yes. That's a total of 4,600 eris," she said.

Basil stared at his display for a moment. Almost three thousand lower than he had expected. He hesitated, then authorized payment.

The young woman called another young woman over to her station, and they conversed in low tones. After a moment, the first woman handed his flexcom back. "Thank you very much, sir." She again consulted a screen out of their sight. "But there is one other thing, sir. All foreign ships must be cleared by security." She smiled politely at them.

Basil's heart skipped a beat. "We just had an inbound security check." Basil touched the flexcom. "This is outbound cargo. Tiran-manufactured goods."

She consulted the display. "All cargo whether inbound or outbound must have a security check. We will inspect at 1400."

A time display showed 1230. "We can't get clearance until 1400?"

She smiled at him. "That is correct."

Cereclo took Basil's elbow and steered him away. "We'll be prepared for security at 1400," he told the woman.

She gave him a perfect bow and a beautiful, wholly artificial, smile.

"We've got some time," Cereclo said. "Let's look around."

Basil followed Cereclo down a pleasant arcade arched with a floral display. They found themselves in a warren of tiny stores, flowers, foods packaged as gifts, clothing, unfamiliar electronic gadgets, and jewelry. After a while, Basil caught up with Cereclo standing in front of a jewelry shop.

"Look at that," Cereclo said pointing to a display window which held a three-centimeter-diameter red gem lit to glow and scintillate as it slowly turned against a black background.

"Red onyx," Basil said. "Beautiful."

Cereclo leaned close. "What do you think it's worth?"

"If it is real, a stone that big would be worth several hundred thousand eris. Maybe more. Especially now that Devir has taken it as his sacred symbol."

Cereclo snorted.

"Don't let anyone hear you mocking," Basil said. "Tiranian culture takes each dynasty's symbol very seriously. The Ziani emperor's sacred symbol was a gold medallion, with highly stylized Imperial script, meaning 'golden aura'…"

"Yeah, I know, double meaning, ora and aura."

Basil guided Cereclo into the tea shop next door. The scent inside was heavenly. Two beautiful women in traditional Tiran attire bowed gracefully and showed them to a table.

Their tea arrived: white cup, gold tea, dark biscuit laid at exactly the same angle across each tiny side plate, a tiny orange blossom, everything perfect.

"Beautiful," Cereclo breathed, nodding at the two women.

They enjoyed the tea in silence for a moment. Cereclo said, "That ship or whatever it was that passed us in lightspace? Demaris said the image looked like a purple flower slowly opening. Probably was a compression wave—seen head-on—of something moving very fast. Here's the image." He keyed his wristcom to holographic display.

"You shouldn't be showing that stuff around out here. Captain Arin said…"

A tiny purple flower appeared in the air above the center of the small table. "Nobody here but us," Cereclo said, but he turned the display off and went back to his tea.

"We almost got blown off into some alternate universe when that monster went by," Basil said. "Our ship's lightspace field, like all ship's fields, has an edge effect. The closer you get to the edge, the weaker the effect, the easier it is to drift out of the field. There's a whole page of symbolics in the advanced course that describes the translight universes, but nobody really understands it, except maybe Mera Reigel. When that ship went by, its vortex jolted our ship and slung that drifting cargo container out of our field and into… somewhere else."

"You like that theoretical stuff, don't you?" Cereclo said.

Basil finished his biscuit. "Yeah, I do. Back at Colresh, one of my instructors said no known technology could drive a ship that fast, but he could model what its field might look like."

"A flower, right?"

"Right."

Cereclo sipped his tea. "Demaris called it a ghost. And maybe it is something drifting through lightspace…"

"I think she imagines too much," Basil said. "My guess is that the new nationalized Cinar has built an experimental high-speed ship…"

"Which will change the balance of power in the whole Curve," Cereclo interrupted. "The old Ramath Defense Force will be scrambling to get that super drive, as will Lord Kaleege and the other deposed royals out on Orane. The major shipping companies too. Maybe that's what this strategic planning session is about."

"What planning session?" Basil asked.

Cereclo looked away. "I shouldn't have said anything." Then he turned his familiar smile on Basil and shrugged it off.

Basil fumed. "I wasn't invited." He paid twenty eris from his wristcom to the tea shop paypoint on the table, and they made their way outside…

Cereclo slapped him on the back again, which Basil was getting thoroughly tired of, and told Basil in a rather supercilious tone, "You'll be invited to the planning session. They asked me for names, and I gave them yours. And Demaris's."

• • •

Aboard *Tawli* at the orbital Tiran Station, Basil fretted and fumed until Tiran security showed up at 1400. They made a cursory check of the seals on one box and were gone. It all took no more than five minutes. *We waited two hours for this?*

Tawli departed Tiran, made her way to the Tiran Gate, and transitioned to lightspace. Shipboard activities settled down to routine. His next off-shift, Basil made his way to the wardroom and drew a glass of the ale he'd designed on the dispenser.

Tiran has a near monopoly on gate maintenance equipment which everyone needs. Tiran needs ora, but her supply is being increasingly disrupted by royalist raiders. Talus and the other big companies are reducing trade with Tiran to honor the RDF embargo. A light cargo load in a C-200 making the Sigma to Karaghia to Tiran and back could turn a nice profit. Except for the threat of privateers.

In his cabin, Basil fell into a sleep marred by dreams of blood-soaked blue, and security police in pale-green uniforms.

Chapter 4

"We transship you three at Epsilon waypoint," Arin said as Basil, Cereclo, and Demaris crowded into a transport capsule little bigger than the three of them. They made a hyperbolic loop from the ship around the center of gravity of the transition gate's internal proto sun, then back out to the maintenance station, which was an unmanned can, used only for the weeklong stays of maintenance crews attending to regular gate calibration. It was surprisingly clean and orderly. Cereclo made tea, and they lay on bunks, waiting their four hours until they would climb back into the capsule and rendezvous with the ship that would take them to planet Rouvi for the Talus Company strategic planning session.

• • •

On planet Rouvi, the campus where the planning session was to be held lay in a mountain valley. The mountains swooped up in dramatic silence against a sky so clear and deep blue it seemed unreal. Evening was spreading across an empty sky where sparks of stars were already appearing.

Basil walked down a manicured pathway among sweet-smelling trees to the lodge. Tall window polarizers were dialed to transparency; inside, a half dozen people sat on carpets and couches around a fireplace blazing with real wood. A tall man with perfect silver hair and a tailored Talus uniform stood at the mantel. The legendary Shuard.

"Come in, come in. You are…?"

"Basil Ajami. I'm an Econ-12 recently on *Tawli*." Others also introduced themselves.

Shuard glanced around at the expectant faces. "I'm Pietr Shuard, of the Special Projects Office." He made a formal bow. "You are the best and brightest at Talus." He smiled. "Hand-picked because you've demonstrated your ability, and…" he raised his hand professorially, "…most importantly, you have imagination, vision, a sense of the future. These next four days will be hard work. But it's important work. Perhaps the most important thing this company will do this year. You will act as facilitators for our senior managers. The senior managers will divide themselves into work groups and select topics to work on. Those topics will include relations with the Orane government in exile, the Tiran economy, ora supplies, RDF intentions, the increase in privateering, the Varil disarray, the growing financial leverage the maintenance facilities on Nokendai and Sourav have, and any other topics they choose. Your role will be to facilitate the discussion, capture the thoughts, consolidate them into something that can be briefed at the following morning's general session, and…" he paused dramatically, "…synthesize within and between the work groups." Shuard looked around the room. "Questions?"

"What do we know about the ghost ship and advanced engine technology?" someone ventured.

Shuard nodded. "The ghost ship. We know nothing beyond what you've already seen—the video from *Tawli*. But…consider how an advanced engine commercially manufacturable would affect economics in the Curve. Each of you has been given a reading list on your com, along with the schedule of sessions and a list of the senior managers attending."

Shuard paused dramatically.

"I'll leave you now," he said. "Get acquainted with each other, decide among yourselves who will facilitate which session and how the resulting findings will be compiled. Each night you should discuss all the findings as they relate to each other and provide a short in-progress report to your individual session first thing the next morning. Remember, time is short, and these are crucial issues for the future of this company."

That evening Director Othman, a portly man with heavy eyebrows, hosted the first-night reception. "To the future." He raised his glass, and the assembled crowd raised theirs. Basil and others started to drink when Othman added with a note of sadness, "And to Varil Company, as it was. A toast to times past."

Shuard solemnly raised his glass, then raised his voice. "And to the future, as it shall be." There was scattered applause.

Basil awkwardly sipped at his glass, found it empty, and snagged a full one from a passing tray. He was exhausted from the journey here, but also elated to be among the senior managers of Talus. Four days to map the future.

After a while, Basil set down his drink and went out the air-door to the wide veranda and the cold, crystalline night air. The shadows of mountain peaks ringed the horizon. Stars crowded the sky. He picked out red giants and many blue-whites, several yellow.

After a moment, he noticed someone standing alone at the stone wall that edged the terrace. It was Demaris. She turned, a frown was replaced by a neutral expression that seemed to Basil very tense. "Hello, Basil."

"I felt like you were avoiding me back on the *Tawli*," Basil said. "Did I do something wrong?"

"No..." She started to say something, then smiled and walked past him, through the invisible air-barrier into the lodge, calling, "Good night."

After dinner Basil and some of the others had the shuttle bus drive them to a tavern in the village. They drank beer in a low, timbered room. Tall blue bottles of beer, small glasses with thick bottoms. One Talus Company guy, after three of the local beers, said authoritatively, "Sure, maybe we should all want to be like Shuard, but I say we shouldn't."

"He's politically brilliant, but so cold, so aggressive."

"I'd call that flexible ethics."

"He's a natural leader, and well-educated."

"He is? I've never seen his resume."

"Giant ego. A political climber. He'll work for whoever gives him the best deal."

"I'll tell you who's the most brilliant guy of our generation: Mera Reigel."

"Continuum Physics? He's from the previous generation. Besides, he's disappeared. The most brilliant guy of our generation is a guy named Piaro. He's a sociologist, designed the Karaghia colony for Lord Kaleege..."

"That's not much of a recommendation."

"The theory is good; there's just been too much corruption in the Karaghia local administration and too much interference from bureaucrats on Orane."

Basil, in a meandering conversation with a girl from Planning and a guy from Engineering, noticed Cereclo deep in conversation with a woman from Talus Headquarters. The beer flowed, the talk got louder, they raised toast after toast. "To the future!" they shouted and meant it.

"Limitless opportunities," someone said. "It's all there before us!"

"Ours for the taking," came a shout from the back of the crowded room.

"No," Cereclo shouted back, "ours for the making."

A long day followed, but the next night, still energized, the facilitators stayed in the lounge at the lodge after dinner. The fire in the fireplace was reflected in the tall glass windows, putting a flickering fire at the base of the mountains in the distant twilight. Wine glasses in hand, people took seats on the carpet, the couches, and chairs.

"Ghost ship?" a man asked. "Think it's more than a rumor?"

"Or a lost Kogon Legion…"

"Alien legion," someone said, and there was laughter.

"Mutants from the killed star planets, the timing would be about right—1,800 years ago…"

A woman scoffed. "No aliens, no mutants from the killed stars, and the Kogon are long gone. What we've seen is a tech breakthrough, disruptive technology." She stood up, a tall woman, a bit older than the rest, in a gray suit.

"How should this company react?" Cereclo asked. He was standing in the erect posture Shuard used. Basil saw people trade amused glances, but the room quieted. "No, don't sit down yet," Cereclo went on. "Tell us what effect a disruptive technological breakthrough would have on Talus Company. That's what this conference is about."

"Alright," she said to the room. "Something that fast can only be a breakthrough in engine technology, so we can immediately narrow its potential sources down to a few: Cinar labs, the rebuild facilities on Nokendai, the Gerash Continuum Institute, and, far less likely, something imported from Xbalc space or Shan space, or even from old Ramath."

"Faded glory," a man interjected. "RDF is not a player anymore, and no Shan have ever come past the Xbalc zone. It's something from the Cinar labs."

"Mention RDF with respect, if you please." It was Othman who'd slipped into the room and stood against the glass wall to one side.

"Sorry," the man said. "RDF has provided—is providing—a lot of stability, but its influence is fading, they are pulling back, and they are using old technology."

"But if they're willing to commit enough firepower to enforce a full-scale RDF embargo of Tiran, that would be more disruptive than a prototype engine," somebody said.

"They are related actions," another voice added. "Despite the Five Families taking half the old Imperial fleet with them to Orane, Tiran still has a significant number of warships. An advanced engine would tip the balance in their favor."

"Right," the woman said. "I'll bet anyone in this room a tavern beer…" There were groans from the crowd. She smiled. "…that what nearly hit the *Tawli* was a prototype developed at Cinar labs on Tiran."

Cereclo strolled to her side. "What should this company's response be?" She started to answer, but he stopped her. "Let's hear from your colleagues first. You there." He pointed at a guy sitting cross-legged on the carpet. "Yes, you. The guy who doesn't like the local beer." Basil found himself feeling irritated at Cereclo mimicking Shuard's commanding presence.

He got sheepishly to his feet, a small man in rumpled clothes. "First, just a point of clarification—I love the local beer, maybe too well." He grinned at a buddy. "One option would be to get as many letters of marque as possible from Lord Kaleege, use Talus ships to privateer the Tiran ships, capture a ship with the new engines, then take it to Nokendai and get it reverse-engineered."

"Bravo." Cereclo applauded. "High risk, high reward. Who else?"

"Me," a woman in the front said. "This company is too small to risk aligning with either side in the Naru/Kaleege conflict. If we align with one side, we'll suffer reprisals from the other. Better to chart a middle course, try to take advantage of both sides. Do Lord Kaleege's trading for him while he's using his ships to fight Naru. At the same time, dry-lease ships to Naru and see if he would be willing to re-engine them…"

Basil saw Othman smiling, clearly enjoying the energy in the room. Basil felt a pride in Talus that he had always been reluctant to voice. He knew he was part of something, something big, powerful, something constructive and good. And he realized for the first time in his life that this feeling was what his father had had with Mehul Construction Company those years in the desert when he had been a little boy.

• • •

Pietr Shuard stood at the glass wall of his luxurious suite looking out at the stars above the mountain peaks. His com chimed. He activated the lights and crossed to the door.

Demaris stood in the corridor. "Your message said urgent…?"

"Come in," Shuard said. He poured two glasses of a dark red wine and handed her one. "Sorry it is so late, but there is an issue that needs immediate attention."

Shuard blanked the window wall and they seated themselves on a low sofa.

"You are acquainted with Cereclo Dathe." It was a statement, not a question.

She nodded.

"He's being assigned a special project. A quick trip with light cargo to Tiran and back. It will be his first command."

Demaris sipped her wine. "I'm sure he will be delighted."

Shuard set his wine glass aside and spread his hands. "It is a special project about which Dathe will not be told all the particulars." Shuard's look was mildly paternal. "The trip is legitimate. But one cargo box will require special handling when delivered to the Tiran elevator head…"

Demaris said nothing. The silence lengthened. Finally, she said, "What role would I play in this?"

"I am transferring you temporarily to Special Projects, with a promotion. Your task will be to monitor the *Rafale*, the ship Dathe will command, and send him a message when the ship is approaching the Tiran elevator. The message will be a code he is to give to Ajisai, the freight forwarding company on Tiran." Shuard crossed the room, returned with the wine decanter, and poured both their glasses full and sat down beside her. "Dathe trusts you, so he won't hesitate to follow your instructions."

"I won't do anything that would put him in danger."

Shuard smiled his creamy smile. "Everything of consequence involves risk. Your friend Dathe will no doubt be pleased at the opportunity to have his first command. And you will also benefit..."

"I don't suppose you'd be willing to disclose what this is all about," Demaris said. "No, don't answer that. I don't want to know."

"That's best," Shuard said. "More wine?"

"No." Demaris set her wine glass aside. "I'll be going now."

"You'll do well in Special Projects, Demaris." He raised his glass in a toast.

The next morning, Basil got to the lodge's great room early, drew a cup of coffee, and stood before the windows watching the first points of fire touch the mountain peaks as the sun rose. Other facilitators drifted in, no one saying much, taking their usual seats for the day's pre-meeting. Basil idly checked his com and, to his surprise, found an urgent message waiting. "Report to administration immediately." The message had been sent twenty minutes ago.

Basil hustled across the campus in the cold dawn air. At the admin office he was handed a secure flexcom. He touched the screen, and his DNA opened the secure lock. "Report to Captain Cereclo Dathe aboard the *Rafale* at Sigma immediately," it said.

Stunned, Basil hurried back to his dorm room, gathered up his things, and went to the shuttle bus stop in front of the admin building. As he passed the lodge, he could see Shuard holding forth to the assembled facilitators.

Cereclo sauntered up just as the bus arrived. "Looks like we've got a priority mission," he said jovially. They got on the bus, and it started down the mountain with just the two of them aboard.

"I'm not supposed to reveal anything until we've left Sigma," Cereclo said. "But suffice to say, this trip is important. I know you hate to leave the conference. So do I." Cereclo frowned at the green pastures brightening with the morning sun.

"You don't seem very happy," Basil said.

Cereclo turned. "I'm happy. Got my first command." He frowned again. "And you've got an acting Econ-13 assignment. I asked specifically for you."

"Thanks," Basil said. "Anything else I should know about this little jaunt?"

Cereclo shook his head and put his confident grin back on his face. But behind it, Basil sensed there was something else.

Chapter 5

Inside the Tiran government center, six men in the indigo uniforms of the Varil Shipping Company sat at the polished black conference table. On all four sides of the room, floor-to-ceiling panels depicted the spectacular view of Tiran City stretching to the horizon in all directions.

But none of the men noticed the view.

A doorway opened as though by magic in one of the vistas of the city. Two guards in black uniforms entered the room followed by a small man in an unadorned gray uniform and a taller man in the gray uniform of the general staff with industrial directorate insignia.

The men at the table snapped to their feet. Naru walked casually to the head of the table and sat down. The taller man stood behind him. Naru's face was calm, his impenetrable black eyes unreadable. For a moment he looked slowly around the table at the men's pale faces, then he stood and walked to the wall and looked out over the image of Tiran City. After a moment, he turned, advanced to the table, and looked at the two most senior managers.

Tension stretched toward the breaking point. "This situation is unacceptable," he said softly. "Varil has thirty ships, yet Tiran faces recurring shortages."

He regarded the tabletop for a long moment then slowly looked around at the six white-faced senior managers.

"You are not succeeding in your task," he said softly. "Varil is losing money and market share."

The most senior manager ventured a comment deferentially. "Royalist military interventions, privateer actions, the threat of embargo…"

Naru interrupted without raising his voice. "I have listened to these excuses long enough. It's time for a change."

The man opened his mouth to speak, but Naru raised a hand and turned to the general staff officer standing beside him. "As of now, Varil is a government entity, a division of the Industrial Directorate. It is your responsibility to return Varil to profitability and eliminate commodity shortages this year."

"Yes, sir." The man bowed.

"Dismissed. All of you."

• • •

On *Rafale* Cereclo introduced Basil to a man named Aras wearing a Talus crew uniform without any specialty insignia. "Basil, meet Aras," Cereclo said with false heartiness. "It would be tough making this trip with only two people. With three we can split the watches and get a reasonable amount of rest." Aras nodded and disappeared below.

To Basil's great relief, the trip to Karaghia was uneventful. He was realizing how much the full responsibility for the economic success of the mission and the safety of the cargo could weigh on an econ officer. The second day out, he resorted to using the sim sleep box every other shift.

He only saw Aras, and Cereclo, at shift change. Fortunately, the boxes of ora were ready and waiting for them at the Karaghia elevator head. Cereclo insisted on personally handling all the communication with Ambai Company on Karaghia. Basil bristled a bit at first, not being authorized to communicate directly with the trading company, but it worked out well. Basil soon found that Aras was of little help loading cargo boxes the way Basil wanted it done. Basil told him to take time off, play his AU game, while Basil did all the box loading himself. Working a double shift, the loading went smoothly, and they departed for Tiran on schedule. Basil retired for some badly needed rest, but his sleep was restless. Even sim sleep could not completely eliminate nightmare images of blood-stained indigo uniforms.

Emergence into Tiran realspace was uneventful. On approach to the Tiran elevator head, Cereclo seemed nervous.

Basil was just coming off-duty, drinking a beer and watching the big board display approach traffic.

"Two Tiranian cruisers orbiting the gate," Aras reported.

"I see them." Cereclo's voice was tight.

"Not much traffic inbound. Lots of traffic outbound," Aras observed.

"Basil, once we dock I want you to go to customs and get the fees paid. Aras can oversee unloading."

"I thought Ajisai, the freight forwarder, would pay those fees."

"That's not what Ops wants this time." Cereclo shrugged the comment off, but Basil could see he was concerned about something. "I suspect they want you to be at the customs office in person in case fees have changed, rules have changed, who knows?"

Docking was smooth and fast under control of Tiran Port Authority. The Tiran elevator head had the most up-to-date docking systems in the Curve.

Basil went to his stateroom, changed into a Talus red and gray dress uniform, and debarked into the echoing port arrivals hall, up two slideways and into the Customs Building now adorned with a huge graphic of Devir exuding fatherly benevolence. The Tiranian women at the desks had the same beige uniforms as before the revolution, but each had a red and black armband with the symbol of the revolution over a line of Tiran script.

Basil went to the desk indicated and put his com with the *Rafale* bill of lading into the reader. The woman at the desk, a classic Tiranian beauty, flexed her fingers in her control field while watching her screen, which he could not see. This went on for a long time.

"Is anything wrong?" Basil asked in Basic.

"Please wait over there," she told him, indicating the long bench against one wall. There was only one other person waiting.

Basil sauntered over and took a seat. He went over the figures and the clearances and the bills of lading on his com. He noticed Ajisai had already accepted all the boxes they'd brought. Cereclo had approved it himself.

The independent trader who had been waiting turned to Basil. "You waiting for clearance too?"

"Yes."

"I've been waiting over an hour," he volunteered. "No explanation." He spread his hands. "But we'd better not complain, right? Then they'd really delay us."

Basil's com chimed—it was the customs agent. "That's me. Good luck," he told the man and went back to the woman at the desk.

She opened a holographic display of the transaction in the air between them. It correctly showed the import cargo, the export cargo, the custom clearances, and the tariffs. The tariff was 10 percent higher than he had calculated, but he paid it, then bowed formally and exited the building.

Outside he stood out of the flow of pedestrian traffic and checked his com display carefully, but all seemed to be in order.

His com chimed an emergency call.

It was Cereclo. "Get back here fast, Basil…"

"Trouble?"

"No. Not yet. But I want to leave as soon as cargo is loaded. We've already been given our exit sequence number."

"How soon?"

"Two hours."

"Has Aras gotten our outbound cargo loaded?"

"Most of it."

Back at the ship Basil found both hold doors open, four boxes loaded, and the fifth and final box waiting on a transporter.

Two Revolutionary Guards were eying Aras coldly.

"What's the situation?" Basil said.

"I think they want an access code for a specific box in the cargo we've already off-loaded and Ajisai has collected. My translator can't deal well with their dialect."

"Where's the captain?"

Aras shrugged. "Up in the control room. He told me to handle it. Or call Ajisai."

Aras made a point of craning his neck around looking for Ajisai. One of the Revolutionary Guards, clearly not happy, made a decisive gesture and started to turn away.

The small woman from Ajisai was hurrying toward them, flagging one of her workers to drive the loader over. There was a Talus box on the loader. She addressed one of the guardsmen in dialect. The conversation went on for a time. Then the man turned away, apparently satisfied. The Ajisai worker drove the loader slowly behind the two guardsmen.

The woman turned to Aras. "Why didn't you give him the number?" she asked rather sharply, tilting her head up at him.

"What number?"

Exasperation crossed her face. Then she laughed. "Don't you people talk to each other? Your captain gave me the code they wanted when you first arrived. I assumed he gave it to each of you. That box was to get special handling. If the RG asks, give them the number, then give them the box."

Aras shook his head and went up the cargo ramp into the hold.

"One box needed a special code?" Basil grumbled. "A code we are supposed to have had. And the box goes to the Revolutionary Guards? No customs clearance? What is this?"

"Wouldn't be the first time in human history that the people charged with ensuring there's no smuggling are the ones involved in the smuggling."

Basil was at a loss for words.

"You wouldn't be interested in a bit more cargo, would you?" the woman asked.

Basil's heart sank. "More smuggling?"

She laughed a short quick laugh. "Not at all. Those two Talus boxes over there are cleared for export, just waiting for available transport. You could take them. Do your company a favor."

Basil's com chimed. It was Cereclo. "Get aboard and close up the hold. I want to be ready to leave as soon as our number comes up."

"How much time do we have?" Basil asked.

"About an hour. Also, the front office is putting a pause on all Talus ships to and from Tiran," Cereclo continued. "We are the last one out for a while."

The Ajisai woman raised her eyebrows at this announcement. "You get those boxes to Sigma now, and your company will probably pay you a bonus."

"Captain isn't going to risk losing our departure slot waiting for us to load more cargo," Basil told her. "He's the nervous type. Besides, your crew is gone. Who's going to load them?"

"You and me." She grinned. "The loaders are right here. Unless your captain decides to slam the hold doors closed on us, we can have those boxes loaded in fifteen minutes."

"Let's go," Basil said. "I'll lock the hold doors open."

An alarm started hooting.

"Can't you shut that off?"

"No," Basil shouted above the din. "I have the hold door locked open, and control is signaling to close it."

"Then we'd better move fast before security comes to find out what the racket is about. You receive the boxes and tie them down. I'll move them into the hold." She scrambled up on a loader and picked up the first box.

Basil went to the cargomaster control station and energized two tie-downs. Within a minute, the first box was sliding onto the rollers, and she had departed for the second box.

Basil worked the box into place, then manually ran a temporary sling over the box to the hardpoints in the deck. Another minute and he had it secured, then went back to the control station, set the second box in place, and attached a sling.

Basil's com bleeped the emergency tone. "Close the hold!" Cereclo roared. Basil sprang up and released the hold door lock. It cycled closed at emergency speed. He had a last look at the Ajisai woman sitting on a loader, laughing.

"Departure alert," the AI voiced. Basil threw himself into his workstation buffer.

The holographic image at the control panel showed *Rafale* departing at the maximum allowable dockside acceleration, barely within the approved timeline.

Basil grinned. *There'll be hell to pay over this little disagreement, but these two extra boxes will almost double our profit margin.*

As soon as the departure maneuver was complete, Basil slid out of his buffer and hurried to the control room.

Cereclo turned away from the main board. "What the hell were you doing?"

"Increasing our profit. Doing the Talus Company a favor by moving…"

"I ordered the cargo hatch closed and you locked it open!" Cereclo snapped. "That's insubordination."

"We departed on schedule," Basil said.

"Don't ever do that to me again," Cereclo said and turned back to the control board.

Basil went to the cargo deck, checked the tie-down on all boxes and the weight and balance calculations by AI.

The shift schedule showed Basil off-duty for eight hours. He drew two beers from the dispenser, took them to his cabin, and drank them in silence.

Gutless bastard. Unwilling to take a chance when it presents itself. And he fumbled the box code for special handling. He gave it to the Ajisai people, so all he would have had to do was notify the Revolutionary Guards that Ajisai had it. Instead he hides in the control room and tells Aras to handle it. Not much of a commanding officer.

And having me go pay customs? What was that all about? I could have given the documentation to Ajisai, and they would have handled the whole thing.

Revolutionary Guards involved in Port Authority operations, in smuggling. Devir's golden revolution is becoming a corrupt dictatorship. History repeating itself.

Basil downed the last of one beer and started on the second one. He recalculated the trip profit with the two extra boxes—20 percent increase.

"That should make the Project Review Board happy. And make Cereclo look like an efficient ship's master," Basil snorted. *He panicked when we were about out of time before departure, and he panicked when the Revolutionary Guards showed up.*

And worst of all, I saw him panic, and he knows I saw him.

On the return trip to Sigma, there was a frosty silence among the three except for the few words exchanged at shift change.

On final approach to the Sigma dock, Cereclo called for a crew meeting.

"Operations sent us a message," Cereclo said without preamble. "Congratulations to all for securing additional Talus cargo at Tiran." He paused, looking away. "Now, back to workstations."

Chapter 6

The chairs at the table in the main Talus Company conference room were for division chiefs, but Basil saw Captain Arin at the table. Along the back wall there were a few empty chairs. Basil slid into a seat beside Cereclo, who did not acknowledge him. Director Othman hunched bear-like in his chair at the head of the U-shaped table. At the other end, in front of the big briefing board, the Talus vice president of trade and the chief of finance were fidgeting, waiting to start. At Othman's right, the chief of Planning said, "Before we start our regular project briefings, we have some awards to present."

Captain Arin called the entire crew of *Tawli* up to the front. The chief of Planning read a crew citation: "...for quick thinking resulting in a significant gain for the company..."

"Well done," Othman said. "Despite the...anomaly...you encountered." He turned to the chief of Planning. "Any explanation for the Varil Company ship situation?"

The chief of Planning shrugged. "None."

Captain Arin and each *Tawli* crew member was given a white paper card with a glowing red company logo on it.

Director Othman addressed the room. "In this company all awards are team awards, because I feel no single person—no matter how talented, or lucky—can make a project successful by themselves. It always takes a team effort."

Back at his seat, Basil surreptitiously ran his wristcom over the logo on the card: an 8,000 eris bonus. He forced the grin off his face, but it crept back.

Basil whispered to Cereclo: "I'm going to present a quick three-cornered trip like we just completed on *Rafale*, then I'll present my alternate maintenance plan. You're going to brief the outcome of our *Rafale* trip to Tiran, aren't you?"

"No," Cereclo whispered.

"Why not?"

"Orders from the front office."

"Why?"

But then it was Basil's turn. He went to the front of the room and briefed a fast three-cornered trip from Sigma to Karaghia: sell parts and supplies for the ora-processing machinery there, buy ora and deliver it to Tiran, buy gate maintenance equipment and deliver it back to Sigma.

"Let me stop you right here," Othman said. He waved the lights up. "I've got a policy memo making its way through coordination. It says that until further notice, no Talus ships will be making any trips to Tiran. We will honor the RDF embargo."

There was silence for a moment.

Basil ventured a comment. "Sir, this project delivers an agricultural product, ora, to Tiran, which could be considered humanitarian goods. I think we can get an exemption from the embargo."

Director Othman smiled but shook his head. "No cargo to Tiran until further notice. Sorry."

The board members shifted and whispered. Basil opened a new display on the board. "I have a second proposal." He pointed to a column of numbers overlaid on an aerial photo of a ship-refitting facility. "Currently Talus has a long-term maintenance contract with the Arixa Yard on Nokendai. Prices on Nokendai are escalating." Basil shifted the display to an image of a re-manufacturing facility under construction. "Three of the major ship maintenance firms, including Arixa, are opening facilities on Sourav III. They are taking advantage of the large pool of skilled engineering worker refugees from the revolution on Tiran." Basil overlaid a column of numbers on the photo. "I estimate we could save as much as 20 percent annually on our fleet maintenance costs…"

"It's a lot farther to go," someone rumbled.

"Twenty percent savings, even with the longer travel," Basil ended.

Several board members were whispering among themselves. Ser Ranmarik, Chief of Engineering, brought up the lights. "This is not a project, ser Ajami. Send your proposal to Engineering for review. Our agenda is full today; we need to move on." The next briefer was already approaching the dais.

Basil returned to his seat. Cereclo was gone. The agenda said the chief of Engineering would be discussing the anomaly encountered by the *Tawli* after four more project briefings. Basil settled in to wait, but his com tingled, a message from Cereclo: "Celebration at the Poem starting now. I'm buying."

Basil slipped out of the conference room.

• • •

The Poem restaurant and bar was the third door down a narrow pedestrian way that dated back a century or more. Basil cut through the small dining area to the back terrace where a simulated stone terrace overlooked a spectacular view of mountains ringing a dark-blue lake with a glassy surface. Mist rose in the distance. The simulation—image, scent, sound, the gentle touch of the breeze—was breathtaking. The tables here were full, dance music played, two couples were dancing. Basil had once been in this room when the simulation blinked off for a moment. It was a bare box five meters by eight meters.

Demaris's golden hair caught the mountain light. She waved for Basil to join her and Cereclo.

"Hello, hero," she said with a smile. She stopped rearranging the pink and white flowers on the table and touched his hand.

Basil, proud and embarrassed, took a seat. Cereclo poured him a glassful of champagne which Basil raised. "To *Tawli*'s profit and to team awards."

"And quick thinking," Cereclo added, making it sound almost like an insult. The distant sound of a bird out over the lake was clear.

"The *Rafale* trip…" Basil started.

"Let's not discuss business, Basil," Cereclo said, scanning the distant mountain peaks. "A communications mix-up, nothing to discuss." He pulled Demaris to her feet. "Let's dance."

Basil's glass was empty, so he signaled for three more champagnes which the automatic waiter brought almost instantly. He tried to enjoy the grandeur of the sunset behind mountains rising out of the distant mist. Demaris and Cereclo stayed on the dance floor for the next song, and the next.

Basil finished his champagne and made his way out of the Poem and onto a slideway to let the storefronts flow past him in the rain that carefully started at the outer edge of the slideway.

Half an hour later, Cereclo and Demaris were strolling arm in arm down one of the narrow arcades behind the docking area.

"You were rude to Basil," Demaris said, admiring the silks in a shop window. The concourse lights began to dim for night cycle.

"Basil talks too much. About stuff he shouldn't. Stuff Shuard told me to keep secret."

Demaris's expression did not change.

They stepped into the Arath Hotel lounge for a drink. They ate dinner there, and talked, but not about Basil or Shuard or Talus Company. Afterward they went up to a room, made love, then lay there in darkness watching a light rain spangle the city lights in the simulation outside the open French doors. "I wouldn't mind working in Special Projects," Cereclo said softly.

They lay in silence for a time.

"Shuard is smart and ambitious," Demaris said finally, her voice soft and flat. "Also powerful, and dangerous. He uses people and he keeps secrets. I don't really enjoy working for him anymore." Cereclo didn't like her tone but could not think of a way to steer the conversation back to something lighter.

She continued, "It's not boring working in Special Projects, but it's not…stable. Not in the long-term." The sound and the scent of rain gently filled the air of the darkened room."I lived on Delta before I came to Sigma to go to Colresh Institute," Demaris said. "It wasn't a very settled life. After I graduated I went to work for Talus, and I like it. But I liked my first few years, when I was an ENG-9 in Engineering, better than this last year in Special Projects."

"Except for your promotion." Cereclo essayed, "Anything important happen at the strategic planning session after Basil and I left?"

But she rolled away from him, pulling the covers up.

Cereclo lay awake for a while listening to the quiet sounds of the city, the rain fading away, the river an almost inaudible murmur.

Beside him Demaris lay curled like a child, hiding in sleep.

• • •

After a time, Basil stepped off the slideway and dashed through the rain to Sagai department store. He rode an elevator up to the top level where there was a complex of small restaurants linked together by a winding white path through an artificial forest done in half-size. He enjoyed seeing the tiny birds and animals—not a virtual display—these were genetically engineered living creatures. A tiny herd of some blue four-legged animals grazed in a two-meter-square meadow. Basil decided on a sleek restaurant decorated as a forester's cabin on Rouvi planet.

The food was great and the beer tasted good, but he could not appreciate them.

Cereclo's a 13 while I'm still a 12 even though we've both been with the company ten years. I haven't had a project approved by the board in two years. My maintenance suggestion will get lost in the bureaucracy in Engineering Division. Cereclo pulls me out of the off-site conference to go on a fast trip of no special importance. Even though he gets himself stressed over a communication mix-up with customs. If I'd stayed at the off-site, I could have made some contacts, maybe with Shuard himself. I might have been able to get a temporary assignment in Special Operations.

He wandered through the nearby stores without seeing anything, then rode the slideway down to dock level and took a seat on one of the long black couches in front of the holographic real-time display of the dock and the ships outside in vacuum. Tiny pastel spheres moved slowly into and out of the docking ports on the side of Sigma Station.

I've been with Talus ten years. Ten years of trips. I'm making a decent wage, but not making many friends. Not really accomplishing anything noteworthy.

After a time he went back to his tiny hotel room and fell into a restless sleep, troubled by phantoms in bloodstained blue.

Chapter 7

The next day Basil went to Talus HQ with some vague idea of talking about his career with Thelis. But Thelis was not available. He checked the master chart of assigned ships and crew, reconfirmed that he was available, and wandered down to the lobby. He thought he glimpsed Demaris's tawny hair inside one of the glass-enclosed temporary offices. He walked that way, heard raised voices, slowed. The office door was partly open. Inside Demaris was standing facing the wall screen which was polarized. Basil heard her snarl "Damn you!" at the screen and click it off. Basil hurriedly turned to go, but she had seen him.

"Basil," she said.

"Sorry…I was passing…"

"Step inside."

Basil stepped into the tiny office and she closed the glass door. No use pretending he hadn't heard her anger.

Demaris sat down in the desk chair, frowning at the blank screen.

"I was just passing," Basil repeated. "I should probably be going…"

"Basil, don't talk. Sit down and be quiet or be on your way."

Basil hesitantly sat down in the guest chair. He watched her click on an auxiliary screen, review something on it for a time, then click it off.

"You came at a bad time." She sighed.

Basil stood. "Sorry." He paused before activating the door. "Anything I can do to help?"

She stared at people passing by. "No, Basil, there is nothing you can do. You just keep working hard, taking ship assignments, doing a good job. And don't ask questions, don't involve yourself in things…" She shook her head.

"I…well…" He bowed and departed.

Basil made his way back to the big holographic of Sigma port activity and took a seat on a bench. He put Demaris out of his mind and watched the tiny replicas of ships. *I've been an econ officer in charge for the last six years. I think I know ship handling and trading in this tiny bit of the Curve. With very few exceptions, the trips I've been on have made money.*

He pulled out his com and looked up ship leasing rates, but he knew he'd have to actually look at the ship and its log to get a feel for what kind of a ship he might want to lease. He called up a com on his wrist screen and began running some numbers. *Tiran badly wants hard currency. They have a monopoly on manufacturing ship and gate maintenance components, but they can't sell all they make because of the embargo. The major companies won't cross the line because of the political pressures from the royalist government in exile and from the Ramath Defense Force. There's a growing shortage of shipping capacity since many free traders have quit hauling freight and are turning to raiding using letters of marque from Lord Kaleege.*

He still had the *Rafale* trip profile in his com. He did a quick calculation of the same trip with half cargo—still profitable. He checked a wet-lease rate on a C-200 and subtracted it from the *Rafale* trip revenue. Still profitable, barely.

He called up Etir Leasing's site: the leasing fee for their smallest ship was twice what he had in cash. *Money can be borrowed, but interest on borrowed money drives profit margin into negative numbers unless I have phenomenally good luck with cargos.*

But there's no harm in taking a look at a ship or two.

• • •

Etir Ship Leasing's office was tiny but, unlike many of the yard-side offices Basil had visited, beautifully neat and well-furnished. The woman at the glass desk was also well-furnished.

"Ser Ajami." She smiled and with a small gesture turned off the AI that had identified him. "Welcome. What can we do for Talus Company?"

"I'd like to take a look at the C-200 you are advertising for lease," Basil said. "Contracting likes for the crew to look over ships before we lease them. Make sure they fit our needs."

"Certainly. Would you like some tea?"

"No, thanks."

She glanced at her screen. "I'll ask a sales rep to come down and talk with you. I see you haven't yet picked up the options on the two C-800s you have on lease from us. Is there some difficulty?"

Basil shrugged. "I'm in Ops, not Contracting, but I haven't heard of any difficulties."

The sales rep, a tall thin man in a pale-blue suit, entered and bowed politely. "Welcome, ser Ajami. I'm told you'd like to have a look at a C-200?"

The receptionist smiled her dazzling smile. "I'll have it opened up for you; number twenty. Just down through the passageway there."

At the entry tube marked twenty, Basil told the sales rep, "I'm just looking, so give me some time to nose around by myself, then we can talk, alright?"

The rep smiled. "Of course, take your time. I'll join you later."

Number twenty was clean and cold and had the familiar smell of aluminum and plastics. Basil went through each of the four holds, carefully looking for any stress wrinkles, cracks at fittings, or welds around the cargo airlocks, or any areas recently repainted that might cover a hasty repair. There were none.

He went through the internal airlock at the safety bulkhead and into the central companionway. It was warmer there.

He looked briefly into the three sleeping compartments: a four-person room for crew, with an adjacent sim sleep cell, one double room for officers, and a roomy single—the master's quarters. He stood in the door of the master's quarters looking at the desk with double display sets, the bunk, the tiny washroom. Then he went up to the control room.

Only the big board and one auxiliary screen were lit.

The recently cleaned black plastic consoles gleamed. The big screen displayed a colorful holographic of the exterior of Sigma and the ships nearby.

New chairs were at each of the control consoles. Both jump seats behind control and nav were folded back. The gunsight over the weapon station was folded up into the ceiling panel, and the panels showed the armaments deactivated. The four spokes of the inertia buffers around each control chair looked like fingers of a cupped hand. Basil turned and made his way back out of the ship.

The rep, whose name Basil had forgotten, bowed to him. "Come on up to the office, Basil."

They rode the slide up. Basil knew that part of Etir's sales strategy was to have their meeting rooms and sales offices overlooking the yard. The view of ships was spectacular—a row of gray and green and orange spheres in an imitation of the pale-orange light from the gas giant planet Sigma orbited.

"Prices have already started up," the rep said casually. "The Tiran situation."

"Up? I would think they'd be going down…more risk…"

The rep activated a big holo on the wall opposite the view of the ships. "Here's Freetrader's buy/sell/lease summary for the last three months. Look at the trend line for small and mid-range ships. Up 14 percent in one quarter."

"I'm surprised." Basil felt his heart sinking and tried to keep his face immobile.

"Well…" the rep said sympathetically.

An office assistant brought in a tray with two cups and an exquisite golden-colored pot of tea.

"I understood Talus was considering leasing one more C-800?"

Basil maintained eye contact while trying not to appear too eager. "I'm interested in something for myself. The 200 looks very good. I'm very interested, but only in a short-term lease, and only in a ship that's not going to cost me time and money in maintenance." Basil paused.

"We've got an attractive maintenance guarantee contract you might be interested in…"

"Don't think so. I don't want the price so high I can't earn-out during the lease."

The rep nodded judiciously, non-verbally sharing Basil's concern, letting him know they would work through the problem together. *I need to learn to be able to do that,* Basil thought.

The rep flexed his fingers in a com field, and numbers appeared.

"Forty thousand up-front which includes insurance. So if you turn a 10 percent profit on short hauls…" he flexed fingers in the com field as he spoke, "…say back-to-back four-week mission profiles, fuel…nice thing about the 200s are their great fuel efficiency…" The bottom line appeared in light purple. "You should be able to cover lease payments and all expenses and still have a 5 percent profit." He grinned. "Depending on how much you decide to pay yourself and your crewmates."

"I'm not greedy," Basil said. "Have to add taxes, export/import duties, but it is an attractive price."

They sat in companionable silence for a time.

The rep let the numbers fade from the screen and activated a holographic reader on the surface of his desk. Basil put his wristcom in the field.

"There's my contact information, and the numbers we talked about," the rep told him. "I know you'll want to talk it over with your crewmates. There's a steady demand for the smaller ships. I'm not trying to rush you, but I will say it's a pretty active market at the moment."

Basil's com chimed. "Sorry, I need to take this."

He put the image on private. It was Demaris. "I'm sorry I was rude to you, Basil. Can we meet somewhere for a drink?"

"Sure," Basil said. "I'm just finishing up here. We could meet at the Sclerus restaurant on A concourse. I think it's about number 2200."

She smiled. "See you there in twenty minutes."

Basil clicked off.

The rep smiled. "Here's a draft lease contract for you to look over. It's our standard contract so legal has already approved."

"Excellent," Basil said. The rep stood, bowed, and Basil left his office.

• • •

Basil and Demaris had a table near the virtual stream and forest that formed the back wall of the restaurant. There was soft music playing. Demaris looked beautiful in the faux sunset light. She raised her glass. "I apologize for snapping at you earlier. A bit of a stressful situation. Don't ask me about it." They drank a toast.

"I'd say Talus management has a pretty high opinion of you," Demaris continued. "You were chosen for the strategic planning session. And your quick thinking on *Tawli*..."

Basil fingered his drink. "Quick thinking? I appreciate the compliment, but I don't feel like what I did on *Tawli* was thinking at all. More like instinctive reaction. OK in emergency situations, but maybe not so good for big decisions."

"You sound like someone considering a big decision now."

He snorted. "I wish I had your ability to read people."

They drank more wine and enjoyed the clear water of the stream flowing past. Hidden lights came on as dusk settled.

"I'm thinking about taking a year's leave from Talus," Basil said, the wine doing his thinking for him. Wine and the intoxicating presence of Demaris.

"Go to work for somebody else?"

"No, work for myself. Try independent trading. See if I can do it."

"You surprise me, Basil. I thought you liked Talus."

"I do. I like the people and I like the work, but I want to try something new. I think I'm ready to try running my own trades, my own ship. Leased ship, that is. I have some money—and with the bonus from the *Tawli* episode, I'm getting close to having enough to lease a 200."

Demaris was silent for a moment, then, "The regs say minimum crew is three. Who do you have in mind to join you in this venture?"

"Haven't decided. Since it is a small ship making short runs, I'm pretty sure I can get a waiver to operate with a two-person crew. Cereclo and I have worked together for quite a while, and I think he might do it, but I'm not sure I want to ask him to take a year off, compromise his career at Talus."

Demaris looked away.

"I don't know," Basil continued. "I don't really want to hire a crew through an agency, but it might be the only choice." He smiled at Demaris. "But I don't need to decide on crew right away. Once I have the money for a lease, I'll work out all the other issues."

Demaris looked at the tablecloth for a long moment, then raised her eyes to his. "I might be interested."

Basil was speechless.

"I'm looking for a change too," she said slowly.

"I'm flattered, but I thought…you working in Special Projects… up there with Shuard and the exec office people. You're on the fast track to promotion."

Basil couldn't decipher her look. "Working in Special Projects is not all that glamorous, Basil. Shuard is a smart, high-profile guy, but he's selfish. He takes all the credit for successes that the rest of us have worked hard to make happen. I don't think my promotion opportunities are any better now than they were a year ago when I was in Engineering." She took his hand. "I'm ready for a change."

"You're serious?"

"Yes."

"Can you wait a year? The lease…"

"I have some money saved."

Again Basil was speechless.

Demaris gave his hand a quick squeeze. "As organized as you are, I'm sure you've got a business plan. I'll need to review it."

He nodded. "Yes, I do. With the big companies honoring the embargo, there's an opportunity right now."

Demaris studied the fine pattern of white on white in the table covering then began tracing it with one finger. The electronic flute music played a tune that had been stylish many years ago.

"Isn't that music the old stuff from…?" Basil trailed off.

Demaris smiled. "Yes. And I've always liked it."

Basil leaned forward. "A small ship, an independent, will be no threat to anyone. Not the Tiran forces or the RDF or the royalists. Low risk…" Basil took her hand in his. She gently removed her hand from his.

"Any action has risk," Demaris said. "But no action also has risk."

The automated waiter poured more wine in each of their glasses. Basil raised his, and after a moment Demaris did too.

"I'll join you," she said.

Basil managed to get his wine down without choking.

"That's wonderful!" he spluttered. "Perfect!"

"You should see your expression," she said and smiled her perfect smile.

Chapter 8

Something was rippling the zero-point energy that sparkled in and out of existence just below the skin of interstellar space.

Basil and Demaris stared at the big board as *Duino*'s image slid slowly along its curve toward the transition point at the entrance to the gate.

"Is that something…?"

"Don't know; maybe nothing," Demaris said from the weapons console. Passive and active sensors scanned realspace nearby, a lumpy volume twisted by molecule-sized bits of matter and veils of gases orbiting the wormhole gate. Gate maintenance equipment kept only the designated entrance and exit lanes clear.

"Keep an eye on it, will you?" Basil said. "I'm going to stay on manual until we're five minutes out. I don't want to burn out the autopilot running this fast with unbalanced thrust." He realized he was chattering so shut up. One more hour to the transition point, then the gate would pull them out of realspace and into lightspace.

A bit of the screen blurred and numbers fluttered for an instant as mass, velocity, emission, and reflection sensors tried to lock. And then it was gone. "Something…but these old scanners can't lock it…" Basil said.

"There!" Demaris shouted. She released the gun locks, and the bar at the top of the screen went from yellow to red. A spark wavered into existence on the board, and the identity numbers beside it fluttered. Two of the six lines filled. "She's fast…"

"…but showing no ID. That's got to be a raider. We've got to outrun him."

Basil advanced power on both engines to 105 percent. The thrumming at the edge of hearing intensified.

The projected course lines from *Duino* and the mystery ship intersected beyond the transition point.

"We'll transition before he has our range."

"Maybe. If everything holds together…" Basil said tightly.

"We're ahead of him. We could scatter mines. He'd have to dodge them."

Basil had the AI run a quick calculation. "Can't. We're too close. The mines would enter the gate after us."

They focused on their tasks, Basil making minute adjustments to their vector; Demaris manning the long-range scan. They watched the numbers flickering on the main board and the two course lines. Forty more minutes to transition.

The raider's course arc continued to change, the projection sweeping toward them. "Damn he's fast!" Basil muttered. The courses now intersected in front of the transition point in the gate. He snapped a glance at Demaris and was amazed to see she was grinning. "Guess we'll get to see how well these old guns perform," she said.

Basil had the AI run projections again: mass, engine thrust, maximum acceptable transition velocity needed, and the relative position of the gate and the debris around it. When he looked up at the main board, only a minute had passed. The course projection arcs still overlaid each other. Accuracy probabilities were still only 90 percent, normal at these speeds, this close to the mass of the gate.

Basil flexed his fingers in the virtual keyboard and did another calculation on his display. What if they vectored to miss the gate? Could they then loop around and transition before the raider could? The intense mass of the wormhole would allow them a very tight turning radius.

Basil worked the numbers, but the raider was running at 0.8X, and the best *Duino* could do was 0.6X. They massed about the same, but the raider seemed to be adjusting his position, not to attack, but to enter the gate first.

"Look at this!" Demaris yelped. The arcs of the two course projections still overlaid each other, but the raider was continuing to accelerate. Basil throttled back to 100 percent power. The raider continued to accelerate.

"She won't be able to match..." he began.

"Watch your angle, Basil!" Demaris shouted. Red alert lights on the board were blinking. Their angle of approach to the transition point was drifting out of tolerance. And an approach out of tolerance could tear the ship apart as gee forces near the event horizon overcame the ship's buffers and subjected the structural frame to massive tidal surges. It had happened to other ships.

Basil let the AI do some alternate calculations, then he pushed select on a course correction that would slow them and let them loop around and enter normally.

"You were the one who wanted to run on manual..." Demaris said. "Get the autopilot back on. There's only twenty minutes left..."

"I know how much time there is," Basil snapped. But he engaged the autopilot. Their shock buffers pushed at them as unbalanced thrust intensified.

"Our friend is still accelerating...damn, there's another one!"

A second ship was wavering and blurring into focus on the board, thirty minutes behind the first one. "Smaller...and not as fast? This doesn't make much sense."

"It makes sense to me," Demaris said. She had the guns targeted on the newcomer. Ten more minutes and they would be in range.

The bigger ship continued to run straight at the transition point. *Duino* would transition in twenty minutes, the newcomer in thirty.

"She's still accelerating! What is that thing?" They watched the lines on the board swinging toward the transition point. Demaris pulled the gunsight scope down and ducked her head into it.

Basil could feel his stomach churning as the buffers compensated for the snaps of steering thrust the autopilot was applying. The frantic thrumming of the engines grated on his nerves as the unbalanced harmonics wavered in and out of hearing. He did another projection on the nav board. If they cut thrust, decelerated hard, would the raiders fly by them without time to change course before the transition? He flexed his fingers and ran the simulation on the secondary inset. He made a mistake, acceleration too high by a factor of ten. He kept staring at the board, watching the lines swinging inexorably toward each other.

The simulation showed *Duino* would be out of range if the raiders kept increasing their speed. "I'm going to try decelerating," Basil said. "I don't know what they're doing, but they will have accelerated past the point of no return by then."

"No! Keep us on course. We'll be in gun-range in five minutes." Demaris pulled her head out of the gunsight. "Five minutes is all I need."

"They're still accelerating. Look," Basil said.

"Why in the hell would they do that?"

"No idea. But they will be able to fire on us if we don't decelerate." Basil flicked through a quick simulation. "Five more minutes…"

"Speed up! I can ripple-fire a pattern in front of him just before we enter the gate." The sound of the engines changed. "Why did you slow us down, Basil?" The numbers on the board showed 99 percent power.

"We're going to burn out the number two engine if we keep pushing it so hard. Besides…"

"I'm telling you to accelerate. Two more minutes, dammit, Basil!" She ducked back into the gunsight.

The lines on the board overlaid each other now. The autopilot flashed and chimed, "Five minutes to transition."

The range sphere showed the first raider, the big one, was within range of *Duino*'s guns. Basil disengaged the autopilot, manually ran up 40 percent deceleration power, and pushed the fire-control override to lock out Demaris's guns. The buffers whined, stressed hard.

Demaris pushed her gunsight up and turned a furious face his way. "What the hell are you doing?"

"We're going around. They're committed to the transition, we're not—they'll pass us faster and out of range. If we go through now, we'll be in this same situation at the other end. A firefight with two bigger, faster ships."

"Dammit! Never lock me out!"

They watched the lines on the board start to diverge. The big raider continued to accelerate, the second ship following. "He's at almost 2X. Way too fast for a safe transition. Hope there's nothing in his way at the other end. Hard radiation is going to be fierce when he exits the gate at that speed," Basil said grimly.

Demaris said nothing.

They watched the board in silence. After a time, Basil started the nav computer on their missed approach calculation.

"Don't you ever lock me out again," Demaris said softly. She clicked her seat buffers off and stomped out of the control room.

Basil set up the approach.

AI said, "Engine synchronization is out of limits."

"Can you override it?"

"Yes, but it will need to be serviced soon."

Basil sat watching the plot of *Duino*'s approach on the big board. He put the engine diagnostics display on the board. His frown deepened.

"Plot an alternate course at the exit gate. To Nokendai."

After a short time the big board displayed the alternate course.

"AI, set that course when we exit the gate." *I'm not going to run the engines out of sync all the way to Karaghia. No repair facilities there. Need to get it fixed before we go any farther.*

For the remainder of the voyage, Basil and Demaris each took their shifts, did their work, and otherwise ignored each other.

It was Basil's shift at docking time. Demaris was nowhere to be seen.

Basil completed the procedure by himself, rather surprised at his own proficiency.

After the Port Authority had confirmed everything was in order, Basil checked the internal master scan. AI told him he was the only one aboard. Demaris had signed out and left the ship with no destination and no return time noted.

• • •

Basil was thrilled when the first shipyard he contacted said they could start on repairs to *Duino* almost immediately.

The shipyard office was a comfortable place with cheerful people.

"We also have some cabins we rent to ship crews for a few days at a time. A lot cheaper than anyplace else around here and quite nearby. We can add the charge to your bill if you like?"

The arrangements were made for the shipyard to do an analysis of *Duino* and compile a list of repairs needed. Basil followed his com to one of the rental cabins and found it to be a neat white house made of native stone just up the hill from the commuter train station. It had a beautifully trimmed hedge along the front and a sweeping view of the bay from the living room in the back of the house. He lay down for a nap and slept almost an hour. Then he got up and wandered from room to room in the house for a time, considered going to the shipyard, but instead took the train to the nearest of Nokendai's many city centers. From the train station he chose streets at random to walk along, hardly seeing the people and the buildings he passed. After several hours he stopped in a restaurant, ate a dinner he hardly tasted, and drank two glasses of wine.

Back at the house the rooms felt very empty.

He drank more wine and again wandered from room to room. Out over the bay the sunset burned deep red. He spoke out loud. "I did what I thought was best. The raiders went on through the gate, they didn't attack us, but if they had, or if they had been waiting for us on the other end, we would not have been able to outrun them with the synchronizer failing. Out-gun them? Maybe. But two against one? I won't take those odds."

Even though he felt worn out, he wasn't sleepy. There was a sim sleep cell in one of the bedrooms, so he removed his clothes, climbed in, and set it for six hours on the lowest setting.

He slept until dawn, but unlike most hours of low-intensity sim sleep, he dreamed. Dreams of frustrated effort, and of indigo stained with red.

The next morning Basil went to the shipyard.

"Want to take a look?" the shift supervisor said. He was a slim, dark-skinned fellow with a Riflik accent. He led Basil past the warning lights indicating a gee decrease.

"How much gee do you maintain?" Basil asked. They walked slowly through the zone. Basil felt like he was rising as his weight decreased.

"About 70 percent standard. Easier to get around, but your inertial reactions are still close to normal. And we don't have to pay the tech for zero-gee time." They started down a curving catwalk. "Lot of people think reduced gee makes it all so easy. I tell them they should come out here and do a full shift's work and see how easy it is."

Up close, the skin of the *Duino* was a reptilian gray-green. Basil reached out.

"Don't touch it. It changes the inductance."

Basil withdrew his hand. "I've never really looked at ship skin."

"Not many people do." The tech pulled an instrument off his belt. "Here, look in this display." The orange hologram showed the subsurface structure—fantastically complex circuits, similar to a biological neural network.

"Your drive system is this network," the tech supervisor said. "Sensors are grown around them." He dialed up magnification. "Right now we've got the dock autosystem supplying a set of input signals through here. Your drives and steering, power, transition, autopilot linkages the AI interfaces with are all responding to those calibration signals.

"You've already replaced our synchronizer."

"Yes, that's the easy part. Now we have a rebuilt synchronizer installed but not connected and calibrated. Once the ship's net has rebuilt itself around the input signals, we'll shift to the new synchro and let the network heal. Good thing you pulled in when you did. It's easy to burn out an engine running unsynced." He adjusted the display and the lines changed to a range of colors. "Should be all dark blue when the system is fully functional. About 40 percent of the network was pale blue and 20 percent was almost green. He snapped the display off and clipped the set to his belt.

"I appreciate you getting us in as quickly as you did," Basil said. "We're independents, cash flow is critical. Maybe leasing this old ship wasn't such a good idea after all."

The man shrugged in the peculiar way that was common on Riflik. "I'd say it was a real good idea. All the big companies are using bigger ships now, 600s and 800s. But these 200s are the best ships Cinar ever designed. This is the design that made Cinar famous. Later, the 600 was the design that let Cinar capture most of the market."

"How long will it take to get it up to spec?"

He shrugged again. "You'll have to talk to the front office, but it looks like about four days. The AI time is the expensive part. Should be able to pull her out of dock the day after that. Then maybe half a day to do the final calibration and full power run-ups. Then close her back up." He unclipped his belt scope again and pointed it at the hull. "Take a look." He pointed with the long fingernail on his little finger. In the middle of the tangle of colored lines Basil could make out a small circle of curving gold lines. "It's the Cinar icon from a hundred years ago. When old Ozun Cinar was personally running the company."

Basil handed the scope back. "You've studied history?"

"Yeah. I like history. Almost as much as I like ships." He flashed his easy grin again. "I like the older ships. They have the elegance of simplicity. The newer ships have more of a modular design, so they don't have the unified style these early models do."

This is interesting, but I'd rather this guy be working on my ship than explaining its history to me.

"The 600 wasn't Ozun Cinar's design, you know. Even though that's what the histories say. All the videos show Ozun in the lab supposedly working on the prototype C-600. And lots of video of the roll-out of the first C-600. You've doubtless seen them. Old Ozun Cinar and his whole team standing in front of the factory in Pica with the first C-600 behind them. But there's one person not in any of those videos: Mera Reigel."

"You know about Reigel?" Basil asked, reluctant to continue the conversation, but interested despite himself. "Wasn't Reigel responsible for the advanced Istan cycle that made 2X speeds possible?"

The tech nodded. "He was. That engine and the 600's modular design were revolutionary. It wasn't long until Cinar had 80 percent market share, maybe more. They dominated the industry until the alliance of trading companies financed the rebuild facilities here on Nokendai. We now provide rebuilt ships significantly cheaper than new Cinar ships." The gee field came up smoothly as they entered the office. "Our market share is likely to increase since Naru nationalized Cinar." He shrugged again. "Cinar's a different company now. Same name, but…"

"Whatever happened to Reigel?" Basil wondered.

"Want some tea?"

They sat drinking strong tea in the dusty customer lounge with its spectacular view of the huge dull-orange sphere of a ship's hull outside in vacuum.

"Reigel was originally from Beria," Basil said. "Became head of the Continuum Physics Department at Gerash Institute…"

"Until Cinar hired him."

"Wonder why he left the Institute? I never got the impression money was much of an incentive for him."

The tech looked thoughtful. "I think he went to work for Cinar because he wanted to see his concepts turned into reality. Only a full-scale shipyard has the money to do that."

Basil finished his tea. "Speaking of Reigel and continuum physics, there's a question that's been in my mind for a while, ever since an incident in lightspace not long ago. I was on a ship when something passed us at incredible speeds, maybe 10X. So fast our instruments could barely track it. But it was real; it just about did us in…"

The tech grinned. "I've heard that rumor. But I can tell you that an Istan cycle engine is not capable of that speed regardless of how small a ship it is driving. I'm not a physicist, but I know Istan engines inside and out. It is just not possible."

"Even with some kind of improved fuel?"

"Not possible," the supervisor said. They exchanged bows. "The office will keep you updated on our progress."

Chapter 9

In one of the small city centers that made up Nokendai City, Demaris stopped in front of the PAE employment office. She half-heartedly perused the flickering display of positions currently being advertised for hire. After a time, she sighed and walked to a sidewalk café with bright white umbrellas and tiny red metal tables, each with a spray of tiny yellow flowers in a black vase. She ordered a coffee.

All my savings gone.

Not Basil's fault, she cautioned herself. *Just bad luck.* But she could not make herself believe that. Not entirely. *He's just too cautious.*

The coffee was hot and sharp.

I'll complete this trip with Basil, but once we get back to Sigma, I'm going to find a different position.

She had just ordered another coffee and happened to be staring straight at the front doors of the PAE offices. The doors opened and a tall man in a gray suit came out and stood for a moment. He turned right and took a step, then turned back to look directly at Demaris.

Demaris sighed, her frown deepening, as the man made his way to her table and sat down.

"Ser Shuard," she said.

"Demaris."

He ordered a coffee and they sat silently for a moment.

"What do you think you are doing?" he asked.

"I need a career change; something other than Talus."

He snorted. "Dramatic way to make your exit. Impolite, to say the least. I was under the impression you enjoyed your work in Special Projects."

"It's not what I want long-term."

He leaned toward her. "You are under a certain obligation, you know."

She looked around at the people passing in the pale sunlight.

"That's part of the reason I need a change…"

"And the reason you should not be making changes without consulting me…"

"You're not…" she shook her head. "Alright."

He smiled a practiced smile. "There are two Talus boxes of equipment to go to Karaghia. It's been waiting four weeks. Too small a cargo to divert a ship to deliver it. Schedules are in disarray since the Tiran difficulties began. You could take those boxes to Karaghia. For pay, of course."

"Our ship is in for repairs. We can't do anything for a while."

"I'm aware of that," Shuard said. "I was at that same shipyard to finalize payment on the armament upgrades on Talus' two leased 800s. While I was there I was told your ship will be repaired soon."

"You're going to hire contract crews from PAE for the 800s?"

Shuard ignored her question. "When your ship is repaired, I'll pay you to deliver two Talus boxes to Karaghia."

"To what do I owe this favor?"

Shuard made a deprecating gesture. "I know a bit about your situation. The ever-generous Thelis has provided you with two boxes of machine tools for Karaghia, and has made arrangements for you to received ten boxes of ora at Karaghia which you will deliver to Tiran. A nice set of starting contracts for a newly independent trader. But now you have a repair bill to pay, and possible delay charges. Two boxes from here to Karaghia could neatly compensate you for your repairs without disrupting your planned trip."

Demaris began carefully rearranging the yellow flowers on the table.

"Anything we should know about these two boxes?"

"Nothing at all." He smiled.

"I don't like being obligated…" Demaris did not meet his eyes.

He held up a hand. "Don't consider it an obligation, consider it the rule of hospitality. When a person is stranded in the wilds, local residents are obligated to offer assistance, since at some future time they might be the one needing help. Give me a minute to draft a standard contract." He opened the virtual display on his com and flexed his fingers in the field. "The yard told me your repairs should be complete in four days. I'll arrange for the local freight forwarder to load those two boxes when your ship is back at the cargo portal."

This guy could talk his way into anything. He's found out our leased ship is being repaired and conveniently has a profitable deal for us…

"And I've included your payment, up-front," Shuard said, closing his com.

Demaris keyed her wristcom and studied the contract for a moment, then closed the display. "Alright, but I need to talk to Basil…"

"Of course. Though perhaps it might be more tactful if I met with Basil."

Demaris's frown deepened. "Why?"

"I want to be assured you are both fully agreed on this arrangement.

Demaris sighed again. "You don't trust me to talk to him?"

"I am quite sure you could convince any man…"

She shook her head and looked away. "Where shall I ask him to meet you?"

"Say nothing to him. I will contact him."

That evening Basil walked through the after-work crowd and up the hill to the house. He stopped at a bread shop and bought two small loaves of something the man behind the counter called "Parment." By the time he got to the house, it was much colder.

He poured himself a glass of wine. The door chimed.

It was Demaris.

"Come in," Basil said, surprised, relieved, and more than a little angered.

She had her travel bag. Without saying anything, she located the bedroom, deposited her bag, and came back to admire the view of the bay. Demaris took his hand. "I'm sorry about…what's been happening. Can we put it behind us?"

Basil took down another glass, poured wine in it, and handed it to Demaris. "Yes, we can. I want to. The shipyard says that the repairs won't take more than five days," Basil said. "Probably cost around ten thousand."

Demaris set her wine aside. "Basil, I'm sorry I snapped at you during the approach to the gate. I thought I was right, you thought you were right. But…" she stood and paced around the room, "…a ship should only have one captain. That's the way it has always been. And for a reason. If decisions have to be made fast, someone has to have authority to make them, overruling everyone else. I know that, you know that, but we…"

"I thought it best…" Basil began, but Demaris shook her head. "Hear me out. Back at the gate, either option could have worked. You chose one. I didn't agree. We are partners in the lease. So I suggest we alternate being captain. I'll be captain from here to Karaghia and on to Tiran. You be captain from Tiran to Sigma."

Basil studied his wine for a moment. "Agreed." Then he smiled and raised a toast. "Let's drink to the good ship *Duino*, and a successful voyage."

They toasted, and she smiled and sat down beside him. Basil kissed her, then poured their glasses full. "Shall we go eat dinner?"

• • •

Basil and Demaris walked arm in arm down the tree-lined street. The restaurant had been uncrowded, the food good.

"I could live here," Basil said.

"No you couldn't. You'd soon be bored. I know I would be," said Demaris.

"We're not going to be driving ships our whole life," Basil replied.

"Maybe, but we don't need to retire already."

"That house there, for instance." Basil pointed at a neat little lavender and pink house with sculpted foliage and a low white stone wall. The corner of a deck and pergola were visible in the backyard. "Cash out our lease, buy a house like that…" They walked on.

"And do what?" asked Demaris, eyebrows raised skeptically.

"Use it as a home base, while we take single trip contracts with PAE or one of the other firms handling professional services contracts. They'd offer us a job in a minute; we know ships and we know trade."

"No, thanks." Demaris smiled. "I want to work for myself, not someone else. Make my own deals. Someday I plan to own a ship."

They paused to examine a small green stone statue at the corner of the park. There seemed to be one in every park, the faces different, but the expressions somehow similar.

"Let's drink a cup of tea in that tea shop."

They sat at a table watching pedestrians passing in the foggy night. "Sometimes, the things we want change," Basil said.

"I've always wanted to drive ships, travel between the stars," Demaris said rather defensively. "Though at the same time I also want…" She paused.

"Want what?" he prompted.

"And what do you want, Basil?"

"Just this," Basil said. "Moments like this. That's what The Way teaches: live in the moment. Surprisingly hard to do."

Silence fell.

"Tell me about yourself, Basil. I don't even know where you're from."

He smiled. "That's considered bad manners in the culture I was raised in—to ask or tell about one's family or birthplace. But, since then, I have learned that in other cultures it is considered bad manners not to ask. The place I grew up, the first place I remember, doesn't exist anymore," Basil said. "It's no longer there, and it's impossible to describe in ways that people can understand."

"Sounds mysterious."

He shook his head. "It's not. Quite the opposite, in fact." He looked at their empty teacups. "But I'd rather not discuss me right now. If you are ready, I'm ready to go home. But first I need to run a quick errand." Basil stepped across to a flower shop and returned with a closed yellow bag.

Demaris said nothing as they walked arm in arm up the street to their tiny rented house.

The house felt warm and good after the night air. Basil dialed the drapes back to let in the spectacular sweep of lights around the curve of the bay. The view filled him with a wistful longing for something he could not name. He took Demaris's arm and walked her to the transparent wall. "I like it here. I like it here with you."

She turned away. "It is nice, but it isn't our lives, Basil. We need to be on a ship, making our mark, before it's too late. Accomplish something before all our time has passed. Do you understand?" She turned away from him then, but when she turned back, she was all smiles. "Now what's in that bag you are so secretive about?"

The lights of the glittering platforms in the bay sparkled pale pink, green, blue, amethyst. "I have something for you," Basil said.

He opened the bag he had been carrying and brought forth a bouquet of pale-orange flowers.

She found a tall green vase for them and put it in the center of the bare wood table. "Lovely."

He put his arms around her. Later they made love with the bedroom drapes open and the lights of the city glowing in the fog outside.

Later Basil woke. *Things are getting better. Or are they just getting more complicated?*

• • •

The next day, as Basil was exiting the train at the city center, he heard someone call his name from one of the sidewalk cafés.

"Ser Ajami!" It was Shuard, looking confident and prosperous as always. He was in Talus dress uniform.

"Ser Shuard," Basil said. They bowed to each other. Basil resolved once again to spend whatever it took to get a uniform as beautifully tailored as Shuard's.

"It's nearly lunchtime," Shuard said. "Could I persuade you to join me?"

"With pleasure."

"Perhaps someplace a little quieter." They made their way to the top of a glass and obsidian tower with a spectacular view of the city and the bay. Basil shuddered at the prices on the holographic menu above the tabletop.

"We'll have a bottle of Ocaura," Shuard told the waiter.

The waiter poured a little of the gold wine into two fragile-looking crystal glasses.

"Raid and trade," Shuard said, raising his glass.

"Raid and trade."

Basil felt himself buoyed by the glory of all that was around him, the view, the food, the wine, and Shuard's bonhomie.

"What brings you to Nokendai?" Basil asked.

Shuard made a small shrug. "Some armaments upgrades on our leased ships. These are unsettled times." He raised his glass to Basil. "I congratulate you on your venture. It takes courage to go independent."

Basil smiled, proud and pleased. "We are trying. But our first venture has not gone well. That's why we are here. Repairs."

"Not many people have the guts and the initiative to step out of the security of a big company," Shuard continued. "But you have. I sometimes think of pursuing that path myself."

"Well, I miss all of the people I knew at Talus, "Basil said. "But I wanted to try being an independent. Before too many years have passed."

Shuard leaned forward almost conspiratorially. "Your timing is good. Things are changing, and that's usually when opportunities are greatest. Most people only think of the negative aspects of the current situation, the embargo on Tiran which will affect trade in many areas…"

Their meals were served, rice and tiny grilled fish on sticks with small sliced blocks of blue-green seaweed.

Dessert was a chocolate and cream confection light as air. A waiter poured the last of the wine into Basil's glass. In the distance white and blue sailboats heeled around the island in the bay.

"Cargos to and from Tiran may not be…trouble-free," Shuard said slowly. "Particularly for the big firms. But my belief is that neither Devir's regime, nor the government in exile, nor what's left of the Ramath Defense Force, will try very hard to stop independent traders from crossing the blockade. It's to everyone's advantage to maintain some trade."

"I always thought you favored the royalist government." The wine had loosened Basil's tongue.

"I believe Lord Kaleege to be an intelligent leader, but I feel he was unable to effect change under the Ziani regime." Shuard chuckled. "The revolution pushed him off Tiran, but I don't rule him out quite yet. In the euphoria of revolution, people on Tiran tended to forget all the good things the Five Families did for Tiran. Two hundred years of steady economic expansion may not be colorful, but people's standards of living improved ten-fold. You're an economist, you know what I'm talking about."

"By most reports, the Imperial regime had gotten rather repressive," Basil said. "The people wanted choice…" Basil began.

"Did they? I submit to you that the people of Tiran wanted direction and stability, not choice. Devir gives them stability and Naru gives them direction." Shuard held up his hand. "Sorry to lecture." He smiled at Basil. "I've enjoyed our conversation, but I must be on my way."

They walked to the elevator and waited, facing a precipitous view down to the street below.

"By the way," Shuard said, "while you are here on Nokendai, I'd consider it a favor to me if you'd give this some thought: we have two boxes here on Nokendai, waiting to be transported to Karaghia. But no Talus ships are scheduled to come here for quite some time. I could arrange to have you paid a simple flat fee, a one-way contract—which might neatly compensate you for the cost of your repairs. Step over here for a moment." Shuard had his com out.

Basil felt his com activate.

"I've sent you the contract," Shuard said. "I know this is happening very fast, but…"

Basil pulled up the contract on his com as a holograph, skimmed it quickly, and nodded. "I accept."

"Fast thinking," Shuard said. "I like that. And I like working with people I fully trust. Information and trust are the two most valuable commodities in the marketplace."

They rode the elevator down, and Shuard bowed and disappeared into the crowd.

• • •

With the repairs completed, Basil activated the loading program for the two boxes Shuard promised. The hold doors were open, the rollaways extended, but the first box did not move. "Inconsistency between the box seal and the manifest," the AI intoned. Basil re-entered the Talus cargo seal code, but the yellow light remained lit. "What's the problem?" Basil queried the AI. "Cannot recognize the cargo box code."

The com clicked. "Basil, we need those boxes secure so we can depart," Demaris said.

"I'm working on it." Basil re-entered the Talus cargo code. The lights remained yellow.

"We only have fifteen minutes left in our departure window."

Basil entered an override code, the lights turned green, and the boxes trundled aboard. *I'll figure this out while we are en route.*

Once the tie-down lights were all green, he hurried up to the control room. Demaris was in the pilot seat. The big board showed the automated departure sequence had already been activated. Basil settled into the nav seat and activated his buffers.

"By the way," Demaris said as they watched the automated departure on the big board, "Shuard has already credited our account for the contract, and I paid the refit bill. We're paid-up."

"Any customs or export duties?"

"The boxes had already been cleared when I filed our departure request."

Duino proceeded smoothly down the departure lane.

Chapter 10

The *Duino* flowed through lightspace en route from Nokendai Gate to Karaghia Gate, a short voyage. Basil sat in the control chair rubbing his thumb along the black plastic edge of the control board. He was smiling.

My ship.

Demaris appeared; Basil transferred control to her.

"All quiet," he said. "That was good luck, running into Shuard, wasn't it?"

Demaris studied her screen. "Luck, yes." Her tawny hair sheened in the subdued light.

"You don't seem very excited," Basil said.

"We need the revenue," she said, eyes still on her control screens. "But the sooner we get the boxes delivered, the better."

"You think there's a problem with the cargo?"

She shrugged. "The documentation is weak."

"Karaghia doesn't inspect, and besides…"

"What's this in the log?" Demaris interrupted.

"AI identified something in lightspace about four hours ago."

Demaris read, "A 20 percent probable sighting of something… unidentifiable." She looked at Basil, eyebrows raised. "You're going to leave that in the log?"

"That's what the regs say we are supposed to do."

"What is Etir Leasing going to do with it? I don't want to waste time having to make formal statements for the security people once we return to Sigma."

"You won't. This kind of stuff is AI-scanned each docking, and extracts are sent to Gerash Institute. They are trying to better understand how lightspace works."

"You should get some rest before we get to Karaghia. We've only got two days scheduled to off-load four boxes and on-load ten."

Basil hesitated, then nodded. "You're right."

He went below, but not to the master's cabin. Instead, he drew a beer and sat in the wardroom and read from Gerash Institute's current research-in-progress postings. Mention of *Tawli*'s near miss with a fast-moving object in lightspace was there. But just a mention, no theoretical explanation. Reading down the list of papers and theories, he found someone speculating that a faster lightspace drive could have produced the waveform seen in recordings for *Tawli*, but another researcher proved it wrong. There was nothing definitive.

Basil clicked the screen off and retired to the master's cabin and sleep.

"We have ten hours until we exit the gate at Karaghia; let's share a meal together. We haven't really celebrated the ship lease yet."

To Basil's surprise and delight, Demaris agreed. They turned control over to AI and retired to the wardroom, drank champagne, and had a premium meal. Buoyed by Demaris's smile and the wine, Basil launched into a long monologue about Mera Reigel. "He became the most distinguished continuum physics researcher of his generation. His theory 'Intersections of Realities' was a breakthrough in understanding the physical laws governing lightspace. Ships have been traveling through gates ever since mankind had spread through the Curve. But most of what was known about gates was empirical knowledge accumulated by unmanned probes, a few brave, or lucky, ship's captains taking their ships into gates, and by years of research on the ancient Kogon documents that describe gates."

Demaris lay back on the wardroom sofa, looking very queenly. Basil talked on. "Mera Reigel was the first researcher to develop a mathematical description of the conditions inside a gate. Which allowed for the calibration of gates, the maintenance of gates, and the design of efficient and safe entrance and exit courses. Reigel was awarded an Emperor's Prize First Class at age twenty-nine. He refined his discoveries in the succeeding ten years, then suddenly withdrew from Gerash and disappeared. The official history was that he had elected to withdraw from Gerash and take up a new life in accordance with Chumon custom. After the revolution on Tiran, the Devir government incorporated Gerash Institute into the Imperial Tiran education system, but Reigel did not reappear in the new organization…sorry, I'm talking too much."

Demaris was snoring softly.

Basil woke her gently and kissed her. She kissed him back. They made love courteously and slept soundly.

His next shift, alone in the control room, Basil opened a screen and rechecked cargo documentation. *I should have asked for proper documentation, but I didn't want to jeopardize Shuard's arrangement.* Basil opened the RDF official site and found nothing about increased cargo inspections, and nothing on the official Tiran site, but the royalist government in exile on Orane had an unusual announcement. "Continued weapons development and deployment by the revolutionary forces occupying Tiran force the legitimate government of Tiran to take extraordinary measures."

No idea what that means.

Duino exited the Karaghia Gate with Basil at the command console, Demaris at the weapons console, and sensors fully extended. After a few moments, Demaris said, "No ships detected."

Basil congratulated himself on *Duino*'s near-perfect exit. Fuel use would be less than calculated. It only took AI a few moments to get *Duino* locked into the correct course for the Karaghia elevator.

Two days later, *Duino* was within visual distance of the Karaghia elevator head. The structure was a dark hulk against the soft avocado and ocher curve of Karaghia.

"No word from approach control," Demaris muttered.

"Elevator is inoperative, no approach control. We contact Ambai Company direct…"

"Elevator inop?" Demaris fumed. "When did you find this out?"

"It's been inoperative for a long time…"

"And you didn't have the courtesy to mention it to me before now?"

"It's in the mission plan," Basil said lamely.

"AI, do a manual docking at the elevator," Basil said. He put a pictorial of the elevator head on the screen. "Twelve docks. Appears to be something in vacuum outside one of the docks."

Demaris pulled the gunsights down. "The gunsights show those masses unarmed and with no propulsion units," Demaris said. "Cargo boxes."

The docking sequence lights flashed; the board cleared to green.

Basil set the external com on the settings for Karaghia elevator head docking and announced, "Independent trader *Duino*, with cargo for Ambai Company."

"Yonna Ble. Ambai Company."

"We have four boxes of machine tools for you, two from Sigma and two from Nokendai."

"We are prepared to receive your freight and provide you ten containers of ora." Basil nodded at Demaris. "We have positioned your first two boxes near the elevator head. Can you see them?"

"Yes, ser Ble."

"The orbital shuttle will be able to make two trips up to you per shift."

Demaris put a calculation up on the big board. Four shifts to off-load four boxes and load ten boxes.

"You can do a manual vacuum transfer, can't you?" Ble inquired.

"Yes. Our holds two and four have multi-purpose receiving tracks. Max box size and mass for our internal equipment is category two."

"As are our boxes," Ble affirmed.

"Standby." Basil put the com on mute. "Dem, if you'll take over the command console, I'm going down to cargo to move two boxes out of hold one so we can move his two boxes in."

On the cargo level, Basil suited up and snapped the master cargo control remote onto his vacuum suit, then opened one hold door and exited into vacuum.

Dem's voice came onto his com. "Ble wants those two boxes from Nokendai set aside. Left at the elevator head…"

"Why? They are in hold one. It's more efficient to move them over to the shuttle first. Just a minute." Basil worked the controls on his suit's remote. "See if you can get Ble to change his mind."

"He's signed off. Said he would be unavailable for the rest of this shift."

There was silence for a moment.

"You could ignore his request," Demaris said. "Send the Shuard boxes down to the surface anyway…"

"I don't want to irritate him. He might start delaying moving ora up to us…"

"It's your call. I see the shuttle approaching."

"Then I need to focus on getting these boxes rearranged."

"One more thing. Ble said he wanted his ten boxes of ora loaded in a certain order—I put it on your screen—the order in which he is delivering the boxes to us."

"Damn! This guy might as well take over as cargomaster!" Basil took a deep breath. "But I don't think we have any choice."

"I don't trust this abandoned elevator we are sidled up to," said Demaris. "Who knows what's in it?"

"I need to get to work," Basil said.

Four shifts later, the *Duino* was loaded and moving down the departure lane toward the Karaghia Gate entrance.

At shift change, Basil waited while Demaris checked ship status.

"Everything's fine," Basil told her. "We are on course and schedule."

She meticulously went through the entire checklist. Basil waited.

"Is there something else?" Demaris said.

Basil looked at the worn texture on the deck. "I feel like I never see you anymore. We could let AI drive for a couple of hours…" Demaris was shaking her head. "Not a good idea. In any case, my off-shift, I'm in the middle of some important game transactions."

Basil was surprised. "Alternate universe? I didn't know you liked that AU stuff."

Demaris gave him a sardonic smile. At the companionway, she turned. "You're unhappy I spend time in AU?"

"A little surprised, that's all. I guess I always assumed people who got involved in games were unhappy with their lives."

"And you think I'm unhappy?"

He tilted his head. “I hope not.”

“I’ve played in AU since I was a kid,” Demaris said. “When I was a kid, we lived on Delta, Mother and me. I had a lot of free time…I learned to like AU.”

She shook her head to end the conversation.

Chapter 11

Duino exited the Tiran Gate into realspace and took her place in the approach lane. A day later they were docked at the Tiran elevator head.

Basil hugged Demaris. "Off-load our cargo, load boxes, and be on our way to Sigma. I've already checked the freight forwarder's inventory and they've got stuff waiting to go to Sigma. Should be out of here in two or three days."

But it didn't happen that way.

• • •

The Tiranian woman in a stylish uniform was very polite. "There is apparently an error in your import." She withdrew to the manager's desk at the back of the room to consult. Basil sat down to wait; forty minutes went by.

Finally, Basil was ushered into a tiny cubicle, given the guest chair, and tea was brought. The translator from the information desk helped him through the long conversation that followed. Various documents were viewed and regulations were referenced, none of which seemed to be what was needed to clear their cargo through customs.

Basil didn't want to leave the room until this was resolved, but he wanted desperately to tell Demaris to stop the ora off-load.

Basil tried to call, but his com just gave him the recorded message that all non-local com was proscribed. He excused himself and stepped into a public com zone, which finally connected him with *Duino*. "Stop the off-load."

"There's only one box left," Demaris said. "And it's already moving…in fact, it's gone. What's the problem?"

Basil winced. "Something's wrong with our customs clearance. I can't tell yet, but I think customs is going to impound the cargo. For reasons I can't…"

"There are some officials here at the ship now," Demaris told him.

"What?"

"They want me to talk to them." She clicked off.

"Damn!" Basil muttered.

He went back to the cubicle, but it was now empty. He stood looking around the room full of desks in neat rows, women in neat uniforms, all industriously busy.

He decided to return to the ship.

He found Demaris alone in the control room. "What did the customs people tell you?"

"They cited several regulations I've never heard of. Something about our route…"

"Did they say what we needed to do to get this resolved?"

Demaris stood up. "Do you think I'd be sitting here if they'd told me what we needed to do?"

With some effort, Basil contained his anger.

"Are they coming back, or do we need to go to customs?"

"I have no idea," Demaris said and stomped off down the companionway.

Basil went to the wardroom, drew a beer, and returned to the control room. *I'm going to assume we'll get this straightened out tomorrow, and can start loading cargo to Sigma.* He opened the Ajisai Company portal on the big board, expecting to see lists of cargo, but instead found himself looking at an intense-looking young woman with very short silver hair. She smiled. "Looking for outbound cargo?"

"Your lot twenty-two to Sigma," Basil said. "What's the delivery date? We might be interested."

"It's not a rush delivery. Four weeks from now." She worked a com. "You're on *Duino*, aren't you?"

"Yes. How did you know? We're unscheduled."

She grinned at him. Her eyes were large and dark.

A window appeared on Basil's screen. "Pay us the fee, and I can let you have these five boxes on consignment. And I'll need about a day's advance notice for customs and to schedule the loading."

Basil did another calculation. "We don't have our cargo delivery payment yet, so I can't make the payment…"

"Let me guess. Your inbound ora is impounded?" She laughed.

Basil bristled. "We're still discussing…anyway, yes, that's the situation. I have no idea why."

Her expression turned serious. "I hate to tell you this, but unless they clear it right through, it's probably never going to be cleared."

"Why? We met all the compliance regs posted on the net."

"That doesn't mean much these days." She studied another screen for a moment. "My guess is that they are unhappy with your stop at Nokendai. They think it is a possible source of contraband weapons. Ora is not the issue. They badly need ora—look at the spot prices—but the revolutionary government is not allowing any trade with any companies sympathetic to the Five Families. And lots of companies on Nokendai are."

"What can we do?"

She shrugged. "Why don't you think about the outbound boxes I mentioned. I'll see if I can think of anything to do about your impounded ora. By the way, my name is Ria."

The next morning, Basil was in control playing with the numbers for the boxes Ajisai had offered. A sullen Demaris came up the companionway, coffee in hand. "If you'd do something other than just sit and think, we might get our cargo out of impound," Demaris fumed. "At least find us an outbound cargo while we're stuck here. You're the econ expert."

"Thanks for your insightful advice."

Lips pursed, she went below.

Another shift went by, and their inbound cargo was still impounded, despite several visits to the customs office. "We could leave the cargo, let Ajisai work it out with customs. It's been done before," Basil said.

"And go back to Sigma empty? And without payment on the ora we brought here? No, thanks." Demaris turned the big board to local pulsecasts.

"Better than sitting here letting docking fees eat us up," Basil muttered. "Maybe we can get an outbound cargo from Ajisai with deferred payment. Leave the ora here as collateral."

"You spend a lot of time talking to Ajisai. Why is that?" Demaris asked.

Basil's pulse started pounding.

"The freight forwarders might give us a hint of how to get our cargo through customs."

"That's highly unlikely." Demaris turned the pulsecast off with a sigh. "I'm going to go talk to the dockside people again," she announced and stormed down the companionway.

Basil sat in the command seat sipping cold tea and trying to control his anger. He called Ria at Ajisai and offered to take the five boxes to Sigma if she would waive the fee until they were delivered at Sigma when Talus could pay the shipping fee. "Ajisai can hold the boxes we have in customs as collateral."

"I'll do better than that. Your boxes are clearing customs now. I'll take your export fee out of that payment."

"How did you…?"

Ria put her com on private mode. "I work with these people every day. And tell your shipmate, what's her name, Demaris, to stay out of dockside business. Her interference and her bad attitude are not helpful."

The five boxes were loaded by shift-end. Basil sealed up the holds, authorized the customs documents Ria sent him, authorized payments to and from Talus, and received a departure clearance in less than an hour.

Basil and Demaris didn't speak to each other except to acknowledge shift change for the trip to the Tiran Gate, through lightspace and two days in realspace after exiting the gate at Sigma.

At the last shift change before docking at Sigma Station, Demaris gave up the command chair to Basil and seated herself at the nav station. "We have better options than taking the scraps the freight forwarders give us," she said tightly.

"We will make a profit on this trip. A slim one."

"Just by chance."

"It takes time to build our contacts in the Tiran bureaucracy…"

"Too much time," Demaris growled. "And…depending on the freight forwarder, to deal with Tiran is risky. If we're going to depend on station-side people all the time, we might as well wet-lease. That way we have no responsibilities other than to get the ship from point A to point B."

"Wet-lease profit margins are less than one percent," Basil countered.

Demaris faced away from him.

"What do you suggest?" Basil said in what he hoped was a conciliatory tone.

She waved a screen to life. It showed a montage of black and red Tiran revolutionary flags, martial music, the determined faces of Tiran workers, the patrician face of Devir himself speaking to an ecstatic audience of thousands. Then a letter of marque faded in, the red and black Tiran revolutionary emblem at the top, Devir's stylish stamp at the bottom. The ship requirements and the compensation scrolled by. Demaris read it aloud. "Ten thousand per month with a bonus for intercepts, and a percent of salvage."

"Salvage! That's a nice word for stealing other people's cargos," Basil snapped. "And eventually getting blown up for Devir's little dictatorship? No thanks. Also, there's the little matter of violating our lease."

"Etir isn't going to care as long as we make our payments and show them some sort of trade log, no matter how fictional."

"Pirate careers are usually pretty short."

"Privateering is different," Demaris said, her voice rising. "You're the history buff—think about the Okun raiders and Andric's group…"

"History is written by the winners, so I'm sure Okun and Andric carefully tailored their stories to omit anything that didn't make good propaganda."

Basil waved on another screen; orange and blue rows of numbers glowed in the air. "Here are the aggregate numbers on shipping to and from Tiran, this year and last year. On the right side is available shipping capacity…"

Demaris surged out of the nav station chair. "Basil, you don't get it!" She slapped the top of the console. "I don't want to scrape by on 5 percent margins. I'm beginning to think I made a big mistake here." She huffed out of the control room.

Basil sat in the command chair savoring the silence of the control room. He waved the big board to the starscape around the ship and sat admiring its cold beauty for some time.

He called up a calculation. They'd be out of money and fuel when they reached Sigma. The payment for delivery of the boxes would cover their trip costs. Basil brought up the lease: a 10 percent early cancellation charge, but maybe he could get Etir to waive it.

Time to start scrambling for a cargo, or call Etir and cancel the lease. I can't single-hand, and I'm not going out with Demaris again. Ever. Hire a crew through JCO, the body shop? Basil opened the JCO portal and started looking through crew resumes, but soon quit. *With no spare cash, any cargos I can find would have to be low-risk which means low-profit margins, which don't interest the better crew people. And hired crew salary would eat up a good bit of the profits. I'd be working hard just to pay the lease payments. And doing it with a crew I don't know and can't trust.*

He got the Etir Yard on the com and initiated the lease cancellation procedure.

"You'd have to do that in person, sir," the Etir AI told him.

After docking, Basil handled the cargo off-load himself, no sign of Demaris anywhere. Then Basil put on a clean shipsuit and went to the Etir office.

He was directed to a small, bare office. A woman in a severe suit with an Etir collar pin greeted him with a perfunctory bow.

With a brusque air she went through the terms of the cancellation, confirmed Basil's identification. A moment later, the virtual scene of prairie wildflowers gave way to the document outlining all terms and charges.

Basil read through it. "Can we talk about the cleaning fee? I'm running out of money."

She zeroed the amount. "How's that?"

"Thank you." Basil nodded. "Fine. Agreed. The *Duino* is at dock 42. Shall I move…?"

"No. We'll handle that. Can you and your crew have all your personal items and electronic files out of the ship by end of this shift?"

"Yes."

"You realize your deposit has been factored into the fees? There's no money left to pay out. Sorry."

Basil nodded.

"Good day, ser Ajami." She stood.

"I wish things…" Basil said as he slowly got to his feet.

"These things happen," she said with a wintery smile. "Better luck next time."

Basil returned to the ship and moved his electronic files to his storage site, then went to the first officer's cabin and collected his few belongings into a ship bag. He checked that Demaris had cleared her own electronics. She had. He glanced in the empty master's suite, and then logged himself out for the last time and walked down the ramp to the main floor of the cargo level. He chose a box-hotel at random and checked into a cubicle just big enough for toilet and bunk. He left his bag on the bunk and went to the bar next door and drank two beers in quick succession.

He felt numb.

After a while, he bought two more beers and took them back to his hotel. His cubicle was well insulated—absolutely silent. He put some familiar music on his com and lay there sipping a beer and staring at the ceiling and thinking of nothing.

Eventually he slept.

Chapter 12

"You don't make my life easy, you know, running off to play independent." Thelis cleared papers off the one guest chair in his office and motioned Basil to sit down.

"Nice to see you too, Thelis," Basil said.

"Now you want your old job back, and an immediate assignment."

"Right and right," Basil said with his most engaging smile. "I submitted a reapplication yesterday..."

Thelis neatened a stack of papers then studied one of his displays. "The company is under some pressure right now."

Basil tensed. "Oh?"

Thelis's fingers flexed, and orange lines of data glowed in the air. "Take a look at this. In the last ten months, Talus shares are off almost 10 percent." Another graph superimposed itself on the first. "Here are spot fuel prices for the same period. Up almost 100 percent."

"We're not hedging?" asked Basil.

"Yes, but we didn't expect the Tiran situation to get this bad this fast. The front office is minimizing low-margin high-risk projects and asking everyone to take a voluntary salary reduction. The senior captains are really unhappy. Their push-back is a work slowdown.

Which makes the situation worse." Thelis smiled. "Except for the junior officers who are now getting assigned as captains on low-cost, low-risk trips."

Basil continued trying to look sympathetic.

Thelis handed him a flexcom. "You may not like this, but here's my suggestion."

"JCO?" Basil said. "They're a body shop."

"But they've got slots right now. Good slots."

The slot Thelis had highlighted was cargomaster position on a ship called *Khios*, Sigma to Nokendai and back. "You submitted my name?"

Thelis lit a dark-brown long-life cigarillo. "I figured you'd be coming to see me. When your reapplication hit our system, I just cross-filed it with JCO. They keep their lists active against our roster. That offer is open right now."

"Know anything about *Khios*?" Basil squinted at the flexcom. "Or Captain Tage?"

Data appeared in the air, some video behind it, basic ship data superimposed on stock shots of the ship, the official company image of an intense-looking captain in front of the JCO symbol. Public relations stuff. "Go to work for JCO for a while," Thelis said, "then come back and see me."

Cereclo was in the lobby when Basil came out of the elevators.

He slapped Basil on the back. "How about some breakfast?"

They made their way onto the uncrowded concourse. Clouds were moving across the sunny virtual sky. They got on a slideway and went down the concourse to where the tourist shops and the galleries and the flower shops and the tea shops began.

"See Thelis?" Cereclo asked.

"Yeah," Basil said. "No-go."

Cereclo kept his eyes on the shops rolling past. "That's tough."

"There's a JCO slot. A shares run from here to Nokendai. I'll probably take it. Ever heard of a JCO captain named Tage?"

"How about here?" Cereclo steered Basil into a bright green and yellow snack shop.

"Actually I have heard of Tage," Cereclo said after they'd ordered. "Rumors are that he's a hothead, a risk-taker, and that half his trips don't make money.""But I assume the other half of his trips make a lot of money, right?"

Iridescent birds and insects droned and flitted among virtual leaves and flowers.

The pale-orange slices of persimmon were a nice counterpoint to the grilled soy and the sharp fermented vinegar on the strips of asparagus.

"How about you?" Basil said. "What are you doing?"

"Got a shot at a master's assignment. I took the coursework on my own time, which helped. I'm sure Thelis told you about the pay cuts, the senior captains' work slowdown. And also about the company now offering temporary master's assignments to guys like me. Every challenge is an opportunity, right?" Cereclo's ebullience was difficult to take, but Basil kept smiling.

"Keep me in mind," Basil said, "I'm going to take that JCO assignment, but I told Thelis to keep my application for rehire active. As soon as something opens up, I'll be back with Talus."

Cereclo nodded. "Junior officers like me don't always have a free hand in assignments."

"I know, just keep me in mind, alright?"

They finished their tea. Cereclo ran his wristcom over the paypoint and they sauntered out of the tea shop into a gusty wind. Virtual rain was coming.

"Sorry to hear your operation as an independent didn't go so well," Cereclo said, studying the clouds overhead. Basil bowed quickly to keep him from continuing the conversation. "Got to go."

• • •

When Basil went aboard the *Khios*, there was no one at the entry to greet him. He went up to control and found Demaris at the nav station. Basil pushed past a couple of crewmen hovering around her. "What are you doing here?"

She turned an empty smile on him. "Same as you, I imagine. Working." She turned back to her control board. "Now if all of you would get to your stations, I have work to do."

In the companionway a thin man in a rumpled shipsuit approached him. "You Ajami?"

"Yes."

"I'll show you your cabin. Stow your gear and get down to cargo. Captain wants to depart immediately."

Captain Tage turned out to be an intense man of below-average height dressed in a tailored shipsuit with JCO insignia and four seniority stripes. "You Ajami?" he said with a swift, bright glance.

"Yes. Basil Ajami, Econ…

"Get this cargo loaded and tied down. I'm departing as soon as I see the cargo indicators go green." He turned and was gone, leaving two crewmen looking at Basil with passive expressions. "What's the problem?" Basil asked.

The two looked so much alike they could have been twins. "Last couple of boxes don't fit," one of them said, waving his hand at the cargo management instruments.

It didn't take Basil long to determine that two class A boxes had been placed in class C tie-downs.

With the lackadaisical help of the twins, he soon had the boxes rearranged, tied down correctly, and both cargo loading ports secured. The cargo management board showed both holds full to capacity with cargo boxes.

The departure alert sounded, and Basil went to his tiny cubicle. *I'll just work my shifts, keep to myself, and get this voyage over with.*

Four days of realspace travel passed uneventfully as did the gate entrance, then four days in lightspace. Basil never left the cargo deck, except to sleep. As the days passed, he met each of the three crewmembers. The slim man he'd met when he first came aboard didn't want to talk. "Born and raised on Sigma. Not much else to tell."

But the twins talked endlessly, mostly complaints, about the trade situation, and about Captain Tage and the way he ran the *Khios*.

"In port we work back-to back-shifts," one of the twins said. Basil had learned one was named Vin, but he could never tell which one was which.

"So no time off while we're in port," the other twin said.

"Tage wants top efficiency ratings and usually gets them. But we don't benefit…"

"So, you probably get good bonuses, right?" Basil asked.

"The minimum allowed by union agreement."

"Why don't you transfer to another ship?" Basil asked.

The twins shrugged so identically that Basil almost laughed out loud.

When Basil next came on shift, he found First Officer Kly talking to all three of the crew. Coffee in hand, Basil sauntered over. "Anything I should know?"

Kly, who never seemed to smile, told him, "Union business. Nothing you need to take your time with." Kly pointedly waited until Basil had retreated out of earshot. Basil read through his JCO contract on his com but found no mention of a union.

Later he asked one of the twins what the meeting had been about. "JCO has a union agreement with all permanent employees.

Doesn't apply to officers. The agreement makes the first officer spokesman for the crew."

Basil was amazed. "First officer is crew representative? On all JCO ships?"

"Almost all."

Just after *Khios* exited the Nokendai Gate into realspace, Captain Tage visited the cargo deck.

"I run a tight ship, Ajami. When we dock and are cleared to unload, I want all crew, including you, ready to work back-to-back shifts until all cargo is off, and prepare to immediately start loading cargo. We'll be full going back too."

Tage turned and marched up the companionway.

One of the twins came over. "He says that a lot—runs a tight ship."

They docked, and Basil and all three crewmen worked steadily, off-loading boxes and loading new cargo boxes. The *Khios* was 100 percent full for the return trip.

The departure alert woke Basil from an exhausted sleep. When he went to the cargomaster station, the slim crewman who seldom spoke was on-duty.

"Why didn't you contact me for custom's approval?" Basil groused. "I'm responsible."

"I think the captain took care of that."

"You think?"

"I'm going off-duty now," the man said and departed up the companionway.

Basil checked the ship's log and found *Khios*'s departure and route to the gate entrance had been approved but nothing about customs clearance. "Not that tight a ship," Basil muttered.

A day later, while *Khios* was still in realspace moving toward the Nokendai Gate entrance, Basil came on shift to find Kly at the cargomaster controls.

"We've got a warning signal in one of the air regen units," Kly said.

Basil glanced at the board where Kly had the ship's air-circulating system displayed.

"Filters clogged?"

"No. Air flow is nominal. AI says the most likely source of the air contaminant is one of the cargo boxes. And the crew tells me they think they can smell something."

They haven't said anything to me, Basil thought. Kly looked at Basil expectantly.

"Alright, here's what we'll do. Check each hold one at a time. Put a man in a sealed suit, with a sniffer inside one hold, raise the air pressure in it temporarily until he can get a reading. Or not. Then do the same with the other hold. We'll find out which hold this 'contaminant' is coming from. If there is any."

Kly gave Basil a look, then departed.

Two hours later, Basil, with the lackadaisical help of one of the twins, had determined there was an airborne contaminant source in hold two.

Kly appeared on the cargo deck again, his brow knotted. "Contaminant levels are increasing."

"The hold access door seals leak," Vin volunteered. "And box seals probably leak."

"Reduce air pressure in hold two…" Kly ordered.

"Wait a minute," Basil snapped. "I'm in charge of cargo operations."

"And I'm responsible for crew safety," Kly snapped back.

"Do not reduce hold two air pressure," Basil told Vin. He turned to Kly. "We will need to be in there finding the box with the problem.

Once we find which box, we'll need to open it, so we'll need the lock code from the owners."

"How long will it take you to find it?" Kly asked.

"How the hell should I know! Both holds are 100 percent full. By moving one box at a time as far forward as it will go on the rollers, we should be able to open the box door enough to get a man inside. It's going to be a slow process. I'll need to work the crew overtime."

"Captain won't like it. Overtime costs money."

"Life safety costs money."

Kly departed.

It took a delicate touch, but with the tie-downs released on a row of boxes, the rollers could move one box at a time forward.

The next shift, Kly and Captain Tage were on the cargo deck, and Demaris was on-screen from the control room.

"I've got two crew members in number two hold with the air sniffer," Basil reported. "We've checked eight of twenty boxes. Nothing so far."

"Steadily rising concentration of contaminant in regen air," Kly said. "Crew has filed a protest, unsafe working conditions."

"From now on they will wear shipsuits sealed up using bottled air," Basil countered.

"Which makes work even slower," Kly said.

"What do you suggest?" Basil growled.

Demaris said mildly, "Could we fully depressurize hold two? We would be losing air, but it would keep the contaminant out of the ship's air."

"Maybe," Tage said thoughtfully. "Leak air all the way to Sigma. Any other suggestions?"

Kly said, "An alternative is to go into orbit around the gate, open hold two, extend rollaways, reshuffle boxes…"

"Ridiculous," Basil interjected. "That would take days of vacuum work…"

"Orbiting a gate is hazardous," Dem said mildly. "That's where raiders usually are. And we would be defenseless with a hold open and boxes outside."

"That's enough discussion," Tage said. "Ajami, continue our present procedure." He fixed Basil with a furious stare. "But I want that contaminant found and identified before we enter the gate. I don't want to be dealing with this in lightspace."

Basil worked a full shift with one of the twins, found nothing, and went off-shift. Sixteen boxes checked, four to go. He had just tumbled into his bunk when the com chimed: "All officers to the wardroom." Basil pulled on his rumpled shipsuit, hurried to the wardroom, and found Demaris, Kly, and Tage there, all looking grim."Recording on," Tage said, then turned to Kly with a frosty expression. "You requested this meeting—state your business."

"Request abandon ship order, captain. The crew is unanimous…"

"What?" Basil interjected. "They've said nothing…"

"Quiet!" Tage told him.

Kly continued, "The crew has made a unanimous request that we place the ship in gate orbit and abandon it while the lifeboat with all aboard can still make it back to Nokendai. A trained salvage crew can attend to the contaminated cargo."

Tage turned to Demaris. "What is the situation with the air?"

"Regen air in system two is outside standard parameters, but we are compensating with the other regen unit."

"Request denied," Tage told Kly, then turned to Basil. "Ajami, the company has provided the lock code and they've been transmitted to the cargomaster control board. You will find the contaminated box, open it, and remove the contaminant source this shift. That's an order. Meeting adjourned."

Basil hurried down to the cargo deck and found Vin at the cargomaster control board. “We’ve found the box,” Vin told him, pointing at the display on the screen. “And the nav officer provided these lock codes.”

“You come with me.” Basil started sealing up his shipsuit.

“My shift is over,” Vin complained.

“I’ll authorize overtime. You come with me.”

They entered the hold and slid along box tops to the identified box. The rollers had opened a space about forty centimeters wide between boxes. Basil slid down to the floor and activated the box lock, then swung the door open as far as it would go.

“What does the sniffer read?”

“Reading just went up 400 percent,” Vin said on his com.

After a minute Demaris said, “Nitrates, small amounts of other stuff…”

“Dangerous?”

“Not at these levels.”

The box was nearly full of smaller boxes. Basil waved the sniffer and light around the available space.

Going to be a slow, difficult job trying to get all the stuff inside this box out and examined.

The sniffer reading increased.

“Seems to be coming from the top of the box,” Basil said. The sniffer light illuminated a cylindrical gray object above the top of the door seal. It had been taped in place. There was a number and several Tiran script symbols on it. Basil focused his com camera on it.

“Call Captain Tage, show him what’s on my com camera.”

Demaris answered, “Captain Tage is off-duty.”

“Can you see this on your screen?”

“Yes. What is it?”

“That’s what I’m asking,” Basil said. “Query AI.”

A moment more and Dem came back on general com. "Military. The symbols are Imperial Tiran. AI is analyzing."

A minute later, Dem came back on. "It's a munition. Air analysis indicates it is unstable and out-gassing…"

Vin cut in on general com. "There's a bomb in cargo! Abandon ship!"

"Negative!" boomed Tage. "Stay at your posts. I'm coming to cargo."

Dem said calmly, "AI says it appears to be an old munition, from before the revolution."

Basil saw the wire going from the bomb to the electronic lock on the box door. "Damn! This thing is wired to the box door lock which we opened. Could it be on a timer?"

Basil scrambled up to the top of the box and slid toward the light at the open cargo door. Vin was nowhere in sight.

"Dem, are you still there?" Basil asked.

"Yes. AI says it's unlikely the bomb is on a timer. What is likely is that it is set to explode when the ship docks and all cargo boxes receive the automatic unlock code. When you opened the box door, you disengaged that circuit. Don't close the door!"

Basil slid to his feet at the end of the row of boxes just as Tage and Kly appeared at the cargomaster station.

"Munition in one box," Basil told them. "But I think we've bypassed its firing system. It is deteriorating…"

"You think you've bypassed the firing mechanism?" Kly shouted.

"AI says…"

"Quiet!" Tage said. "Leaving the box door open, we'll proceed to Sigma. The air…"

"Are you crazy?" Kly shouted. "We abandon ship now."

An alarm started blaring. The lifeboat had been activated.

"Who did that?" Tage shouted at Kly.

"Any crewmember is authorized to activate the lifeboat in an emergency."

“I have not declared an emergency!” Tage shouted above the racket.

“I am!” Kly shouted back. He started up the companionway.

“You get in that lifeboat and you’re a mutineer!” Tage shouted.

Kly kept going.

“You’re demoted to crewmember!” Tage shouted up the empty companionway. Tage turned to Basil. “Ajami, I’m putting you in charge of those mutineers. Get on that lifeboat. At Nokendai take them to the JCO Office or Security, I don’t care which. I’m taking this ship to Sigma.”

“I volunteer to stay aboard,” Basil said. “You can’t single-hand her all the way…”

“No, Demaris has already volunteered to stay aboard with me. You’re in charge of the crew. You have good crew relations; now’s the time to use them.”

The lifeboat launch countdown started.

Tage pushed Basil forward. “Go.”

Basil hesitated for a heartbeat, and then bolted up the companionway and scrambled aboard the lifeboat just as the hatches began to close. He slid past occupied stasis pods, tumbled into an empty one, and activated buffers. When the pod’s indicators showed the lifeboat was on course for Nokendai, Basil activated the pod’s stasis field, glad to have his consciousness soothed for the empty hours until they reached Nokendai.

• • •

Basil stumbled off the lifeboat, still groggy from stasis. Four Nokendai security troops in pale-red body armor were there in the over-bright lights of the security arrivals area.

Kly and the three crewmembers were standing in a little knot.

“We could have died on that ship,” Vin snarled at Basil. “Now our shares have been forfeited…”

"We've been cheated, and you're responsible," the other twin said.

"Me?" Basil exploded.

"We are filing charges against JCO, Tage, and you!" Kly added.

"Let's go," one security guard said, waving toward the row of small cubicles. "Individual statements."

When Basil was released, he immediately went to the JCO office and signed a contract release and was credited with the pay he was due.

My contract with JCO is terminated. I have no responsibility for that crew and none to Tage or JCO. I never want to see any of them again.

At the passenger terminal, Basil found there was a ship leaving for Sigma within the hour. "All that's left is a stasis pod," the clerk warned.

"I'll take it," Basil said.

After docking at Sigma Station, Basil found a pulsecast several days old, reporting "The *Khios* Incident." Apparently Demaris and Tage had pushed through to Sigma, parked the ship in the security area, and reported they had found a sabotage device in one box. Tage and Demaris were being hailed as the heroes. There was no mention of the crew or who might have planted the device.

In the immigration scan tunnel, the barriers closed around Basil, and he was shunted to an inspection area where robotics checked his body and his belongings. Two immigration officers then escorted him to a small, windowless room with a table and two chairs.

"What's this all about?"

"We need to ask you some questions," one said as they departed.

Chapter 13

Eventually two men entered the room. One man stood while the other one sat opposite Basil. They told Basil to describe his time aboard *Khios* from the time it departed Sigma for Nokendai until now. It took a long time. He was prompted for details, and occasionally a date or time was corrected by the AI listening in, but eventually his statement was complete enough for the recording being made.

A muscular woman in a gray security uniform entered. The interviewer gave up his chair and left the room; the guard stayed standing behind Basil. The woman and Basil looked at each other for a long time. He'd never seen anyone with so little expression. Maybe her strength enhancements produced this effect, or maybe she used it to intimidate.

"That munition was Tiran Imperial military, more than thirty years old. Our analysis of the triggering device indicates it was intended to explode when the ship docked and boxes were unlocked."

She speared Basil with a look. "You unlocked that box before docking which is what saved the *Khios* and a Sigma West dock. Should we thank you or suspect you of complicity?"

"Complicity?" Basil huffed. "To blow myself up?"

"You may have had a plan to delay the unlocking until you could exit the ship."

"I didn't," Basil said.

She stared at him for a moment more, then stood. "You can go."

In the Talus building, Director Othman walked a short woman to the elevators and bowed politely as she stepped onto one and departed.

"I need thirty minutes without interruption," he told the staff in his outer office.

Then he closed the door to his office and sat looking at the virtual view of waves on an idyllic beach. *The crown prince sent his own personal envoy,* Othman thought. *I must still be held in some regard at Lord Kaleege's court.* Her message had been short: he was to make a Talus ship available at Tiran as soon as possible. At Tiran, it would add special cargo then depart immediately for Sigma.

Othman put the Talus ship schedule up, now in some disarray since he had instructed Operations to honor the RDF embargo. He selected a C-200, the *Rafale*, and wrote the trip outline quickly: Sigma to Karaghia to Tiran and back to Sigma. He glanced at cargo lists. Something could be quickly assembled. He sent the information to Thelis personally, including instructions, "Tell the ship captain to contact the freight forwarding company Ajisai when he reaches Tiran. Follow Ajisai's instructions exactly." Othman smiled. *When I first started the company, I would do trip designs, and redesigns, every day. Those days seem very distant. I owe Lord Kaleege a return favor, several return favors. He helped me get Talus started. I will do this favor, but I don't like it. I don't like having this company involved in the growing difficulties between Devir and Lord Kaleege. Difficulties which will only get worse with Naru running the Tiran economy as though it were his own personal company, and the crown prince on Orane building up a war machine to retake Tiran.*

He spoke into the silence of the bare room, "I have made Talus my life, but maybe it is time for a change."

Six levels below Othman's office, Basil walked into the Talus building lobby. The familiar red and gray color scheme had never looked better. Reflected in the polished brass of the elevator trim, Basil saw he was smiling.

He made his way to Thelis's cluttered office. Thelis had his door closed, but soon opened it.

"Hello, Thelis," Basil said uncertainly.

Thelis motioned Basil to the guest chair. The room went anechoic as Thelis activated the silencer.

"You know why I'm here. But I can come back later..."

Thelis took a deep breath. Basil grew uncomfortable at Thelis's look.

Basil said slowly, "I want a position here at Talus as soon as possible. If my efficiency report from JCO is not that good, I'll take a down-grade...you know about the *Khios* incident."

"Yes," Thelis said. He seemed to have difficulty concentrating. After a moment, he took a breath and said, "Let's see what we can find." He activated a screen which a few seconds later showed Tage's report.

"Not too bad," Thelis said. "He rated your management skills the weakest."

"It was a difficult crew."

"I can guess," Thelis said. "I know the union's influence on JCO ships." He switched the screen off. "You don't make my life easy, Basil. Your decision to go off with...I don't remember her name... and turn independent with no contacts..."

"I know you did us, me, a big favor with cargo..."

Thelis waved his hand. "That's history. Just by chance, I happen to have an opening right now that fits your qualifications. A C-200 run from here to Karaghia to Tiran and back. It would be a temporary cargomaster assignment, but not a down-grade..."

"I'll take it," Basil interrupted.

Thelis shook his head. "Basil, that's what I'm talking about. You need to think things through before you make snap decisions." He shrugged. "But in this case your decision is good. You know Cereclo Dathe. He's got the temporary assignment as master on this run. One crew, a man named Noteth. The front office says this ship needs to depart as soon as possible. Looks like cargo is already loaded and Cereclo and Noteth have already signed in. Get moving."

• • •

The two days in transit to the Sigma Gate entrance passed pleasantly, as did the next days in lightspace. Basil felt tensions relaxing that he hadn't even known he had. Sitting at the command station, alone in the control room, he savored the silence. It was good to be back—back on board a well-maintained ship, Talus' familiar procedures, Talus crew. He'd not appreciated how well-maintained Talus ships were. The *Rafale* was a nice, clean C-200, engines recently overhauled, environmental systems rebuilt, interior cleaned and refinished.

He and Cereclo and Noteth exchanged a few words at each shift change but no more than that. The second day in lightspace, Cereclo lingered after his shift ended. He and Basil shared silence for a time in the control room, then Basil essayed, "It's good to be back with a company where we all have confidence in each other." Basil squinted. "Though a work slowdown doesn't improve management–employee relations. I hope there's no talk of unionizing. That would be the end of Talus as a good place to work."

"This work slowdown has provided a nice opportunity for me." Cereclo grinned.

"I didn't think you were that high on the seniority list."

"I'm not. This is a rush mission, and I was available. There is no project review board approval. Thelis didn't say it, but he implied it was a directive from Othman himself."

"I guess that's why we are running with so little cargo," Basil mused. "What if we convert from salary to shares. Say…2 percent?"

"Leave it alone, Basil. Let's just accomplish the mission as designed," Cereclo said. "Also, Thelis told me to remind you not to get too close to crewmembers. That was noted in your JCO efficiency report."

Basil took a breath. "Yeah."

Cereclo grinned and slapped Basil on the shoulder. "Shouldn't be a problem on this trip, right?"

Basil laughed. "I assume the elusive Noteth is an Alternate Universe game person?"

"Right."

The shifts passed, pleasantly uneventful. At shift change one day, Cereclo cornered Basil in the wardroom. "What do we know about Ambai Company?"

"Ambai's one of the biggest ora growers and processors on Karagia. They've been in business since recolonization. About thirty years."

"I thought Karaghia's been inhabited for five hundred years," Noteth said.

"It has," Basil said. "But about two hundred years ago, during the Ziani family war of succession on Tiran, trade to Karaghia was cut off. Karaghia devolved back to subsistence."

"How many settlers? Originally."

"Peak population before the war was estimated at close to a million. When Kaleege bought Karaghia thirty years ago and sent the current colonists out, they estimated there might be two hundred thousand left, some out in the bush, some in coastal towns. Language had changed. Technology devolved down to hand tools. Fortunately a fair amount of the original infrastructure was made with ferrous alloys rather than composites, so the locals could salvage it for tools, and weapons. No energy sources other than fire and wind, with one notable exception. The mass driver and shuttle remained operational—left over from Kogon days, self-maintaining. But the locals had no reason to go to orbit, so as far as I can tell, it remained unused until the new colonists started exporting ora again, about twenty-five years ago."

Basil put a visual of the planet up on the wardroom's small screen.

"Pretty, isn't it?" Basil said. "One of Lord Kaleege's selling points for the bond issue that funded the recolonization was that ser Piaro had designed the economy and written the business plan. I've read it. It's a fairly famous study. Piaro's one of the top two or three thinkers in economic design…"

Noteth was fidgeting…"Sorry," Basil said. "I get excited about this stuff."

"But the colony failed two hundred years ago and had to be restarted, right?"

"Right. Kaleege's staff floated a couple of rounds of successful bond sales to get the thing going. But he and five of the Tiran gentry, his cronies in the Imperial court, own all the voting stock. They remain the absentee landowners. Each colonist team leases a hundred thousand hectares, then they're appointed lord protectors and have to swear an oath that they're practicing members of the state religion." Basil grinned. "You know where Kaleege is from. They are supposed to earn-out the infrastructure investment on income from the ora exports. Kaleege's syndicate and Kaleege himself put a pile of money into this place. One of the economic reports I read years ago said over 50 billion eris. Shipped a bunch of machinery out here, had Ildara Company drop the elevator into place, installed the orbital power and com networks and a bunch of surface infrastructure—monorails and such—to move the ora."

"That was thirty years ago?"

"Yeah," Basil said. He sipped his tea and stared at the planet slowly turning above them. "Things never really seemed to take off, though. I don't know why. Karaghia just kind of limped along, breaking even. Even during that period when ora prices almost doubled, you never saw Karaghia exports pick up. Then came the trouble on Tiran, and I'm sure Kaleege has more important things to worry about than Karaghia. Most recent reports on the datanet says that the colonists are in debt to Kaleege's Karaghia Corporation to the point they will never earn their way out. About half the machinery for ora planting and harvesting has broken down. Hand-picking, using native labor, is now cost-competitive with machines." Basil waved toward the cargo holds. "But the processing mini-mills are still working. That's why we've got all this OMI stuff on board. The locals living in towns near the plantations soon realized it was a lot easier working for the plantations than hunting or fishing or farming, so thousands of them are now employed by the plantations. And a huge bureaucracy has grown up, calling itself the Karaghia government—none of which is really needed. The plantations are autonomous states, above the local laws, if there are any." Basil smiled. "In the one and only follow-up report on the Karaghia Colony, the study team characterized the local bureaucracy as corrupt, incompetent, and filled with nepotism."

Cereclo stood. "I was just curious about the company we're going to be dealing with. I really didn't need a history lesson."

• • •

Rafale exited lightspace at the Karaghia Gate and began a standard approach around the pale-yellow sun that Karaghia orbited.

"Anything around?" asked Cereclo.

"Nothing moving except us."

"Good."

"We're right on the profile. In fact, we should arrive slightly ahead of schedule." Basil got up out of the command chair.

Cereclo set his tea cup down and slid into the command chair. "Have you talked to Ambai?"

"Ambai has a recorded message saying they'll return our message soon, whenever that might be."

"Backwater planets," Cereclo said. "AI, dock us at the elevator head."

"Alright," Cereclo said. "Prepare for docking in four hours. Ser Ajami and ser Noteth off-load and load cargo as soon as the ship is secure at the docking point. Karaghia elevator is out of operation, so they'll be bringing boxes up to us with a shuttle."

Noteth groaned, "More handling time."

"Yes, and you'll be on cargo-handling detail until we get cargo off-loaded and on-loaded."

"Overtime," Noteth stated.

"Yes. Read your contract," Cereclo snapped. "Any two shifts in a row gives you overtime for the second shift. And that's what you'll be doing."

"What about time off to go planet-side?"

"Not this trip," Cereclo said. "I want to get on our way to Tiran as soon as possible."

Noteth departed.

"Something strange here," Basil said. "Ambai is moving ora to orbit with shuttles instead of an elevator, which means higher costs. Demand for ora on Tiran is very high. Both those factors should drive prices up, but they haven't." Basil tilted his head toward the mild-looking planet. "But there's still a good profit margin in shipping Karaghia ora to Tiran. We could negotiate with Ble for a few more boxes. We have room for them, so if Ambai has them available at the same price…"

"No, Basil. Our instructions are to get the six boxes of ora we've contracted for to Tiran as quickly as possible. Who will we be dealing with at Ambai?"

"Manager is a guy named Yonna Ble." Basil activated his desktop display. A company summary came up then dissolved to a hologram of a sandy-haired, thin-faced man of indeterminant age. He was in Ambai Company uniform with the company flag behind him, a forced smile on his face. He introduced himself, and talked in glowing terms about Ambai's ora production."This tells me nothing," Cereclo said. "They still haven't answered our query?"

"No. But that recorded message from Ambai yesterday said they have two boxes at the elevator head ready for us to load." Basil activated a holographic display and pointed. "I'm going to start loading," Basil said. He suited up, opened the cargo hold door, and started moving the first box of ora into place. He'd just finished getting it into place and activating its tie-downs when his com chimed.

"Change of plans," Cereclo said. He sounded rushed. "I need you up here in control…"

"I've only got one box loaded…"

"This is urgent," Cereclo repeated. "Stop what you're doing and get up here."

Basil controlled his irritation, closed the hold doors, unsuited, and checked the tie-down on the first box. Then he went up to control.

"What's this all about?"

Cereclo looked shaken, then put a smile on his face and a second later changed it to a frown. "We need to be secure. I told Noteth to suit up, in armor, and go over and check that abandoned elevator."

"That will take hours," Basil said evenly. "I thought you wanted to load and unload as quickly as possible."

"We don't want any surprises."

"Surprises?"

Cereclo turned to him. "Who knows what or who might be hiding out in that hulk."

"We need to be secure," Cereclo said over his shoulder as he hurried down the companionway.

Basil shook his head and sat down at the command console. There was an amber signal on one of the com settings. Basil clicked it to reset. Cereclo had apparently received a coded message and left the com link open by mistake.

Wonder where he went in such a hurry?

Staring at the view of the planet on the big board, a thought nagged at him. The coded message had self-erased. But the sender's code was still there when Basil had reset it. Curious, Basil opened an inset screen and checked the Talus general directory. The suffix was for the Special Projects office.

I guess they warned Cereclo there might be some kind of threat to Rafale *hiding in the old elevator head.*

"Noteth here," the com said, and an image formed on the big board: the dark hulk of the elevator head occluding most of the pale-green curve of Karaghia now looked ominous.

Basil watched Noteth push out of the *Rafale* lock for the manway beside one of the cargo locks on the elevator head. "Guy on Tertia said he'd been here," Noteth said. "Said he'd climbed this elevator all the way up. A hundred kilometers of stairs carrying air. But weight would diminish…probably take…oh, 750 hours, water would mass a kilo a day. Course you could take a recycler, if you could stand the taste, but those things aren't light either…"

"Knock off the chatter," Basil said.

Noteth entered the personnel hatch. Someone had hand-painted "12" in white beside the hatch.

"You read me inside?" asked Noteth.

"Yeah, clear. What's it look like?"

"Dark and no air. I'm going up to the operations level."

After a few moments of breaths, scrapes, and grunts, Noteth's hand-light flashed around in incomprehensible arcs. "Nothing," Noteth reported.

"Alright," Basil said softly. "Go back down to the cargo level, take a close look around the dock nearest us."

"Right," Noteth said.

"Then get back to the ship. Let's get those boxes moved."

"Take a look at this!" Noteth gasped. The suit camera picture on the big board was a moving black and white glare—something shiny.

"What is it?" Basil said.

"Somebody in a bubble suit."

"What are they doing?"

"Nothing. They're dead, long dead, desiccated corpse—one leg is blown off," Noteth responded tightly.

Basil could make nothing of the images coming from Noteth's suit cam.

"He a local or off-worlder?" Basil asked.

"Local, I think."

"Any other bodies?"

The picture on the big board jumped and flickered.

"No. Nobody moving around, no power, no air, no control board indicators still active."

Basil thought for a moment, then told Noteth, "Take the emergency alert beacons from your suit and set them to trigger if anyone comes out of the elevator anywhere along this side of the dock level. Then get back to the ship. It would take too long to do a thorough search. We'll let AI monitor the elevator. You and I need to get boxes loaded."

Chapter 14

The shuttle screamed down through Karaghia's atmosphere from day to night to day again. Basil sat in the control seat watching the automated systems bring the shuttle down from orbit. It was a utilitarian vehicle, two seats and an empty cargo space. The ride down was equally utilitarian, sharp deceleration, a plasma glow that soon dissipated, the nose-up reentry attitude moderating to glide attitude. With a sonic boom to announce its arrival, the shuttle lined up on the single runway and touched down with a jolt.

When the control board showed they were parked at the freight loading zone, Basil released the side hatch and stepped out into a pink dawn rich with humid air and the scent of foliage.

Basil felt his sinuses contract then relax as his immunity implant neutralized his body's reactions. There was a sealed box with Varil insignia nearby and an untended loading machine. Several hundred meters away was a weather-beaten arrivals hall. No one around, nothing moving.

Behind him the shuttle's stubby wings clicked and popped as they cooled. Basil jumped when the shuttle started up on wheel power and guided itself to the box loading station at the head of the mass driver.

"Backwater planets," Basil muttered and started walking toward the arrivals hall carrying the pay processor from *Rafale*.

The glass doors of the arrivals hall were locked. Inside, Basil could see a dozen gray metal desks piled with papers, wooden chairs made of dark wood, cabinets along one wall. No people in sight.

He opened his com, but there was no signal, so he sat down on the concrete steps of the building and watched the purple light become a deep blood-red and the cloud bottoms shade from gray to gold.

Eventually he heard footsteps inside.

A man in local dress opened a door, waved Basil inside, then withdrew. Basil started through the identity scanner which was apparently not switched on. An official in a rumpled gray uniform waved him back with much incomprehensible muttering. Eventually the machine was switched on and Basil walked through. He put his com over the scanning plate, but no lights lit. After a moment, the official waved him through and pointed to the exit.

Outside, the day was already hot. A dark-blue car with Ambai insignia was parked at the curb. The driver in blue Ambai uniform politely waved Basil into the car which was comfortably air-conditioned. The driver handed Basil a flexcom and wheeled the car out onto an empty road. Basil activated the video on the flexcom: "I am Yonna Ble," a sandy-haired man said. "Ambai manager here on Karaghia. I look forward to meeting you when you arrive at my plantation. The car ride to the plantation will take about an hour. Unfortunately, the communication system here on Kara is in disrepair. Your com will not work here on the surface which is why I asked you to meet with me in person."

We could have discussed this over the com coming through the elevator head. Instead I have to go to him. Just to pay him for six boxes of ora.

The road ended abruptly at the edge of a town of weathered stucco buildings. The car wound through streets crowded with pedestrians and carts and ancient ground-cars. The people favored bright-colored clothing, reds and yellows mostly, with intricate patterns. Many of the women balanced baskets on their heads. Soon the car was through town and making its way down a road between geometrically perfect rows of what Basil assumed were ora plants.

Basil took out his com and studied the profit profile for their trip. Then he recalculated it for seven boxes of ora instead of six. Profit increased from 6 percent to 8 percent.

After a while, Basil dozed. When he woke, the car was pulling up in front of a sprawling white building surrounded by scarlet flowers in stone planters.

A thin, pale man with sandy hair stood at the door. “I'm Yonna Ble,” he announced with a formal bow.

Basil followed Ble down a long corridor paneled in dark wood. They eventually reached a large room open on one side to a courtyard with more scarlet flowers in planter boxes.

A low table had been set for a meal for two. Ble slumped into a rattan chair while a serving girl poured wine into two glasses and Ble raised one. “Welcome.” He drank down half the glass. “Try some of our local wine; it's surprisingly good.”

“No, thanks,” Basil said, his irritation beginning to show. “It's morning for me. I'd like to get our business transactions…”

“You can take time for some breakfast, surely.”

Basil realized he was hungry and acceded. The meal was a series of small dishes of unfamiliar foods of exotic colors, all of which turned out to be delicious, as was the wine. The meal ended with a cool and creamy sweet. Ble stretched his legs out and lit a cigar, offering Basil one. Two servants in pressed white uniforms with blue Ambai crests cleared away plates. A serving girl in a red and gold sarong refilled their wine glasses.

“The cargo you brought from Sigma has been properly transferred and you've received payment?” Ble said in a bored tone, more statement than question.

Basil activated the pay processor. "Yes. Delivered, accepted, and paid by a firm called," Basil squinted at the image, "Theonax, I think." A holographic image of an insignia with notations as to the transaction appeared in the air above the pay processor.

Ble glanced at it without much interest. Basil collapsed the image. "Processing equipment seems to always be in disrepair," Ble mused. "Always costing time and money to repair. Not like the shuttle and launcher…self-repairing. Some ancient technology, I'm told."

"Kogon," Basil said. "Here is our consignment payment for your six boxes of ora." Basil put another image in the air which Ble read and nodded his assent.

"At the airfield I noticed another ora box," Basil continued, "with a Varil logo on it. Is it intended for Tiran?"

"Yes," Ble said. The serving girl poured his wine glass full again. "It was scheduled to be picked up weeks ago. I have no idea what the delay is."

"As you probably know, Varil has been nationalized, so their schedule will probably be a bit uncertain for a while."

Ble inclined his head. "I don't keep up with events on Tiran."

"We could add it to our cargo. It would be at the Tiran elevator in ten days," Basil said, trying not to sound eager.

Ble seemed to be drowsing.

Basil compiled a shipping order and put the Talus logo and text up holographically. "Same rate as the six boxes for Talus." Basil said nothing about the small additional payment made directly to Ble for "expedited handling" but he was certain Ble saw it.

"Agreed," Ble drawled.

The house was a little overly warm and humid for Basil, but fans turning overhead kept it comfortable. Or maybe it was the wine he'd drunk.

"Culture is not one of the virtues of this place," Ble explained. "The locals have spent three hundred years perfecting puppet shows, lacquered wood, and woven baskets." He shrugged.

"But the economy must be stable," Basil said. "Demand for ora is steady."

"Yes, but the growing and processing of ora with antiquated equipment, local labor…all plagued with corruption…"

He motioned to the serving girl, and she came and knelt by him. He touched her hand; her face remained expressionless.

"Blood red," Ble muttered. Basil lifted his wine glass. The light from the open veranda made the wine glow. Ble snorted. "Beauty is everywhere."

This guy's already drunk.

"Nothing much happens here," Ble slurred lightly. He reached to touch the girl's hand, but she moved away gracefully.

• • •

"You want a contract to haul that stray Varil box to Tiran? Fine. You have it."

Basil quickly called up the contract and put it in the air near Ble, who nodded at the hologram, and the deal was done. His eyes seemed to glaze behind half-lowered lids.

"We had some excitement a year ago," Ble picked up in a conversational tone. "One of Lord Naru's cruisers in orbit, a military contingent on the ground out near the Lion Coast." The girl refilled Ble's glass. "Called that because some of the rock formations reminded an early explorer of a lion's head. I've not been there myself. The ever-pressing business of growing ora occupies my time, you know." Ble's tone dripped sarcasm. Basil didn't know whether to smile or not, so chose not to. "The Imperials spent several months out along that barren coast, doing whatever they came to do. And then for a couple of days there was much activity, shuttles riding the mass driver up to orbit, military cargo lifters roaring overhead. Then they were gone; all very secretive."

"When can I get a ride to orbit?" Basil asked, closing the pay processor. Ble stifled a sigh, energized a virtual keyboard, and made a notation. "Schedule is in your com."

Basil was dismayed to see the next conjunction was not for three hours. He closed his com and drank the last of his wine. The silent girl in the red and gold sarong appeared and refilled it.

"Are you in that much of a hurry to get to your ship, to get to Tiran?"

"I appreciate your hospitality, but I don't want to intrude…"

Ble laughed.

"Perhaps I could have your driver take me past one of the ora processing facilities on my way back to the airfield."

"I don't recommend it," Ble said. "Agricultural processing plants have little sightseeing value. And if you are looking for local culture…well…"

Basil finished writing up the report on the Ambai ora load for Tiran. The wine tasted great. He drank another glass and admired the scarlet flowers in the planter boxes in the courtyard.

This place really is paradise. Or could be. Ble watched him, and the locals in the room watched both the off-worlders with expressionless faces.

"This plantation is certainly beautiful," Basil said. He accepted another glass of wine.

"A comfortable enough prison," Ble muttered. "But always under watchful eyes."

Basil looked down and away from the serving girl's face. "They understand Basic, I assume."

"Sometimes. When they choose to."

Basil hesitated. "You aren't seeking a transfer?"

Ble said nothing, looking pensively into his wine glass. "That is no longer possible. Tu vir."

"Is that a local phrase?"

"A phrase of many meanings. It sometimes refers to a color, deep red. Sometimes it may mean 'a bond of blood,' and unbreakable… no matter. I will stay here. My plantation provides livelihood for many people…I, we, are responsible for lives, such as they are, as this economy devolves into a barter society…watched over by… those who want stability." Ble's words drifted into silence.

Baffled, Basil said, "I don't fully understand your meaning. This is a beautiful place. Ora is important…" Ble was not listening. He touched the hand of the serving girl, and she didn't pull away. Ble and the girl were motionless for a moment under the eyes of the two servants standing at a respectful distance in their immaculate dark-blue Ambai uniforms. Then she pulled her hand away and left the room. Ble roused himself. "Come to my office, and I'll authorize the shuttle to haul the Varil box to your ship." Basil finished his wine and followed a wavering Ble down a corridor to a roomy office overlooking ora fields and the distant mountains. Ble sat down at an antiquated electronics set and flexed his fingers in the control lights with surprising alacrity.

A moment later, Basil's pay processor chimed with the contract and the shuttle schedule. "I've put a manual hold on the shuttle departure," Ble told Basil. "I assume you will want to ride it up to your ship. Read this code into your com. It will open the shuttle launch gate and authorize the shuttle to launch."

Basil did so.

"Now," Ble said, "I have other things I must attend to. Return to your breakfast, your wine. Enjoy the comforts of this house. You are free to stay as long as you like." He bowed. "It has been a pleasure meeting you."

He went out into the corridor where the girl in the red and gold sarong was waiting.

• • •

Basil collected *Rafale*'s pay processor and walked slowly down the corridor to the front door of the house. Outside, the sunlight on the rows of ora was harsh.

A driver in Ambai uniform opened the car door, Basil climbed in, and they departed.

Basil woke when the car slowed and turned off the road at an ora processing facility. There was no one around. The driver said something Basil's translation software could not handle. He stopped the car and turned to look at Basil for a moment, then repeated what sounded like "tu vir." The driver held his hand out, fingers closed, then slowly opened them. He seemed to be pantomiming a question.

"I don't understand," Basil said. The translation software on his com told him nothing.

The driver got out of the car and walked to the shade of one of a row of large silvery tanks. Basil noticed there were three locals in yellow and red clothing standing in the shade. Basil tensed. *Should I have brought a Saris?*

The driver came back to the car and opened his hand. On a small piece of yellow and purple cloth lay a tiny red onyx, burning like fire in the sunlight. The driver said a few unintelligible words, wrapped the stone in the cloth, pressed it into Basil's hand, got in the car, and they drove on.

Basil put the stone in his pocket and sat watching the ora fields flowing silently by.

At the airfield, the driver opened the car door and stood expressionless while Basil got out and stood awkwardly for a moment. "You'll want payment…?"

The man's expression did not change, then he bowed politely, got back in the car, and departed.

I'll figure this out later, Basil thought.

The code in his com got Basil through the security gate at the base of the shuttle launcher, then up three flights of steel stairs to where the shuttle lay on its launch rail. Inside, it was stifling hot. The shuttle confirmed he was aboard, and that a cargo box was aboard, then doors closed and sealed. Basil settled into the control seat and activated buffers. *These old mass drivers are still functional after how many hundreds of years?*

After a number of jolts, the shuttle was in launch position, and the mass driver slung the shuttle forward at three gees, then there was an instant of free fall before the reaction drives fired with a roar. The vibration and noise were deafening, but mercifully short.

The shuttle navigated itself to *Rafale*. Once the shuttle autopilot chimed that it was correctly parked, Basil sealed his shipsuit and crossed to the ship.

Neither Noteth nor Cereclo were anywhere to be seen. Basil notified AI to bring the box aboard. "Non-Talus ID," AI informed him. Basil punched the override, and the box was trundled aboard and the exterior hatch closed and locked.

Cereclo's face popped onto the screen. "I'm initiating departure now…"

"I need a little more time to check all box lockdowns and recalculate cargo stowage…"

"Do that en route," Cereclo snapped, and his image disappeared.

Basil hurriedly checked box tie-downs, then sank into buffers as the departure alarm sounded.

Chapter 15

Basil found Cereclo in the control room. "I need to talk to you privately," Basil snapped.

"We're ready to go," Noteth said. "You want me to notify Ambai?"

"Why bother?" Cereclo said. "Let's go. Basil, we can talk as soon as we're on track outbound."

Noteth activated the AI which steered *Rafale* clear of the elevator head. Readouts showed the number two impeller had a slight energy loss. "I see it," Cereclo told Noteth. "Proceed." They proceeded down the standard track around the star toward the Karaghia Gate entrance.

"Something out there, captain," Noteth said. "Could be a track…"

"Extend the array," said Cereclo. The big board image changed with the greater magnification. An orange spark flickered at the display's pixel limit. After a minute, it disappeared completely.

"Nothing scheduled inbound, according to Delta Station," Basil noted.

"Which is out-of-date info," Cereclo responded.

"Raiders?" Noteth speculated.

"With the array extended, we are making a pretty big signal in the zero-point energy field. Makes it easy for raiders to spot us."

They studied the board for a minute.

"AI, what's the energy needed for them to align to attack us?" Cereclo asked. Lines appeared on the plot. "Not feasible unless they mass a lot less than my estimation," the AI said. "I assumed gunship mass and power."

"Retract the array, but keep a virtual track on that ship," Cereclo ordered. The big board went back to a diagram of the Karaghia system with a single red point far past the gate entrance. *Rafale*'s image was moving precisely along the gate approach track.

Cereclo turned to Basil. "If you have something to discuss, follow me down to my cabin. I'm going off-shift."

In the master's cabin, Cereclo shoved wrinkled clothing aside and sat on the bunk. He waved Basil to the chair. "Basil, I didn't pull us out of Karaghia just to spite you," Cereclo said. He sounded tense. "You might as well know; I've got orders direct from Special Projects to get to Tiran fast."

"Any idea why?"

Cereclo shrugged. "I'm not supposed to be discussing the message."

Basil stood. "Alright. I'm going on-shift." He returned to the control room. Noteth had already logged himself off-shift.

"Dammit. Supposed to hand off the ship to me, in person, before leaving control. He knows that."

Basil logged himself in and ran through the shift change check list. Everything was in order. *Rafale* was on a high-speed track toward the gate.

"Anything change with that unknown object?" Basil queried AI.

"Entirely out of range now."

Halfway through his shift, a coded message appeared in the master com for ser Ajami. "Not Cereclo?" Basil muttered. He double-checked it, but it was for him only. He activated the coding shield and read the message. "Proceed to the Tiran elevator at best speed. Once there contact freight forwarder Ajisai and do as they instruct. Special cargo." It was from the Talus Executive Office.

Basil acknowledged receipt, and the message erased itself.

Rafale arrived at the Tiran elevator without incident. In the *Rafale* wardroom, Captain Cereclo handed Basil and Noteth flexcoms. "These are the current Tiran regulations for all foreign ships docking. Read them and put your imprint on them—the national police require a copy on file from everyone aboard." Cereclo looked at them. "You can go ashore for four hours at a time, during which time you'll likely be followed by the secret police. If you get into trouble, you are presumed guilty because you are a foreigner. We have a departure slot at 0200 two days from now, and we are not going to miss it. In that document you'll see that the Port Authority AI is now under military control, and any ship missing their assigned departure is subject to search and seizure. And the ship is impounded until a new departure is assigned and confirmed. There's also a penalty fee." Cereclo gave Basil and Noteth a meaningful look. "We're not getting ourselves in that situation. Ser Ajami, keep me informed as to customs clearance, the import and export duties, and the cargo transfer progress both off-loading and on-loading. The Ajisai rep is supposed to already have our info."

"Additional cargo?" Basil asked.

"No," Cereclo said.

Basil nodded. "As soon as Ajisai gives me the cargo handling times, I'll coordinate with departure control…"

"I'll take care of that," Cereclo said. "I've already got numbers from Ajisai. You concentrate on keeping Ajisai moving."

Basil left the ship, fuming. *This temp command assignment has gone to his head.*

• • •

A small woman with very short silver hair and gray-green eyes was waiting, hands on hips, when Basil opened the hold doors. “I remember you,” she said. “Came here on an independent, and before that you were in Talus uniform. Now you’re back with Talus?”

“Yes, I’m Basil Ajami, back with Talus.” He nodded a tiny bow. “And you’re Ria, still with Ajisai.”

She bowed. “And you’re late.”

“No I’m not. I’m on time, and we need to stay on time.”

“Then we’d better get going. Your captain already has our estimates. Where is he?”

“Gone to get our departure slot.”

“He should have let me do that. It’ll take him twice as long. Anyway…” She signaled to her crew to start moving boxes.

Basil nodded toward the *Rafale*’s master cargo management station. “You want to take it, or shall I?”

“My people can do that. Open the codes.”

Basil did so.

“You and I are going to customs…”

“I need to be there in person? I thought you folks handled all that.”

“Not anymore. The rules have changed.” They rode an uncrowded slideway to the glass doors of the customs complex. “Lots of things have to be done in person these days. Security. Got your data?”

For the next two hours, she led him through the warren of offices in the customs and duties section of the arrivals deck, producing data files on request, waiting endlessly in some offices, reworking data while officials waited in others, always with a smile and a thank you for the polite and stultifyingly bureaucratic army of clerks in multicolored uniforms.

Finally, the last set of glass doors slid closed behind them, and they stood in a large receiving and inspection hall. The air was too warm and smelled like a hundred unfamiliar cargos. Ria pointed. "You're outbound cargo has been approved as planned." She tapped his com. "That symbol there. Remember it." Basil tried to fix the Tiran character in his memory. She consulted her com. "My crews are right on schedule moving your inbound cargo, but won't start loading outbound until…tomorrow first shift. I didn't think you needed expedited service—it's expensive—so I only asked for single-shift work. Expedited service often gets flagged for special inspection by security. You don't want that. Load cargo tomorrow, and we'll be right on schedule. Your differential grav controls for the holds work, don't they?"

"They work fine."

She flashed him a smile. "My crew just about has your inbound cargo off the ship. And right on time at shift-end."

Basil looked around the wide concourse. "Any place around here we could sit down, drink some tea? I owe you that for walking me through today's bureaucracy."

She took his arm. "It's time to eat." She led him down a slideway to the row of automated taxis. Ria said an address, the door slid closed, and the taxi slid up the track silently.

"I've never seen so much bureaucracy," Basil said. "No, correct that, I have seen this much bureaucracy. On Karaghia. But there it's just a pointless, disorganized mess. Here it seems highly purposeful. Though I thought perhaps the revolution would make things a bit less complicated."

She snorted. "We now have Revolutionary Guards. The people with red and black armbands. They are a law unto themselves."

"I'm not surprised," Basil said. "A revolution destroys all authority; it doesn't just replace the previous authority with a new one, as most people think. After revolution, there is only the rule of power, not the rule of law."

"You a history student?"

"Economist, but macroeconomics is about the psychology of large groups of people. Which is also history," Basil said.

They glided to a stop, and the taxi door slid open.

Basil and Ria joined the dense crowd waiting on the train platform. The Tiranians were silent, well-dressed, courteous. A train stopped every minute, and hundreds of people boarded and exited. Ria and Basil were packed into the train almost face to face.

They stepped off into a windy night scented with the smell of ocean. Shop lights were a gaudy rainbow of pinks and mauves and lavenders against a cloudy evening sky.

"This is the real Tiran, the old Tiran," Ria said as they walked down a street only three meters wide. There were no vehicles. "The food is good here, and the beer. You do drink beer, don't you?"

Basil nodded.

"Good. I don't trust men who don't drink beer." They walked for a moment in silence. "Two hundred years ago," Ria continued, "each of these train stops used to be a fishing village. As the city grew, the villages became suburbs, but never very affluent. The better suburbs are at the end of the peninsula. That's where all the people on the train were going. But I like it better here in the old section."

She slid a wooden door aside, and they stepped into a low-ceilinged restaurant. On the left, an old man bowed to them and then retired to the kitchen behind a blue curtain. There were four worn plastic tables and four wooden booths with well-used cushions and reed mats. They took a booth. Faded pictures of fishing boats and serious-faced fishermen were haphazardly stuck to the walls. Ria said something in Tiran to the old man. The video on the wall showed a woman in Imperial-era clothing singing against a stylized backdrop of tiny pink flowers and deep-blue sky. "What is that music?" Basil asked. "I heard it at the docks too."

"It's old stuff from a couple of generations ago. Simple and sentimental…" Ria grinned. "Out of fashion these days. I like it."

The old man shuffled over with a tall silver bottle lettered with angular black Tiran script. He opened the bottle and poured beer into each of the tiny glasses.

They toasted each other and drank the tiny glasses empty.

"What do these bottles say? Long live the revolution?" Basil reached for the bottle, but Ria pushed his hand away and poured his glass full herself.

"It says fresh-brewed for summer flavor. They're big on seasonal things here. The custom here is that you don't fill your own glass. I fill yours, you fill mine."

Basil poured hers full.

"Weren't you partners with a woman when you were here as an independent?"

"Yes." Basil looked around the tiny restaurant again.

"Ah…"

"How long have you been on Tiran?" Basil asked. "This beer is excellent, by the way."

"Four years, except for the half year I was off-world during the worst of the fighting."

Basil nodded. Outside the wind had risen, fluttering under the old wooden eaves.

"Can I ask you a question?" Basil said.

"You can ask."

"I'm a little concerned about gratuities. I've got about 1 percent budgeted, but you haven't said anything. Should I be paying someone?"

"No, don't even try. Ajisai will handle all that."

"Don't tell me the revolution has swept away all that sort of thing."

"Hardly..." She frowned. "But it's a very complicated and convoluted business. Old societies like this one tend to evolve very rigid courtesies and insults." She poured his tiny beer glass full again. "The revolution eliminated all that in theory. In reality it just went underground and it changed. Hard to know what the rules are these days. But I will say that the revolution accomplished some good. There's no street crime, there's no petty theft, there's no danger from robbers breaking into your apartment. I seldom even lock my apartment...it's nice." Her smile faded. "But off-worlders are never really fully accepted here, no matter how long you've lived here." She drank her beer down. Basil refilled her glass.

The alcohol was sinking into his blood. Basil noticed her quick, sure movements, her smile—beautiful hair if she'd rescript her implant to let it grow longer.

"Did Captain Cereclo talk with you?" Ria asked, her eyes on the woman singing on the video.

"No. He read us some Tiran regs." Basil hesitated. "And he mentioned we needed to depart quickly. On schedule. He'd received a message from Talus headquarters."

She eyed him, then nodded. "Yes."

The old man brought two plates of tiny grilled fish on wooden skewers and another bottle of beer. They ate in silence for a few moments.

"Your company has volunteered you to help me tomorrow," she said finally.

Basil set his fish down carefully. "I'm happy to help. But you've told me cargo handling, customs, rules and regs have gotten complicated lately. I should leave it to you, to Ajisai."

"Your captain has your departure slot assigned." Ria tapped her com. "Took him all day, but he got it done." She laughed her silvery laugh.

"What kind of help have I been volunteered for?"

"Your company seems to think you are smart and able to think on your feet, which is why they recommended you."

Basil made a deprecating gesture.

"That recommendation is straight from your company's director, Othman, I think his name is," Ria said with a grin. "Confidential, you know."

Basil snorted. "Confidential and you already know about it? Can't be that confidential."

"After your ship departs, it won't matter."

Emboldened by the beer, Basil said, "Well if you won't talk about what I am supposed to do tomorrow, let me pay you a compliment. Your eyes, very pretty. You've changed the color."

"It's considered impolite here to discuss someone's appearance."

Basil reddened. "Sorry. I meant it as a compliment. The color, seems different, very nice."

Ria laughed her quick laugh again. "I've set my implant to change my eye color slowly and continuously. It's amazing how people, my friends and acquaintances, notice something is different about me, but they can't name what it is."

"Speaking of small changes," Basil turned his glass in minute increments of a circle, "I think I'm ready for a change. Maybe."

Ria laughed again. "Maybe doesn't sound like ready. I've heard a lot of young officers make that statement. Usually they talk about going independent. You've done that already, and you're back with Talus. Talus is a good firm."

"Yeah. Reputable. Reliable. Conservative."

The wind boomed outside. The old man brought another bottle of beer.

Ria poured both their glasses full. "Well maybe this trip will bring you some recognition." Basil, lost in thought, didn't notice the look she gave him. "How's your captain doing?"

"Cereclo? He's doing OK. Been a little anxious lately."

"Understandable."

Basil puzzled over that for a moment. He found himself admiring Ria's profile in the dim lights and pulled his gaze away. "He's a young captain," Basil said. "Nervous. And with the situation here on Tiran…"

"Well…" she said, not looking his way, "…hope he's not too nervous."

Cereclo gets a coded message from Special Projects telling him to get to Tiran fast. So what?"So give me a hint as to what we're going to be doing tomorrow," Basil said. He knew the alcohol was talking for him, but he couldn't seem to stop. "Additional cargo?"

"Yes, sort of," Ria said, frowning. She studied her beer for a moment then drank it.

Basil found himself admiring her hair, her face. He downed his beer in a gulp. She refilled his glass then abruptly stood up. "I need to be going."

I've offended her. Basil started to rise.

"No, you stay here," she said with a smile. "Finish your beer, take your time. I'll see you tomorrow. Straight up this narrow street to the first corner, then left to the train stop." She flashed him a smile and was gone.

Chapter 16

The shift change tone woke him. His com said he needed to be at the Ajisai office in half an hour. Basil dressed quickly.

At the exit airlock, Noteth was waiting. "Cargo off-loaded. Two boxes of Sigma cargo loaded. Captain said to tie everything down ready for departure, but also be ready to take on more cargo." Noteth paused expectantly. "I'm going off-shift."

"I'm heading to the freight forwarder to see if more cargo is available."

Noteth shook his head and wandered off.

Basil hurried to the Ajisai offices.

Ria was waiting, impatience all over her face. "Let me scan your shipsuit ID," she said curtly.

Taken aback, Basil said nothing while she ran a specialized scanner over the data port woven into his shipsuit.

"Two of your boxes are aboard," Basil said. "But we can handle more. Our captain is eager to depart, but if we could quickly get…"

Ria smiled tightly. "Let's get this errand done, then we can talk additional cargo." Basil followed her down the street to the train station where they boarded an automated train.

At a building similar to others around it except for a stone arched entry, Basil followed Ria off the train and up to a nondescript entrance built into the stonework.

The Tiranian signage seemed quite beautiful to Basil. He imitated what Ria did at the security screening, machines and guards scanned him, and he passed through. He followed her down an empty corridor to one of a bank of small elevators.

The elevator slowly descended. "This the recon out-processing facility?"

"Yes, among other things. This is Valsi Prison. For political prisoners…"

He turned on her. "You brought me into a prison! Under someone else's ID!"

Ria smiled. "You are temporarily assigned to Ajisai. Although it's not too hard to get into a prison…"

"You lied to me!"

Her smile faded. "No I didn't. You've been briefed by your company people…"

"I have not."

She patiently said, "I assumed they had. Talus Company…"

"I'm walking back out of here. Taking my chances…"

"No you are not!" Her grip was tight on his arm. "The best way out is to stick with me, stick with the plan. If you try something else, it will compromise me, which I'm not going to let you do. Got it? Last night I gave you plenty of time to voice your misgivings, to review the plan. You said nothing."

"I knew nothing."

"Not my fault."

The elevator stopped, the doors opened, and they walked out into a gloomy corridor empty of people. Ria led him to a steel stair. They descended into gloom.

• • •

Basil and Ria advanced slowly down a dark corridor. On both sides were rows of steel doors in frames. A DNA lock was attached to each door with a smear of epoxy.

Also on each door, three characters had been hand-scrawled in Tiran script. Basil looked at Ria, who nodded uncertainly. They heard movement.

Ria studied the scrawled Tiran script on the door on the right. "That's it—number 733."

She pulled a scan/lock out of her pocket and held it over the lock until it clicked. Inside the dimly lit cell an emaciated form sat on the floor, eyes closed. The eyes flickered open; the mouth mumbled something unintelligible. With Ria's help, Basil got the filthy form to his feet.

Ria unpacked a shipsuit and with considerable difficulty got the ragged figure into it. Sealed up to the collar, he looked almost passable. He continued to mouth sounds. Basil and Ria linked arms and helped the old man down the corridor. The stairs were difficult, but they made it up to the elevator level.

"There's water in the shipsuit e-pack. You should drink some," Ria told the old man. "You are Piaro, right?"

The old man sucked some water up the tube, then pushed it away with a shaking hand. "Piaro, yes. Who are…?" His voice faltered.

"Your rescue. Save your voice. In a moment we need to walk out the front door. We can't assist you passing through the security interlock. We all need to look like employees. There's a guard at the exit security who may be able to help, but don't count on it. We get off the elevator and walk through security and out the door. Five minutes of effort is all that it will take. But if you stumble or fall, or do anything except walk straight through the automated security system, we are all in trouble."

The old man seemed to be gathering his senses.

"You understand?" Ria asked. "Let's take a moment before we get on the elevators. Straighten yourself up. Keep an alert appearance on your face. Tiranians aren't very adept at recognizing off-worlders' faces. Their AIs are better at it but not that much better."

Ria motioned Basil to let go of the old man. "Walk a few steps. Then turn and walk back to us."

Piaro did so, tottering a little.

Ria straightened his posture. "Look forward. Don't make eye contact with the guards or the AI ports. But don't look down or away. Be confident. We are Ajisai employees here on legitimate business."

Ria used her ID to call the elevator down.

"These IDs and the false data in the AI in their system will be deleted at the end of this shift which is in just a few minutes. We need to be outside the building before then.

The elevator arrived. Two guards stepped out.

Piaro stumbled back, Basil supporting him.

"What's wrong with him?" one said, eying Piaro.

"Injury down below; we're taking him to the aid station," Ria said. She and Basil half carried Piaro into the elevator. The door closed and it started up.

"That was close," Ria said. She put her face close to Piaro. "You're going to have to walk out of here on your own. A real injury wouldn't be carried out the front gate. It is not far, maybe a total of fifty meters. You have to do it on your own."

Piaro straightened. "I will."

The elevator doors opened at the street level. Piaro and Basil followed Ria into the exit walkway. Transparent panels and automated doors were constructed to form a two-chamber exit in which only one of the three doors could be opened at once.

Ria handed the duty officer her com and said something in Tiranian. He laughed.

Piaro was standing easily; Basil held his breath.

The duty man waved them in front of the recognition scanner. Basil went through first, his heart pounding. If they were recognized now, they were trapped. Then into the second chamber. Guard booths lined both sides of the gate complex. The last doors slid open silently, and he walked out past the ancient gate and into the uncrowded street.

Piaro came through next, eyes straight ahead. Exiting the last door, he started to crumple. Basil caught him.

Ria joined them, and they made their way out onto the uncrowded street.

"Another twenty meters," Ria said.

Basil and Ria continued to half carry Piaro, around a corner, then another. People didn't stare, but Basil could tell they were looking. "In here," Ria said. They ducked into a cluttered shop selling inexpensive children's clothing. They went down the narrow aisle and into the back of the shop. In a room that seemed to be someone's living space, Ria opened a cabinet and took out three shipsuits. They were changing clothes when an old woman came in and said something to Ria in Tiranian.

Now in different shipsuits, Ria and Basil assisted Piaro out the back door of the shop, down a short alleyway, to the street, and to where there was a short row of automated taxis. They slid into a taxi where Piaro slumped against Basil. "He's out. Exhausted."

Ria said an address to the taxi which rose up to the tramway and fitted itself into the flow.

The taxi took them to a quiet street lined with residential towers.

Basil couldn't rouse Piaro, so he carried him into the empty lobby. Ria led the way down a corridor and unlocked a room. Basil deposited Piaro on some cushions in the living room.

"When do we go to the ship?" Basil said.

"A change of plans. The old woman at the shop told me the national police are patrolling the departure gates up at Tiran Station. We need to lie low for a time. And we all need rest. This safe-house has a sim sleep box in the other room. You go get two hours' sleep. I'll tend Piaro. Then you watch him while I sleep."

Basil was too tired to argue.

Basil woke, disoriented, then climbed out of the sim sleep box, dressed, and went into the other room. Ria was watching Piaro where he lay.

"He's alive," Ria said. "Doing better, but too frail for sim sleep."

Ria pulled the old med-patch off Piaro's thin arm and put a new one on. "I upped the dosage a little; he won't wake for a while."

"I'm leaving," Basil told her.

Ria shook her head. "No you are not. That's not the plan. Three of us go together up the elevator to…"

"You can help Piaro along by yourself. I need to get back to my ship. I want no further part of this."

Ria confronted Basil, her eyes smoldering. "You were briefed on the plan; you are in the middle of it. You can't walk out now. All our lives now depend on…"

"I was never briefed."

"That's your story."

They stared at each other.

"My organization is assisting Talus in this, not the other way around," Ria snarled. "You are a Talus employee, and you want to quit halfway through? Ridiculous!"

"I'll tell you what's ridiculous: Talus Company is supposedly involved in some covert plan to smuggle Piaro out of prison and off-world? Ridiculous! Talus is a trading company."

Ria held her hands up. "I won't talk about this anymore. I have got to get some rest. You watch Piaro for the next two hours."

She stomped off to the bedroom.

Basil sat staring at the glittering towers of Tiran City. From time to time he checked on Piaro, who seemed better—regular breathing, the strain on his face relaxed.

After a time, Piaro woke and sat up, clearly disoriented.

"I am Basil Ajami. Econ officer on the Talus Company ship *Rafale*."

"I am Piaro. Economist," Piaro said. "Thank you for saving me."

"Don't thank me; this is her operation." Basil nodded toward the bedroom. Piaro's rejuv patch had turned blue. Basil rummaged around in a cabinet and found a well-stocked first aid container and put a fresh patch on Piaro's arm. "Feeling better?"

"A little."

"We have a couple of hours. Ria is resting." Basil made tea for both of them and they sat silent, looking at the lights of Tiran City.

"I know a little of your work," Basil told Piaro. "Very distinguished. I'm puzzled that the lead economist for Lord Kaleege would come to Tiran," Basil said.

"I didn't come here voluntarily. The royalist government sent me to Karaghia, to try to reign the plantation managers back in. Since the revolution, Orane has been preoccupied with other matters, and the plantation managers have been running things their own way. The Karaghia economy has stagnated. The managers are paying the locals in scrip. That violates the constitution I wrote for Lord Kaleege. Scrip is slavery. The workers go into debt, then they are indentured. It's happened many times before in history." Piaro sipped his tea with a shaking hand. "Sorry. I am talking too much. But to answer your question, Tiran military captured me. They have covert teams on Karaghia, it seems. My guess is that they will try to take control of a plantation or two, ensure a supply of ora for Tiran, and perhaps reduce the supply to the royalists."

He fell silent and soon was dozing.

I could walk out right now and make my way back to the ship, Basil thought. *But do I want to endanger the lives of Piaro and Ria? Is she even telling the truth about the danger?*

After a while Ria appeared, sleepy-eyed from sim sleep. She woke Piaro, put her com in front of his face, Basil's face, and her own, then flexed fingers in the control field. "Good. Our three IDs are still in the Port Authority AI. Which will allow *Rafale* to depart with the same five crew the Port's AI thinks she arrived with. But we need to lie low until our people find out what's causing the security alert…"

"Look," Basil interrupted, "I have no intention of lying low. I want no more part of this. All I want is some additional cargo…"

Basil's com chimed and he answered.

It was Cereclo. "Troops came on board. My docking permit has been pulled. Got to get in the departure line now or they'll impound the ship!"

"What for?"

"Get aboard now, Basil." Cereclo's voice was tight. "I'm pulling the ship out of here with or without you." Cereclo clicked off.

"*Rafale* has been directed to leave," Basil said.

"What!" Ria shouted. She jumped to her feet, rousing Piaro. "Your ship called you on your com?"

Basil nodded.

"Then we need to leave here right now." She hoisted Piaro to his feet. "That call will be traced and will alert security."

They scrambled out the door and down the empty corridor.

"They ordered him to leave," Basil gasped at Ria. "He has no choice."

Ria turned a furious face to Basil. "He's abandoning us! You people at Talus are completely irresponsible!"

The three of them hurried down a narrow shopping arcade to a taxi pickup point and slid into the first empty car. Ria tapped in the departure terminal of the elevator and held her wristcom over the plate, and the doors closed. Then they had to sit and wait while the machine reconfigured for three people, but eventually it rose up to the tracks.

Ria activated her com. "Makes no difference now that the secret police monitor these calls."

The taxi doors slid open, and they joined the crowd in the elevator hall. They inched forward with the queue and eventually packed into one of the hundred-person elevators.

On the concourses there seemed to be uniforms everywhere—police, military, security, Revolutionary Guards.

They found their concourse and walked through the automated scanners with the rest of the crowd.

"*Rafale*'s at number forty," Basil said, trying to keep his tone conversational.

"Call your ship," Ria said. "Tell them we are two minutes away."

"Security monitors?"

"Doesn't matter now. Backup plan…"

Basil called Cereclo. "We are two minutes away."

"I can't wait!"

Basil clicked off.

They jostled through the crowd, half dragging Piaro. Ria kept a determined smile on her face, walking fast and confidently…As they passed a row of kiosks, a man in civilian clothes stepped forward and started to speak. Ria dived at him, knocked him to the carpeted deck, and rolled to her feet. The crowd parted for an instant. Ria tore Piaro from Basil's grip and shouted, "Get to gate 20!"

Basil pushed forward into the crowd, but Ria and Piaro were out of sight.

He turned and sprinted to gate 20 and flashed past the automated security gate and up the ramp into the unfamiliar ship.

"About time!" a crewman snarled. He slammed the hatch closed and hit the emergency pumpdown cycle, then led Basil to a vacant four-bunk crew cabin. "Get into buffers. We will be accelerating hard."

Basil lay down on the bunk and engaged buffers. He stared at the emergency evacuation instructions on the bottom of the bunk above him.

That bastard Cereclo abandoned me! And Ria and Piaro.

Chapter 17

Basil woke still tired, showered, dressed in a shipsuit from the machine, and drew a cup of coffee in the wardroom. A tall thin man stood at the adjacent drink dispenser, his back to Basil. "I am Isel," he said without turning, "Captain of the *Deokar*." He was carefully monitoring the settings for a cup of tea which the machine eventually produced.

Isel wore a formal officer's tunic rather than a shipsuit. His immobile face above the military collar gave him a very autocratic look. He gestured Basil to have a seat across from him.

"I'm told you are qualified in ship handling," Captain Isel said.

Who told him that? Is he Tiranian spy?

Isel's colorless eyes searched Basil's face. "You don't need to fear me. I am being paid to transport you to Karaghia."

"I'm grateful for your help," Basil said slowly, trying to get his mind fully engaged. "Can I ask who is paying?"

"Better you don't."

Basil sipped his coffee. "There were…others…trying to leave. Do you know…?"

"I know only that all shipping scheduled for departure at times near our departure slot departed as scheduled."

Basil took too big a drink of too-hot coffee and coughed. "Talus ship *Rafale*?"

"All ships."

"I need to return to Tiran," Basil said flatly.

"If your crew skills are acceptable, I'll carry you as a working crewmember for pay, but I urge you to reconsider. Naru's police are efficient. In their eyes you are a known subversive. When you return to Tiran you will be monitored. Anyone you contact will come under suspicion. The police will give you free rein, since in effect you will be helping them identify more conspirators."

Basil finished his coffee.

"I dislike offering unsolicited advice," Isel said, his eyes steady on Basil's, "but I will risk doing so. If you return to Sigma to seek revenge on your colleague who abandoned you, that will not be to your advantage either."

"It is hard not to feel…anger."

"Anger, and revenge, are seldom constructive."

Despite the coffee, Basil felt his eyelids drooping.

"You need more rest," Isel said. "Then I will put you to work. Take two hours sim sleep, then report to the control room and take the tutorial at the nav station. I would like to have you stand a shift in the control room. I will trust you, and in turn, you can trust me. Agreed?"

Basil woke once in the sim sleep chamber, the nightmare image streaming through his mind: a bloodstained blue-uniformed body lying face down, short silver hair above the blue uniform collar.

He woke feeling better and reported to the bridge and introduced himself to Cargomaster Tanda. Tanda was a small man with black hair cut very short and an expression bordering on anger. He did not return Basil's bow, so Basil went to the nav station and waited. Tanda sat motionless at the command console. After a moment,

Basil got up and went over to him. "Could you log me in and call up the operating tutorial?"

Tanda flexed his fingers in the control field. "There. You are logged in and the tutorial is open."

Basil stifled his anger and set to work. The control room was quiet. Tanda sat motionless. The hours went by.

Basil was pleased to see that the maintenance records were up to date and that a full level three overhaul had been done a year ago. *Deokar* was a well-maintained ship, as good as anything Basil had seen at Talus.

Eventually Basil worked through the training exercises and began studying current operations. The trip plan showed a two-jump trip to Orane. *Once I pass through Oranie security I won't be able to return to Tiran. Well, I'll deal with that later.* Basil noticed the cargo was a light load of agricultural equipment.

Basil approached the sullen Tanda. "The trip plan shows a two-jump trip."

"Yes?" Tanda said.

"To Orane. Agricultural cargo to Orane?"

Tanda deigned to meet Basil's eye. "We will change our plan at the waypoint. Our destination is Karaghia."

Tanda turned his attention back to the big board.

"Karaghia would have been a direct jump. Why the two-jump…?"

Tanda stood. "Captain's orders. My shift is almost over. I'll turn control over to you for these last few minutes. If you are ready…"

Basil snorted. "I'll take it."

Tanda departed.

Basil's shift was uneventful.

Next shift change, Basil rose early to make his inspection round of the ship before relieving Tanda in the control room.

Isel was in the wardroom drinking tea and reading.

"Captain, I see our trip plan is a two-jump to Orane, but Tanda informs me we will alter it at the waypoint and proceed to Karaghia instead."

"That is correct."

After a moment's silence, Basil continued, "May I ask why we are taking a two-jump route on what is usually a direct trip? And carrying cargo that Tiran export authorities know full well would not have any use on Orane?"

Isel nodded. "This route preserves the illusion of honoring the barriers Tiran and Orane have set up between themselves."

"You are familiar with Karaghia," Isel said—a statement, not a question. Basil was still a bit disconcerted by Isel's impassive face and unmodulated voice.

"I have been to Kara several times," Basil said cautiously.

"There is an interesting fact about Karaghia that you may not know." Isel closed his book. "The Ziani family tomb is on Karaghia."

"I had no idea."

"The current government on Tiran does not publicize that fact." There was the slightest hint of a smile on Isel's face. "Devir's revolution, like all revolutions, wants to erase the past."

"Why would the Ziani dynasty place their tomb on an agricultural planet?"

Isel rubbed his neck. "I believe it is because the Imperial family believed their spirits needed to be near ora—the elixir we all use. 'Golden aura' was the Imperial family's honorific."

He likes to tell stories. "No Ziani monuments in the parts of Tiran City I have seen," Basil said. "I suppose Devir did a good job of clearing them away."

"Except the one at Sogeru Center," Isel said. "Which was so big that Devir's government did not want to spend the effort to remove it, so instead remodeled it to commemorate the revolution."

Basil snorted, "Very efficient."

"Dictatorships usually are."

Silence fell between them.

Basil finished his beer and drew himself another one. "I don't mean to be too inquisitive, but I noticed…I wonder…that we seem to have crossed the Tiran blockade easily enough."

"It is not uncommon in mankind's war-torn history for some parties on each side of a conflict to maintain communications with each other, often through a third party. If done well, those open lines of communication can reduce risk of the conflict escalating, which would not be to either side's advantage."

"You are in communication with the royalists?"

Isel said nothing.

"Why doesn't each side just communicate directly?"

"If something goes wrong, both sides can deny responsibility."

A dangerous game, Basil thought.

Isel closed his book. Basil noticed it wasn't actually an ancient book as he'd supposed but some sort of electronic device.

"I am an enthusiastic reader," Isel said. "Ever since I was a boy." Isel rubbed his neck and Basil saw there was something tattooed there. "I often think of those long-ago days."

"I enjoy reading," Basil said, uncertain what Isel meant. "But I enjoy non-fiction. Fiction is just what someone makes up. Histories are fact, science is fact, political science and economics—all interesting non-fiction."

"What are facts?" Isel said. " Histories are edited and re-edited. Scientific theories are found to be incorrect. New discoveries are made. Political and economic theories are revised."

At a loss, Basil groped for something to say. "I much appreciate you taking me off Tiran."

"I enjoy talking with passengers," Isel said, sipping his tea. "I once had an interesting passenger going from Karaghia to Tiran. I don't enquire about passengers' business, but if they want to talk, I will listen."

A valuable trait in a spy, Basil thought.

"This man's passion was continuum physics. He tried to articulate some of it, but the concepts do not communicate well in Basic. Only mathematics. Strangely, he told me he had been on Karaghia on a meditative retreat. On an unpopulated desert coast somewhere, he said he had found enlightenment and now wanted to put it to use. He mentioned Chumon Gate. Are you familiar with the mythology?"

Basil nodded, but Isel explained anyway. "One sets aside all of the objects of one life, passes through the gate, and takes up a new life. There is an ancient gate, on Beria, but the act of discarding all possessions and beginning a new life can occur anywhere. Purging oneself of possessions, and unproductive thoughts, memories, and emotions." Basil was intrigued to see a faint smile on Isel's face.

"I assume the enlightenment he found was as unexplainable as continuum physics," Basil said.

Isel nodded and fell silent and seemed reluctant to continue. Basil resolved to clear his mind of hate for Cereclo. *Forget about all that. Get back to Sigma, go back to work for Talus. Walk through my own Chumon Gate, become a different person. Spy or not, I envy Isel's calmness. A quiet life, his own command.*

But he could not keep from remembering…*My friend who betrayed me…and Ria who lured me into the plan. No…I could have refused to help, but I decided to join her, a decision that will haunt me.*

"Sorry, my mind was elsewhere," Basil said.

"I suspect your mind was on your hasty departure from Tiran," Isel said.

"I…yes, it was. Sorry."

Isel's look was sympathetic, but he remained silent.

"I think anyone would be hurt by betrayal," Basil said finally.

"An error can look like betrayal…"

"An error!" Basil snorted.

"A decision made in haste, under stress. A decision that is later determined to be cowardice or courage. Any of us can make errors." Isel rubbed his neck. "Military organizations train people to react automatically so that they will not make errors in moments of stress."

Basil thought about this a moment. "But that can be taken to the extreme. The old Tiran Imperial Guards, for example. Fanatics. Sworn to defend Ziani and the empire at any cost. That seems like conditioning, not training. A wrong decision made in advance, indoctrination."

Isel looked at the pattern in the wooden tabletop. "That is Devir's version of history. From another perspective, unswerving loyalty is usually considered a positive trait. As is a sense of duty despite the odds."

"Even when in service to the wrong cause?"

"It is sometimes difficult to determine whether a cause is right or wrong," Isel said mildly.

"Eliminating the Imperial Guard was one of the few things the revolution did right," Basil said. "Why they tried to reconstruct a few, I don't know. Probably just so Devir could appear to be merciful."

Later, as Basil tried to sleep without a sim sleep session, he recalled Isel's words: *Was Cereclo's decision right or wrong? If he had waited, gotten us all aboard, he would have missed his departure slot, security would have impounded the* Rafale, *and all of us would now be prisoners charged with espionage.*

Next shift, Basil went to the control room a little early. *It's time I got to know Tanda a bit better.*

Tanda was there in the control chair. He did not acknowledge Basil's arrival.

Basil sat in the weapons chair. "I understand you had an interesting passenger some time ago. A continuum physics expert. Captain Isel said he spent much of his time aboard in conversation with the AI."

"Yes," Tanda said. "He was rather aloof."

Like you, Basil thought, but said, "I admire those brilliant researchers, exploring the frontiers of knowledge."

Tanda heaved a sigh, then expostulated, "Love of knowledge is admirable. Pure research is admirable. But in the physical sciences, large sums of money are often necessary to build the tools that prove a theory, whether on a cosmological scale or on a subatomic scale…"

"Like continuum physics," Basil said, irritated at Tanda's pedantic tone.

"Obviously," Tanda snapped. Basil cautioned himself to quit interrupting. *Tanda likes to lecture.*

"The easiest place," Tanda continued, "often the only place, to find great sums of money to build machines that prove or disprove a theory, are in the weapons budgets of dictatorships like Devir's. New theories proven, technological breakthroughs, are welcomed as long as they can be weaponized. Scientists become obsessed, willing to sacrifice their principles just to get money to prove their theory."

"But research, and the technology it produces, bring many benefits," Basil said. "This ship, for example. Cinar shipbuilding drew the best minds in the Curve."

"Today things are different."

No they are not, Basil thought.

Tanda stood and left the control room. Basil moved to the control chair and logged himself in.

Oh well, I tried. But I still don't like the guy.

Basil's shift was uneventful. He went to his cabin, tried to sleep, failed, and went to the sim sleep chamber.

Before going to the control room for his next shift, Basil stopped for food and coffee in the wardroom. Isel was in his customary seat reading from his com, his ever-present cup of tea at his elbow.

Basil ate, drank coffee, and against his better judgment decided to ask Isel about Tanda.

"Captain, this is none of my concern, I know, but I am curious…" he sipped, "…curious that if Cargomaster Tanda is as unhappy as he seems…" Basil sipped more coffee, "…why doesn't he seek an assignment on another ship?"

"Are you applying to be his replacement?"

"No, no, not at all, I'm just…he seems ill-fitted for this assignment."

"He was assigned here, not of his choosing."

"Can't you ask that he be reassigned elsewhere?"

"I prefer he stays."

Basil nodded, though he didn't understand.

Isel continued, "I believe part of his task here is to spy on me. I prefer having a spy I know than one I don't."

Basil opened his mouth then closed it. *I need to learn to keep my mouth shut.*

Chapter 18

Basil, trying unsuccessfully to sleep, heard the alert chime. When he got to the control room, Isel was already there. The big board was bordered in red, showing a predicted intercept.

Basil settled into the jump seat and engaged his shock buffer. He sipped coffee in silence and looked at the two fans of vectors from *Deokar* and the unidentified ship. Basil brought up a back plot on his own screen. Raiders often orbited exit gates in non-ecliptic orbits, allowing for a disabling missile shot as they passed by the victim. But this ship was in an ecliptic orbit, converging fast.

Isel advanced power to 90 percent. "This acceleration will increase the fuel needed to decelerate at the Karaghia elevator head," the AI advised. Isel said nothing. The line showing the raider's probable track was still converging on *Deokar*. The ethereal sphere around the *Deokar* icon on the big board showed the estimated range in which a disabling missile would be effective. Basil remembered reading in the maintenance log that *Deokar*'s engines had been pulled and a level four overhaul done a year ago. They might be able to outrun the raider, and they would only have to outrun him once, after which the two ships would be on diverging courses, impossible for the raider to swing around and re-engage.

"Engines to overdrive," Isel said.

"Potential engine damage," the AI said.

"Understood," Isel said calmly.

Isel's acceleration might allow them to outrun the raider, but they would overshoot the Karaghia elevator. Then Basil saw Isel's strategy. Increase speed, outrun the raider in a hyperbolic approach that would loop them around Karaghia's sun then back to the elevator.

It might work.

"Missiles," the AI stated. On the big board four white lines emerged from the enemy ship. Their projection converged on the *Deokar* icon.

"Another signal," the AI announced.

Basil, Isel, and Tanda stared at the big board in silence. A pinpoint of white had appeared between *Deokar* and the exit gate.

"What is it?" Isel asked softly.

"Unknown," the AI replied.

The signal began to elongate on one side, its color shifting white to purple.

"Unknown signal is overtaking…" the AI began.

Suddenly there was a lateral thrust as though *Deokar* had swung sharply past a very dense object. Shock fields punched Basil's chest then faded. Red lights flashed across the master plot, and the master board went dark for a second, then relit. The white point of light was now deep red and moving away from *Deokar*.

"Captain, I'd like to put a replay on the big board," Basil said.

Isel nodded. Basil put the replay of a ripple in the star field behind them emanating from a purple dot that faded to black.

"Something passed us," Basil said, "moving so fast the scan could not track it properly. It damaged us as it passed."

"Going where?"

Basil flexed his fingers in the control field. "Possibly Orane."

"You've seen such a signal before, ser Ajami?" Isel asked.

"Yes," Basil said.

Isel stared at the big board for a time. "Was it ever identified?"

"No."

Isel advanced power. The big board flared red. "Engine damage," the AI stated matter-of-factly.

"Fire a screen of antimissiles," Isel ordered. The AI complied. And four short green tracks sprang out toward the approaching missile but faded quickly as they swung wide.

"Emergency acceleration!" Isel snapped. "Regardless of damage! Hard starboard and down." The drive units emitted an earsplitting howl. Basil's shock fields strained against the acceleration forces, overwhelming the gee field compensation.

Basil saw Isel advance the power on both engines. A monstrous shuddering shook the ship, and he slid the power back down. "Two minutes," Basil said.

Isel was silent, his hands working the controls. A missile fan lit the screen, and for a moment Basil thought the raider had fired, but it was *Deokar*'s own dorsal battery firing. The missiles curved off into the hydrogen haze.

"Enemy ship appears to be attacking us to destroy, not disable," Basil said.

"Eject cargo, captain?" Tanda asked.

"We've lost some hull integrity, captain," Basil cautioned. "Could rupture…"

"You and Tanda get into the lifeboat," Isel said. "This enemy is not a raider. It's a royalist warship. Intent on blockading Kara."

Tanda climbed out of his buffer. An audio alarm blared, "Danger! Personnel unsecured!"

Four long paces and Tanda was at the ladder. He scrambled up it.

"Go!" Isel told Basil.

Basil saw the pair of *Deokar* missiles emerging from the haze. They would destroy both the enemy and *Deokar*. In less than a minute.

Basil grabbed the overhead access bar and flung himself into the lifeboat. As the hatch swung closed, Basil thought he heard Isel say something.

A huge fist punched Basil in the back. Darkness flapped before his eyes, and the dim lifeboat cabin became a flickering red and black whirlpool. He gagged and sagged against the shock harness. After a time, clarity returned. *I'm still alive,* Basil thought.

The lifeboat appeared to be undamaged, the red emergency lights were off, and he could hear an orchestra of audio cues as the main board reset itself. Basil worked his left hand. Nothing seemed broken. "Tanda! Are you OK?"

The screen was dark. They were in the gate. Basil lay still, letting his heartbeat slow. *Isel's doomsday shot must have worked, missiles fired in a short hyperbolic orbit behind the gate's protosun, emerging in the electronic noise of the star, closing on the raider at incredible speed, too fast for their defenses.*

Now the raider is only a mist of radiation. And so is Deokar, and Isel.

After a time, Basil deenergized his buffers and crawled forward. Tanda was alive, but just barely. For some reason he had not gotten into his buffer correctly.

"No medbox," Basil whispered to Tanda, "but there is some painkiller." Basil administered a dose and soon Tanda's features relaxed a bit.

The next time Basil checked, Tanda seemed almost lucid though clearly in pain. "Hurts…my left side…"

Basil administered another dose of painkiller. *Three days to Kara.*

Tanda's monitors showed his heartrate erratic. The auto-diagnostic indicated he was sinking.

Basil returned to his bunk and lay there trying to think of nothing. But he found himself remembering the scent of cinnamon from Isel's tea, the yellow glow of lamplight on wood.

After a time, Basil again checked on Tanda and found him muttering again. "Isel was complacent, overconfident. I warned him." Basil leaned close. "He thought I was a spy, but I protected him…nobody liked having Guard recons around, but…" Tanda's voice drifted into silence. His monitor showed he was very weak, respiration shallow, heartbeat irregular.

Basil returned to his bunk and lay staring at the exercise regimen stenciled on the bulkhead overhead.

Isel a re-conned Imperial Guard! And me babbling about the evils of the Guard to a man who had once been one. A man who saved my life. Twice.

When Basil next checked Tanda's monitor, he was dead.

Basil confirmed again that the AI had the boat on course to the Karaghia elevator head. Then he lay on his bunk for a while in darkness.

Basil slid back into the control seat and checked the course, then, restless, went back to Tanda's bunk and switched off the health monitors. He switched the boat's gravity off and pushed the body into the airlock.

In slow motion he watched his hands push the big green button that locked the inner door. He set the recycle to retain air in the lock. When the red button for the outer door lit, he stared at it for a long moment and then pushed it. Noiselessly, Tanda's body disappeared into darkness. Basil chewed a tranquilizer and stared at the sparks of light on the screen. *Isel a re-conned Imperial Guard. Tanda not a spy. How little we know people.* Basil slept, ate, and watched the stars. Ria's silver hair and gray-green eyes came to his mind. He put that thought aside.

Time passed. Eventually the lifeboat screen detected the massive structure that was the orbital end of the Karaghia elevator.

But as he approached closer, the boat's screen resolved several ships at the elevator head, and the elevator head strangely dark.

The lifeboat automatically selected a docking port on the elevator, and successfully docked.

Basil tried his com, but it didn't seem to be able to connect. He left the control seat and energized the entry hatch on the top of the lifeboat. Indicators showed atmosphere in the connecting airlock. Basil drifted up into the airlock but was not able to get the lock to cycle.

He pulled down on the manual operating lever, which was stuck, then braced himself full-length against the loading arm mounting bracket and managed to free the lever. He pumped the door open and slid in, then awkwardly pumped the door closed again and pulled down on the inside air dump.

Basil's suit showed twenty-two minutes of air left.

Basil manually opened the inner hatch and slid weightless into a dark corridor. There was a dim emergency light twenty meters away. He pushed past junk left in the corridor and around the huge automated bulk cargo handling equipment. A cable left across a dark corridor caught his helmex and spun him into a wall with a clatter. He slowed down and drifted gently through the dimness.

Past more litter, there was a distant glow in the corridor. Basil stopped. Several suited figures flicked past a distant light. He moved forward. At an intersection, a flex tunnel had been connected. Inside the translucent plastic, a person slid something along toward the airlock where the tube's outer skin had been glued. The elevator end of the tube was glued to a bulkhead hatch. Basil backtracked down the dark corridors until he figured he was opposite the hatch. He swung the manual hatch open. Temporary light strips had been stuck onto the wall of the elevator corridor. Basil went in, then slid between steel girders and onto the top of an elevator box. It thrummed under his gloves. He grabbed handholds as the steel box started down the shaft. His suit gauge showed twenty minutes of air remaining. The box clanked and bucked as it slid over the induction magnets that would accelerate it toward the planet's surface 150 kilometers below. Basil held on tight. The box was not made for humans to ride, and the computer that drove it would optimize its descent to generate power for the capacitors that drove boxes up the adjacent shaft. Unless the box was carrying something fragile, the computer might use high-gee decelerations. Basil pulled his mantra up, relaxed his muscles, and prepared for anything.

With a huge jolt, the box floated free and gently began drifting toward the surface of the planet. A short, sharp acceleration pushed a cable he was lying on into his bellly. He tried not to move to keep the cable from abrading the fabric of his suit. In freefall, the box fell toward the distant surface of the planet. Basil's suit gauge showed fifteen minutes' air supply left. He tried to calm his breathing. The mesh of girders gliding past gained speed. In the distant blackness past the edge of the planet, the imminent sunrise was a line of gold.

Deceleration began and went on interminably. But it was manageable.

When the box rolled onto the curved receiving track, the lateral deceleration almost slung Basil off the box. Then the box was inside the receiving station, sliding down a track. Behind him another box was coming toward him on the track.

Basil rolled off the box and onto the track. He ducked into an alcove that held four huge electrical terminations. He prayed they were well insulated.

The next box rolled over him, clearing his helmex by two centimeters. His air was gone. He clicked the release and swung his helmex back, gasping Karaghia air.

He waited until a box cleared the next handling flange then darted through and ducked down into a maintenance manway as the box rumbled by overhead. The manway hatch was not latched; he swung it inward and tumbled down the shaft and onto a steel catwalk ten meters above the concrete foundation. There was a rusty ladder there. He scrambled down the rungs to the dew-wet weeds. Insects flitted away, and the scent of green growing things was strong. Sunrise was painting the rusty steel gray and yellow. Above him the tower stretched up into the sky past the vanishing point. He staggered down the row of hedges to a copse of lantern trees and collapsed in the dirt under their gentle shade.

His head began to ache. Planet-side atmosphere. He fumbled for nose plugs in his shipsuit pocket but found none. *But I was here on Kara not long ago; my implant will be able to quickly adjust to this air full of scents and dust and pollen.*

After a time, he got to his feet and crept along the hedges to a gate. He crouched in the shadow of the hedge for a long time, studying the plains that stretched out before him, the mountains beyond. To his left was an excavation and two new prefabricated buildings. Three utility dirt-movers were parked between the buildings. Basil ran to the corner of the building then ducked under one of the massive dirt-moving machines. The red clay on the tires was fresh. These vehicles had been used recently. It would be fully light soon; crews could begin arriving anytime. Basil needed to get far out onto the plains as fast as possible. From two sliding doors that formed the end of the second building, an unpaved road led to the excavation. It would be much faster walking down the road than through the tall yellow grass, but he didn't want to chance meeting anyone.

He skirted the open excavation and started through the tall weeds. The dawn over the still plain was very beautiful, but Basil didn't enjoy it. A kilometer beyond the excavation, the grass was sparser, and he sat down under a lantern tree to rest for a time and amazed himself by falling asleep. When he woke, it was full morning.

Chapter 19

Basil lay under the lantern tree for a long time. The breeze was warm and soft, bringing the scents of the sunbaked savannah. He watched clouds tracing their shadows over the yellow and green plain.

He tried the navigation setting on his com but got nothing. *Karaghia repeaters don't work*, Ble had said. *I don't know who's on the elevator, but I can't trust them. I'll walk to the Ambai plantation. Ble is not trustworthy, but dealing with him will be better than dealing with complete strangers while I figure a way to get off Karaghia and back to Sigma.*

He walked all day along the foothills, skirting the mountain range.

Over each hill he hoped to see the even rows of ora plants, but there was only more savannah. At night he ate a protein bar and bedded near a scree of rocks.

He woke at dawn realizing he was hearing seabirds crying. He was so sore he could barely move. Shipsuit utility boots were not made for walking. By midmorning he had reached the ocean.

He watched waves rolling into the tumble of giant rocks where the mountains met the sea.

I've gone too far.

He made his way along the giant rocks, then up them a little way. Finally, exhausted, he found a level spot in the shade of some ferns. It was some time before he recognized that he was hearing a tiny spring running between the rocks. He drank, then drifted into sleep where he lay.

When he woke, he painfully got to his feet and made his way down to the tidal pools at the base of the cliff. The moss in the still pools was brilliant green. Tiny fish hung suspended, then flicked away. A few red crabs, small as one-eris coins, browsed the pools' edges. He put his suit glove on, caught one, smashed it on the rocks, and pulled its legs off to reveal white flesh. He sucked it out, then killed and ate a dozen more. The other crabs continued their business, undisturbed by the fate of their colleagues.

The wind was increasing and the tide coming in. He crawled up the rocky slope and dozed in the sun. When he woke, the sun was setting and the wind had turned cold. The ocean stretched to the horizon.

He creaked to his feet and drank from the spring then made his way up the rocky slope. At the crest he looked north. The last mountain—lit orange in the setting sun where the range dipped to the ocean—had a headland. *I have food here, and water. I'll rest for a day then go back and find Ambai.*

The wind was strong and the waves were whitecapped to the horizon. He clambered back down the rocky slope and found a cave.

He probed a small pile of litter with the toe of his boot and realized it had once been something living. Bones gnawed clean, a bit of cloth. The tough fabric of a utility suit. Suddenly fearful, Basil turned off his light and scanned the darkness outside. The waves still boomed in the distance. The stars were bright.

Whoever this was, their corpse was long dead.

When he woke, the ocean was dark, roaring with wind and waves. He lay still, heart pounding, listening for what had wakened him. After a time, he realized the black marks on the roof of the cave were from smoke. There was a cluster of dark rock at the opposite side of the cave. Someone had had a fire there. Saris pistols wouldn't harm rock or ceramic or metal, but they would heat organics like driftwood.

Using his pistol, Basil got a fire started and sat watching the flickering orange light. The salted wood occasionally hissed green and purple.

Basil visualized the map he had seen. The elevator had been located a relatively equal distance from the five plantations on this continent, which meant the next plantation would be about two weeks' walk if the countryside was the same.

Basil sat in the firelight and watched the flames flicker. After a while he slept. When he woke, the wind had stilled. He gathered more wood and rekindled his fire. Then he watched the moons set at the rim of the ocean.

As he smoothed the sand, his hand touched a small object buried in the sand. It was an archaic com. He fingered it until it activated, then flexed his fingers in the fan of light, trying some standard passcodes. The screen showed old-style Tiran Imperial text which Basil could not decipher. A warning light flashed, low charge. Basil recharged it from his own com. *This old-style com is the same as the one Isel used.*

Basil scrolled past incomprehensible text. The last entries were pictures of sunsets over the ocean. The two bleached moons in a night sky. A fire flickering in the mouth of a cave, this cave.

The dead man's voice was a guttural whisper. Basil scrolled down through the days.

It seemed to be a chronicle of life in a construction camp.

Are all our lives this inconsequential? he wondered. Some was in Basic: daily reminders, prayers for his ancestors and the emperor, a list of things to do, exhortations to himself to maintain his physical health, gossipy comments about coworkers, the status of the work. He and his squad-mates were assembling prefabricated buildings out on the empty plains of Karaghia. Basil scrolled ahead to scenes of confusion. The guardsman had apparently left the recorder on as he ran. He was running with his comrades from an attack by hovercraft in standard military marking. Basil thought he understood the Tiran date superimposed on the pictures—it was before the revolution had begun. *But why would Imperial forces attack other Imperial forces?*

The next scene was a view of the empty plain, similar to the ones Basil had crossed. And then the rocky coast, the headland in the shape of a legendary animal. The cave, then views of a sunrise over a calm ocean, a storm, a sunset. The pale moons above a black and silent sea. Then nothing more.

Basil turned the com off.

In the first light of dawn, Basil walked to the spring and filled his flask with water and collected some sticks of wood. Animals scuttled away in the dim light.

Basil got the com out again and studied the days just before the attack. There was an open-sided warehouse under a soft sun. The pictures were now from a waist-high perspective; they were jumping and swinging as though the camera had been hung on a belt while a person went about other tasks. A squad of Tiran troops in gray utility uniforms using construction equipment loaded a twisted piece of wreckage the size of a tube-car onto a multi-wheeled truck. The men all had the same narrow features and height of the Imperial Guard. They finished loading the twisted metal, covered it with a shroud, and the truck moved off. The scene moved to a warehouse where the truck was stopped.

Basil dialed back several days. Harsh sunlight, construction excavators working, five of them, digging a massive step-sided pit. Trucks drove up and down the stepped road hauling out dirt. Then a view from the top of the pit as a huge tracked crane lifted an object onto a truck.

The date changed. The sides of the warehouse had been enclosed. Numerous vehicles crowded a makeshift parking area. A platform had been erected. Around it, many people were gathered. An official car pulled up and several men got out and were greeted with deference by a knot of soldiers in Imperial gray. The men passed by and entered one of the warehouses. Basil stopped the record, ran it back slightly, and stopped it again, freezing the three men just before they entered a warehouse door held open by a soldier.

One of the men was Mera Reigel.

What would a continuum physics expert be doing in the Karaghia desert?

Basil tuned the com off. *This com has value. I may be able to trade it. No, better to leave it here. I can find it later. Tell Ble about it, make a deal.*

• • •

The second day walking north, Basil found the road, a straight line pointing toward the distant mountains. It was much easier walking. Basil hoped to reach the low mountains in three days, when he estimated his water would run out. But the road led him instead to the ruins of an abandoned camp in the afternoon of the second day.

Basil approached the fallen buildings cautiously, but the silence was unbroken. The buildings were not that old, perhaps ten years. At one side of the cluster of buildings was a huge open pit, its sides spotted with grass and scrubby trees. There was water at the bottom, but its color was strange, so Basil did not walk down the stepped road. There was quite a lot of debris among the buildings, and he found an open-topped steel tank that had collected rainwater. There were many animal tracks near it, so Basil assumed the water was drinkable. He forced himself to take only a small sip as a test, then he retired to the shade of an empty room to see if his stomach would accept the water.

He woke with a start. There had been a sound. He slid his pistol out and clicked the dial around to burn. He crept to the doorway and looked across the empty space of the warehouse. The roof had fallen in across one corner. When he stepped outside into the sunshine, they jumped him.

Native arms circled his throat. Another twisted his right arm back and shook the gun free. They hustled him to the ground and tied his arms back with practiced efficiency, then backed away. He scrambled to a sitting position.

"What is this? Who are you?" he grunted in Basic. They watched him for a few moments then dragged him into another room where several more natives squatted. One of their members was heating something in a small brass pot over an open fire.

"I want to go to the plantation. I need your help."

They ignored him. The cook poured some kind of a drink into small ceramic cups, and they squatted, drinking it. Then they stretched out for a nap.

The hours passed.

When the day had cooled into late afternoon, they began a trek across the prairie. After nightfall they reached a circle of off-world tents around a fire. There was an off-worlder sitting in a camp chair in front of the fire. The men stood back with Basil while the leader approached the off-worlder and said something too low for Basil to hear.

The off-worlder came over and asked in Basic, "Who are you?"

Basil told him the truth.

Basil's bonds were released, and he was shown into the tent. "Sorry you were treated so badly by the locals, but we have not yet fully reestablished order here."

The man seated himself behind a camp desk. He regarded Basil with the coldest blue eyes Basil had ever seen. His smile was engaging, his expression and his gestures were animated. But his eyes remained cold.

The man glanced at his desktop display. "You came here on a lifeboat from a ship, an independent trader, en route to Karaghia. That ship was destroyed. Your lifeboat took you to the elevator. You rode it down to the surface, correct?"

"Yes."

"Why didn't you contact our people at the elevator?"

"I wasn't sure who was the proper authority here."

"So you set out on foot for a plantation? A plantation whose manager you know from a previous visit?"

"Yes."

"But you didn't find the plantation?"

"Correct."

The man studied Basil for a long moment. "I can tell you who the proper authority is here on Karaghia. It is the Tiran royal family Kaleege. We are reestablishing that authority. You'll ride our transport back to the elevator and exit Karaghia. Let me have your com."

Basil handed it to him.

"This temporary pass allows you three days on Karaghia. We will transport you to the elevator."

After several hours' wait, a military transport rumbled up and unloaded a squad of royalist troops. Basil showed an officer his pass and boarded the transport. A trooper in Kaleege blue uniform sat across from him. The afternoon passed. There was little to see out the slot windows of the armored transport.

At the facility at the base of the elevator, Basil followed a sour-looking solider down corridors to a room full of half a dozen uniformed folks at temp computers set on field desks. "This is Jana," a man said with a wide and artificial smile. "She'll out-process you." He turned and strutted away.

"Pompous ass," Jana said, glaring after the man. She eyed Basil's shipsuit. "You an independent?"

"Detached duty from Talus Company. If you check their inactive rolls you'll find me listed." Basil angled his com to the receptor on her computer.

"You're an Econ officer?" she said. "I want to get into econ."

"It's a good field. With the Tiran situation there are lots of opportunities…"

She shot him a look. "Not around here there aren't. Most people are working hard to get the status quo back…"

"Which is exactly the time to go in the opposite direction…"

"Talus looks like a pretty good company to work for. You've got a standing authorization for a 3C ticket back to Sigma from anywhere."

"Can I get a commercial lift to Sigma?"

"Better than that. With Talus vouching for you, we'll give you a lift on a troop carrier going back to Sigma. You'll be assigned observer watches, help the crew as assigned, but you'll be back at Sigma within two weeks." She glanced up. "If you can leave immediately, *Karada* departs orbit in four hours."

"I'm ready now."

"Not so fast. First look at the crest over there and read the loyalty oath. We need to get you scanned for eye and voice print."

"A loyalty oath? To Lord Kaleege?"

She laughed. "That's right."

"Are you guys trying to eliminate slavery or enforce it?"

"If you want to ride on one of Kaleege's ships, you have to

join the team. Don't worry, all orders read that way. You are in the service of Lord Kaleege until he elects to release you." She pulled a flexcom out of her machine. "Which will be when you hit Sigma." She flipped the com over to show him a map. "Here's the departure point; get over there now." She turned back to her work.

Soon Basil was standing with his departure group on the tarmac at the foot of the great soaring arc of the elevator. Evening light was spreading across the sky, shading from royal blue into magenta and orange. The evening was still.

A royalist officer made an announcement from the top step of the departure terminal entrance. The troops sitting on the warm pavement got to their feet, shifted their gear, formed a line.

Basil was one of the first of his group to board what looked like a new utility car. He filed all the way to the back and took a seat in the last row near the end. The car started up the elevator track.

Chapter 20

Basil woke from a doze, looking for the clock usually set in commercial elevator cars to tell passengers when they would arrive. There was none.

A soft sway ran through the car. The troops in the rows ahead of him craned around to see what was happening. The utility car they rode had no windows, only the tiny port in the exit door. It swayed again. A soldier near the door got to his feet and peered out the port. The car lurched, and gravity evaporated. The soldier floated up, rotating slowly until he grabbed a stanchion.

A babble of talk rose. The car suddenly smashed left and down and the lights went out.

"Something's hit the elevator!" somebody yelled.

"It's an attack!" somebody else yelled.

Basil ducked down to seal his footgear and pull his shipsuit gloves out of their pocket. The seat ahead of him slammed into the top of his head. But it had saved him. He could smell the stench of cut meat and blood in the darkness before he sealed his helmex. Basil became aware of a great tear in the side of the car two meters from where he sat. He scrambled out of his seat, grabbed a reaction pack from the row on the back wall, and contorted through the ragged opening into vacuum. The tangled elevator was all around him. A cloud of dark shapes hung in front of the huge green and ochre curve of Karaghia.

The elevator dock was only debris. The truncated end of the elevator was still in slow oscillation. Basil slid his arms through the loops of the reaction pack, clicked on inertial guidance, and moved away from the debris. He hung from the pack as it accelerated gently upward. The ranging radar beeped intermittently, asking if he wanted to lock a target.

It was a few seconds before Basil realized the pack's double tone was indicating an object very close. There was a black arc occluding half the stars above and behind him. It was huge and it was close. The gauge showed a thousand meters' distance. Basil pressed the button, and the tone changed to target lock. It had found an airlock.

He began to think he might live.

As he closed on the ship's hull, he noted ragged tears and ripples in the mottled pale-purple hull.

No choice. He had nowhere else to go, and the shipsuit pack would run out of air in about half an hour. He tried to slow his breathing.

Ten minutes later, he slid through an emergency airlock and into the corridor where only the emergency lights glowed. There were no sounds. It was cold, but the hull was still holding air. Basil made his way to the central shaft through a gee field that surged uneasily. He went up three levels to control.

There were two dead bodies in Tiran military shipsuits lying at the bulkhead entrance to the command center. There was a mutter, a voice. Basil crept to the bulkhead and peered into the room. The main board was lighted, showing Karaghia nearspace; control stations were lit. The status lights above the board were a filigree of reds and greens.

A black shadow was backlit against the display of the Karaghia system. Someone was sitting at the command station.

As Basil approached, the figure turned an age-lined face toward him. A second passed, then recognition burst into Basil's mind. "You're Mera Reigel!"

The old man raised a Saris pistol and aimed it at Basil. The gee field pulsed, the old man's hand wavered. Out of reflex Basil swept the pistol away.

Basil pointed the pistol at Reigel, who shrugged. "In thirty minutes Kaleege's flagship will arrive here. I've reset the weapons powerplant on this dreadnaught to explode, vaporizing him and me. Your threats are meaningless."

Basil put the pistol to Reigel's head. "You'll tell me a way off this ship…"

Reigel cackled a laugh. "Or you'll kill me? No point in threatening me. And where do you intend on going? The elevator is now inoperative. I've seen to that." He paused. "But prior to detonating this ship, I will be releasing the artifact that powered this ship. It is too important to be vaporized." He shot a glare at Basil. "You can ride it."

"What are you talking about?" Basil pocketed the pistol.

Sheer smiled a ghastly smile. "The price you pay for your escape is to listen to a story. We have time. I won't release the artifact until Kaleege is so close that his weapons won't be able to track it."

Basil stood, thinking furiously. *I can't go back to the elevator. Now what?*

Reigel lapsed into a sing-song mutter. "Several years ago, I came here to Karaghia, to the mountains along the coast, to find The Way. Instead I came across the greatest find of our generation. I had spent many weeks trying to quiet my mind, but was unable to smooth away the sadness I felt." Reigel's eyes closed for a time. "My daughter Sora left me a note when she killed herself. Her daughter had been killed in one of the royalist raids on Tiran. She said because her daughter was dead, her soul was paralyzed. In a world fighting itself, she wanted only peace. That is why I left Tiran and Devir's great revolution. I was seeking only obscurity and an unclouded mind. But out along that desert coast I found an artifact technologically more advanced than either of the two colonial civilizations on Karaghia could have developed. Curiosity overcame my desire to find peace. But to have the resources to investigate this artifact, I needed the Tiran shipyards. So I became Kapil Sheer, convinced Naru and his idiots in black uniforms to fund the effort to bring the artifact back to Tiran and set it up in a proper lab. The special weapons directorate became my laboratory. Naru wanted the artifact made into a weapon. I wanted to investigate the concepts behind its awesome power. We made a bargain."

The deck heaved sharply and subsided. The thrumming came again, more insistent now. Reigel heaved himself to his feet. His yellow eyes searched Basil's face. "It is time for you to depart.

"My coworkers in the special weapons directorate know of the existence of this artifact, so it can't be uninvented. But it can be undiscovered. I have learned that certain control settings will cause it to return to a star system at the edge of Xbalc space. The Kogon knew of this artifact. They used one of their sunkillers to poison planet 985 to hide the artifact. How it came to Karaghia, no one knows."

They staggered down the corridor in the pulsing gee field.

"It is Kogon then?" Basil said, curious in spite of himself.

"I think not." Reigel activated a power door which pulled back a short distance and jammed. They squeezed through. The cargo bay in the center of the ship had been fitted with a web of ceramic struts, several of which were splintered.

"Through there." Reigel indicated a way through the forest of beams.

At the center of the nest of beams was a twenty-meter-long white cylinder floating free above tracks that pointed aft.

Reigel opened a hatch on the dull white cylinder, revealing an ordinary medbox fitted with some additional controls.

"Get in and secure yourself in the buffers," Reigel told Basil. "When this vehicle reaches its destination it will orbit for a few hours then descend to the surface. The planetary surface is a poisonous dust hell. Get out while the cylinder is orbiting. There is an abandoned research station in orbit. With luck you can reach it and survive there until someone finds you. Now it is time for me to eject this cylinder from this ship then give the great Lord Kaleege his due."

Basil got in.

As the hatch closed, Basil heard Reigel whisper, "It is time for me to die. I hope there is no afterlife."

Chapter 21

Buffers at maximum could not fully counterbalance the acceleration. Basil felt consciousness being torn away from him in gasping ragged tears. He fought for breath, watched the instrument's glowing green sparks blur and haze into blackness as he lost consciousness.

He woke in freefall.

The capsule scraped against something and Basil froze, his heart pounding. With buffers on, the capsule felt like it was motionless, but if he released the buffers and the boat accelerated, he could be killed. There was a change in air pressure as a hatch unsealed.

Heart pounding, he released the buffers and opened the medbox.

A woman's voice. Human. The tone was cautioning. A man answered, disagreeing, impatient. The capsule hatch swung open, and the two figures peered in. They were wearing ship's utility suits, standard issue; the chest script was unfamiliar. They had their helmex flipped back and were speaking in a language Basil did not recognize. They both carried guns.

The man backed away and signaled Basil to follow. The other figure stepped to the side to keep her field of fire clear. The air was warmer in the space that looked like a ship's hold, or the loading dock of a station. He detected the familiar smell of storage containers, and a mix of other scents he couldn't identify—ship's air, not station air.

"We have to get out of here," Basil said. "I am not controlling this capsule. It could accelerate at any time."

They looked at him uncomprehending and herded him down a passageway. There was unfamiliar script stenciled on the hatchways they passed.

"Where am I?" Basil croaked. He cleared his throat and said, "What ship is this?"

They marched Basil to a small room with a table and four chairs. And there they waited.

Basil said after a while, "I'm a refugee, not a threat."

Two others came into the room. They were wearing dark-blue utility uniforms.

"Who are you and where did this lifeboat come from?" one said in accented Basic.

"I'm Basil Ajami, Talus Company, based on Sigma Station. I am an Econ officer. I escaped fighting at Karaghia in this capsule. It came here under its own automatic programming."

They looked at him without expression. Finally, one said, "You have entered Xbalc space without authorization."

"This lifeboat was auto-programmed—I had no control over its destination. I am a non-combatant, escaped from a warship at Karaghia. I would like to return by first available commercial carrier to Sigma Station, in Ramath space."

Two more officers, this time in gray uniforms, came into the room, and there was a lengthy discussion. They all had the same shade of skin color, the same black hair and modest height, the same slim noses. A handsome people.

After a while they moved him to a detention cell.

Basil woke from a surprisingly sound sleep. He was brought a tray of food and a cup of water. The food was unexpectedly good. He ate it all. Time passed.

Two uniformed Xbalc motioned him out of the cell. In another room, two Xbalc, one male and one female, were sitting at a table. Basil was seated on the other side.

The woman said in accented but clear Basic, "Describe how you came to be here."

Basil told them.

They looked at him, expressionless.

"I would like to return to Ramath space, Sigma Station. My company, Talus, will fund the passage."

They left the room. Time passed. Eventually two Xbalc, one armed, escorted him to a separate security system and motioned him to walk through the scanner. It exited into a utility room where another guard waved him into an exit capsule, which immediately departed for the surface. After a harrowing ride down, he stepped out into a mild day. There was no one in sight, only a large concrete surface, an open-sided shelter with half a dozen wooden benches, and distant green hills. At one corner of the paved area, a large sign in Basic said to walk to the reception center. A footpath led off into the countryside.

Basil stood for a moment, enjoying the sunshine and the breeze.

No choice.

He set off down the path. On either side were small fields of a low crop, broad green leaves in neat rows, gray-brown soil in the furrows between the rows. The path wound on into a forest of dappled sunlight on russet-brown leaves. At a clearing Basil paused and noticed in the distance the pale blue of what must be an ocean. The sun was approaching the horizon.

Hope the reception center is close. I'm exhausted, and I'd hate to have to spend the night in the forest.

Pausing for a moment, he heard a silvery tinkling in the forest to his left. He stood motionless and the sound came again, like drops of clear water falling into a still mountain pool. He followed the sound through the woods and soon discovered a low wall made of white stones. Through an open, arched gateway he could see a small stone house. A windchime was making the gently tinkling sound. There were no vehicles in sight, and no people. As he hesitated, the door opened and an off-worlder in a worn white utility suit came out and stopped abruptly when he saw Basil. The two men stood staring at each other.

Finally Basil said, "Basic?"

"Go back to the main trail," the man said in Basic. He pointed into the forest. "The reception center is a thirty-minute walk in that direction." His accent was familiar.

Recognition dawned in Basil, and with it, anger. "Cereclo! You abandoned me at Tiran Station."

"Basil," Cereclo said, shaking his head. "What are you doing here?"

"I was in a…lifeboat…that strayed into Xbalc space. Their security forces sent me here."

"Go back to the path. Turn right. The reception center is about half an hour's walk. You can make it before nightfall."

Demaris stepped around Cereclo. A gleam of sunlight lit her tawny hair.

"It's Basil Ajami," Cereclo said unnecessarily.

Basil found himself apologizing. "I'm sorry to intrude…"

"Come in," Demaris said.

"He needs to go check in first," Cereclo said.

"Rest first." Demaris led Basil through the house and out onto a stone veranda with a spectacular view of the forested valley.

They sat down on a worn wooden bench in the shade of a tree. There were short plants with purple flowers growing on both sides of the bench.

Weariness fogged Basil's mind to the point he began a rambling dialogue. "I came into Xbalc space on a vehicle. It has an advanced drive of some sort. If someone can analyze it, duplicate it, it could mean a leap forward in ships' engine design..." He stopped talking, wondering why he had said what he had.

Demaris smiled a tiny smile. "Others may find it, Basil; not you."

He watched the breeze ruffle the treetops.

"You'll come to like this place," Demaris continued. "The Xbalc are not cruel. They have provided us this area of this planet and assured that we have the necessities we need. They leave us alone." She studied the distant horizon. "They do not furnish us with ora, but that cannot be changed. We work at the farm. It is a comfortable life here. But we can never leave."

"Is it enough?" Basil said. "Once on Nokendai you told me it was not."

The chirring of insects was softening as the sun sank behind the trees on the far side of the valley.

"I've changed," Demaris continued.

Silence stretched between them for a moment.

Cereclo sauntered out onto the veranda. "I'm off. Final review of the section three irrigation system is this afternoon. Back in a couple of hours." He turned and went out through the gateway.

"He's angry," Basil said.

"You are a reminder that we can never leave. He spends a good bit of time in the village," Demaris said, "attending council meetings, organizing things. He likes doing that. He likes to feel that he is accomplishing something." Demaris gave Basil a tiny smile. "And it is his excuse to spend a little time away from me." Demaris ran her fingers through the purple flowers beside the bench. "It is my fault he is here. Remember when Shuard pulled Cereclo and you out of the offsite planning session for a fast run to Karaghia then Tiran? That was one of Shuard's smuggling ventures. Smuggling red onyx into Tiran and using the profits to buy influence within Devir's government, within Sigma Security, and within Kaleege's court. Cereclo didn't realize what was going on, but I did, and I said nothing. Later Shuard blackmailed Cereclo by threatening to expose him to Sigma Security as the one doing the smuggling. And later Shuard pressured Cereclo to leave Tiran without Piaro, and you. I should never have let Cereclo become involved."

"How did you and he end up in Xbalc space?"

"Remember when you and I ran across Shuard on Nokendai? He said he was there overseeing the installation of updated armament in two C-800s for Talus. He later hijacked those two ships, took them to Karaghia, and turned both ships over to Lord Kaleege, in exchange for a position on Kaleege's military staff. Cereclo and I were among the crew members in that hijacking." She shook her head. "I knew Shuard was deceitful, but I had not thought he would turn all us crewmembers over to the RDF for shipment back to Sigma and trial as pirates. Cereclo and I escaped in a lifeboat and crossed the frontier into Xbalc space."

"There is no way off this planet?" Basil said.

"None. I am resigned to that fact. Cereclo is not yet...comfortable with it."

Basil's eyelids were drooping with fatigue. But Demaris clearly wanted to talk. Maybe to confess.

"Here, in exile, is the place to follow The Way, to walk through Chumon Gate, to put aside striving for things that are not satisfying. To live simply." She turned her remarkable gray eyes on Basil and smiled a more genuine smile. "Let me tell you why I feel this way. Long ago my mother lived on Delta Station. She lived alone, working for the Port Authority. My father disappeared in the war. When I was eighteen I was accepted to Colresh, to the navigator course, and moved to Sigma, although I would visit Delta several times a year. That's when I realized how simply, how frugally, my mother was living. Her apartment was small and tidy, almost bare. Once I asked her if she didn't want to move into something bigger, something better, and closer to other people. She said she had all she wanted. Her health was not good, residual effects from some lung infection she received during the fighting on Jais, but she never complained. I came for one of my visits toward the end of my senior year. She and I knew it might be the last time I would see her alive, but we did not discuss that; we spoke only of positive things, of the daily activities of our lives. And then I returned to Sigma just as I had a dozen times before. I never saw her again. She died just before I graduated."

Why is she telling me this? Basil wondered.

"When I came back to clear out her apartment, I remember feeling sad that she had left so little behind after so many years. Standing in that neat little apartment, I remembered a conversation my mother and I had when I was about eight years old, the first year we lived on Delta. A woman had come to visit her, a friend of hers from Jais before the war. I had crept into the room to sit on the floor nearby, listening to these two ordinary-looking women talking over cups of tea. They talked about wartime and post-war food shortages, how they had been raped from time to time by soldiers, the confusion, the lack of water, the pointless conscript work, how lost people had been when the city was without law, and without purpose. Only the power of the soldiers had any meaning."

Demaris stopped talking and got to her feet. "I remember my mother telling me, 'What matters most is being allowed to live your life in peace, working, and being with those you love.'" Demaris nodded to herself then smiled and helped Basil to his feet. "You are exhausted. Stay here tonight. Tomorrow Cereclo and I will walk you to the reception center." She led Basil down a short hallway to a small room painted creamy white with green trim. There was a rolled-up futon on the mat floor and in one corner a tall pale-green vase with a single orange flower in it.

"My mother was right, Basil. Time and peace to live our lives quietly are the most precious things we can ever have."

Basil sank onto the futon and into sleep, feeling as though he had come home after a long journey.

Chapter 22

A light woke Basil.

"In here," someone said in Basic.

Basil sat up. Two men in black utility suits stepped into the room. They spread out along the walls, guns pointed at him, while a third man indicated that Basil was to come with him.

"What is this?" Basil asked.

"You come with us."

Basil was herded out to a black rad-absorptive air-land craft in front of the house. Cereclo and Demaris were already in it.

"Move! We're only one step ahead of an Xbalc squad."

Basil and the two men jammed in, the door slid shut, and they thrust off into the night sky. Basil heard Cereclo say, "If they take us to RDF jurisdiction, we're dead." Basil tried to turn, but they were jammed in shoulder to shoulder. And he didn't know what to say anyway.

The AL rendezvoused with an orbital, and they were hurried inside under blackout conditions and shown acceleration couches. Basil lost sight of Cereclo and Demaris.

The orbital lifted off.

Later, Basil, in a clean RDF shipsuit, was shown into a conference room on the RDF warship. He started toward an empty seat near the back but was redirected to a seat near the front. A holographic display showed a deep-red star crinkled with sunspots, its disk warped by a dozen gigantic flares. The small conference room quickly filled to overflowing. Three senior officers came in, and juniors relinquished their seats and stood along the back wall. A short man in a gray-green RDF shipsuit that Basil identified as a Special Forces uniform, ground operations, went to the front of the room and clicked the display off. "With your permission, sir, we'll get started."

The commander nodded and a new display appeared, a surface mission trajectory diagram. Most of the acronyms were unfamiliar, but Basil gathered it was a search-and-retrieval mission, inside enemy space. Find and retrieve the capsule Basil had ridden. There was no discussion of cost/benefit balances, no description of strategic pros and cons, but there was a risk assessment. And that assessment indicated only a 40 percent chance of success.

"To summarize, Xbalc IV and 985-II are currently in this alignment, which will work in our favor. From this point two air-land craft make a hyperbolic approach and high-deceleration reentry to 985-II. The search team deploys and assesses the situation at the probable location of the device, right here." He changed his display to a com-generated detail of the surface of a planet. It appeared to be a city. "This depiction is speculation. The teams assess the situation and make a go/no-go call as to whether to try to retrieve the device or to withdraw and regroup. If a no-go, the team returns to the air-land craft and to orbit. If a go, the team forms a perimeter and the second air-land moves up and loads the device, then both craft return to orbit where the RDF-40 intercepts. We make a high-speed acquisition and immediate departure along this track." His display changed to the system diagram. A line showed a high-acceleration exit to the transition point. "A ten-hour jump from there will bring us to rendezvous with the RDF-63 in neutral space. The air-land craft with the device aboard will be kept in trailing configuration inside the ship's field, but not in the transport cradle, in case the device detonates."

Someone snorted, "A hundred meters of space won't make any difference if that thing detonates."

"Knock it off," the commander said. "Questions?"

"Can we load the device in that environment without being detected by the enemy?" a man seated in the front row said. "Last thing we need is to lose a team to either the environment or the Xbalc."

"Estimated mass is less than ten tons based on trajectory and deceleration analysis. The suits and the air-land crafts will handle up to twenty hours on the surface."

Somebody else in the crowd spoke. "Do we have intel on Xbalc movements on the surface?"

"No. But we know they sent three D-class boats into atmosphere yesterday."

The senior officer, a commander, stood up looking at Basil. "I'd like for you to describe the device. You are the only one here who has actually seen it." Someone shoved a graphics box into Basil's hands.

Basil did his best to sketch the object as he remembered it nestled in the warped structure of the *Ahn Mehan*. "Was the *Ahn Mehan* destroyed?" Basil asked when he was done.

"Entirely. Along with the royalist ship *Karada*, with Lord Kaleege himself aboard."

"It housed the override controls for the capsule," Basil explained. "Without those controls, the capsule will respond to its own internal preprogramming."

The assemblage looked at each other for a moment. And all eyes eventually went back to the commander.

"My orders are to retrieve that device, and that's what I intend to do."

The sub-commander stood up. "Sir, the second air-land, the one carrying the device, will be unmanned. If the device activates while it is aboard, we will let it go where it will, using the craft as a tracking device. Unless the Xbalc intercept it, which they may do."

"Enough discussion," the commander said. "Time is critical. We know the Xbalc tracked the device to the surface and that they were coming for ser Ajami yesterday. They may already have deployed a team to recover it. If the Xbalc intercept you on the surface, they will attempt to capture you, and if they can't, they will file a diplomatic protest which our government cannot excuse. We are in their restricted space. If you cannot retrieve the device undetected, then you are to withdraw before the enemy detects you, is that understood? If word of this mission reaches RDF opponents in the council, it will be very bad for all of us. Now I want the team suited up and moving out."

As the room began to clear, Basil awkwardly stood looking around. A frowning sub-commander came up to him. "Follow me."

They went down three decks. Basil was surprised at how narrow the companionways were. They stopped at a ready room where six men were suiting up in military anti-radiation armor. The sub-commander disappeared.

Two crew members in shipsuits led Basil to an armor rack, backed him into the suit shell, and began to quickly close the armor around him, adjusting size as they went.

That's when he realized he was expected to accompany the team to the surface.

A stocky man in armor, helmet off, turned to Basil. His name display said Stilo, with a rank notation that Basil couldn't interpret.

Stilo scowled. "Sir, you should know that I strongly object to you being a part of this team. You are untrained and unfamiliar with tactics and equipment. You will do exactly as I instruct, and you'll do it without discussion, is that clear? I will not allow you to compromise this mission."

"I object to my going just as much as you do, believe me," Basil snapped.

They shuffled aboard an ALT and set their buffers. The lock closed on red combat lights. There were no ports or screens. Basil could feel the minute shifts in the buffer as they dropped away from the ship and entered atmosphere.

Stilo came on the intersuit com. "Suit power is the middle indicator in your chin-screen." It showed 100 percent charge. "The suit powerpacks will run the AR generators for about six hours, that's all. Once we get to 50 percent, I'll give you a go or no-go about continuing. Once we are at 25 percent, we return to the ALT and immediately return to orbit." He looked around at the five of them.

"That's only going to give us a couple of hours on the surface," one team member said.

"That's all we've got."

A holograph appeared in between the suited figures in the dim light. "Here's where we'll set down. We put a recon probe in there—undetected, we think." He changed the display, and Basil strained to make sense of a geometric network of lines and circles. Stilo's red indicator dot came to the center of a nest of concentric circles. "Mass, gravitics, and emissions spectrometry indicate it may be here. But since the surface is unexplored and the environment is thick with emitters, we are not sure. It is also highly corrosive and toxic. But at least this area appears to be sheltered from the high winds that continually scour the planet."

The display clicked off.

After a rough landing, the ramp door of the ALT opened, and Basil followed the team out into a dark world of streaming dust. His display showed dark shapes in the near distance. Basil followed his teammates. It was difficult walking in the dust.

The dark outlines ahead shimmered in the darkness, and dust drifted and ran, although in the heavy suit he felt no wind. The AR suit's field effects had a slightly blurring effect on his peripheral vision. He knew it was mostly his imagination, but from time to time the shadows seemed to move at the corner of his eye. Com had been silent for a long time. He plodded ahead past the drifting dust, the huge empty ruins.

"The Xbalc came to this point, we think." Stilo's voice was flat over the com. When the voice cut off it was dead silent. After a minute he came on again. "Check your internal guidance."

Basil brought up the display.

"Check your sector then back to this point," Stilo commanded. "Twenty minutes, no more."

Basil followed Stilo along a ramp that led up to one of the colossal structures. The screen was blank. They plodded up the great ramp, turned left into what might have been a room.

"This is strange, spooky." Basil realized he had spoken out loud.

"No com. Unless you've found something. Or unless you're declaring an emergency."

Basil plodded along. They entered a long hallway. There were shapes along both sides. Basil and Stilo approached. In front of the wall was a ten-meter-tall shape. And beside it another, and another, down the length of the corridor.

They paused. Stilo was checking the composition. This close, Basil could see in visible light. The smooth dark shape of the stone, the streaming dust, long, misty sand. But the surface of the shape was not smooth; it was dimpled all over.

Basil's display turned amber and flashed slowly. His suit detector chimed—a large mass, at the limits of his suit sensor's range. The signal was intermittent. And another reading, maybe drive emissions—not a full signature though.

"Stilo, I've got something, coordinates L-30. Permission to investigate, five minutes only."

"Go! Five minutes max," Stilo snapped.

Basil moved quickly through the streaming dust. Ahead were two columns. His scan told him they were structures that looked like open gates. He trudged through them. A plaza was beyond; the buildings to the left had collapsed. The signal was stronger now.

Black figures seemed to move in the dimness beyond the rubble. Basil kept moving. The building ahead had a curious smoothness above the rubble at street level.

Again something moved in the haze. Basil blinked, but the shapes remained, four Xbalc moving single file toward an opening in the rubble. Basil froze, then slunk back to the nearest wall and into the first opening. Those figures were not mirages.

"Stilo," Basil whispered. "There's somebody here besides us."

"Everyone!" Stilo's voice crackled on the com. "Withdraw to the rendezvous point immediately. Keep out of sight. We may have company."

Basil stared at the hazy plaza, his imagination painting it with Xbalc in every shadow. But nothing moved except the streaming dust. His heart pounding, Basil crept back along the broken walls, past the gate, then turned and trotted as fast as the AR suit would allow.

At the plaza they quickly boarded the ALT, locked down the hatch, and boosted for orbit.

After they rendezvoused with the ship, there was a sub-commander in the dressing room to meet them. As the deck crew was assisting the team out of their AR suits, he updated them, "While you were on the surface, we detected anomalous sensor readings both from the planet and from low orbit. Our assessment was that we were seeing a 20K-class ship in orbit and it had deployed multiple armored probes to the surface. But detection is difficult in that environment, so assessments may be erroneous. In any case, you would not have had time to locate the artifact, rig it for transport, and lift it to orbit without being detected." The annunciator clicked. "We will orbit for approximately ten minutes then accelerate out. All crew to stations."

The sub-commander exited the ready room, and the team filed out after him.

Stilo showed Basil to an empty bunk. "Take this bunk. Your gear has been stowed here." He waved at the locker below it. The rest of the crew took to their bunks and activated buffers. Basil followed suit.

"There'll likely be a debriefing as soon as we stop accelerating," Stilo told him.

As he activated the buffers, his display came on, the face of Commander Biaraf. "Ser Ajami, we will hold a debrief as soon as we are safely away. Plan to attend."

Basil woke. A subaltern was shaking his shoulder. "Need you to come to med center, ser."

Basil followed the young trooper to the med room.

A tech with medical insignia motioned him to the lone bunk. "Going to have to ask you to make your mission assessment report under analysis."

"This is not what I want to do, you know," Basil said as he lay down on the bunk.

"Sorry," the tech said. He popped Basil's shoulder with an injector and rotated the autohypnosis mask in front of Basil's face. Basil felt himself floating in zero gee, euphoric. He held back laughter. The patterns on the screen in the mask had given way to a kind woman's face. He felt as though he knew her but could not quite remember under what circumstances they had met. After a while he realized he had been having a lengthy conversation with her, answering her questions as they led this way and that. He was beginning to feel a bit restless; the bunk was not that comfortable.

The med tech rotated the mask away. Basil swung his legs down.

"Sorry that took so long, but my orders were to go to level three."

The chronometer told Basil he had been lying on the bunk for more than two hours. He was suddenly exhausted, from the interrogation, from the strain of the mission. "I've got to go lie down for a while."

The tech turned away from his editing screen. "Commander says you can rest until transition, six hours from now. Then be in the wardroom for the debrief."

Basil stumbled back to his bunk and fell asleep instantly.

He was soon being shaken awake.

"Now what?"

"Commander needs to see you in the wardroom."

Basil got up, straightened his shipsuit and made his way down the narrow corridor and up a level to the wardroom. Commander Biaraf was seated at the long table. He smiled his affable smile and waved Basil to a chair opposite him. Tea was served. Basil drank his down. The tea was not particularly good, but Basil was grateful for anything hot and stimulating to counter the cloudiness in his mind. The technician poured his cup full again and left the room.

"I wanted to express our thanks for all you've done, ser Ajami," Commander Biaraf said. "I'm sorry about asking you to be auto-interrogated, but I needed to get my after-action report off, and what you've seen—both on the mission and before—is central to what we are trying to do here. Tried to do here." His smile turned rueful. "My report states we failed to retrieve the artifact. Did not even locate it with certainty. But we did confirm the presence of Xbalc forces here."

Basil sat, silent.

"Before we transitioned, I received feedback on my report. I think you might be interested in hearing our analysts' conclusions."

"I would," Basil said. It was difficult to speak clearly.

"They believe the vehicle you rode from Karaghia into Xbalc space is a Kogon drive of unknown design, but capable of an order of magnitude more speed than even the best Istan drive units now being manufactured. Yes, help yourself to more tea if you like."

Basil got another cup of tea and sat down again. "So will the RDF risk an incident with Xbalc forces to retrieve the artifact?"

"No." Biaraf glanced at the right sleeve of his perfectly fitting uniform, flicked non-existent lint off the service bars. Basil wondered how many years of service those bars represented. "The artifact may have great military potential—it almost certainly does—but our analysts," his tone was less than complimentary, "feel the Xbalc military will not be able to convert it or duplicate it for military purposes for at least ten years. We are in the process of deploying sensors that will monitor its location and activity. It has a very distinctive emissions signature I'm told."

"And sometime during these ten years, I assume the RDF will attempt to retrieve it," Basil essayed.

Biaraf shrugged. "That decision will be made at headquarters. The ten-year timeline is based on the assumption that the Tiran weapons division has lost the key man involved in reactivating the Kogon weapon." Biaraf fell silent for a moment. "Out of curiosity, since you are apparently the only person outside of Tiran with direct knowledge of this weapon, do you share that opinion?"

"You have the results of my interrogation," Basil said.

Biaraf smiled. "I want to hear it from you."

Basil drank the last of his tea. "I am no expert on ancient weapon systems. I will say that Kapil Sheer was of the opinion that this artifact was unique, so probably not easily reverse-engineered."

Biaraf leaned forward. "You have had contact with Kapil Sheer? Do you know his whereabouts?"

"Quite likely dead. He was aboard the Tiranian warship that caused destruction at the Karaghia elevator head."

Biaraf busied himself for a moment with his com input, then handed Basil a small flat flexcom. "Our thanks for your assistance. And a note from your employer. We contacted them when we removed you from Xbalc space."

Basil read the terse officialese. "…services rendered during the time period…" He felt a smile break through the stiffness in his lips.

Basil looked at the second notation. Under the Talus Company logo was a personnel reassignment, directing him to report aboard the Talus ship *Ecliptor*, now on-orbit at Karaghia.

"Karaghia," Basil said.

"Yes, Karaghia." Biaraf stood up. "There is no efficient way to get you to a station, so you can make your way there on commercial transport, and we are passing by Karaghia, so we will deliver you personally. Approximately forty hours from now. You're welcome to take the observer's seat in control, otherwise kindly stay out of the way of my crew." Biaraf smiled thinly, stood, and turned to go. "And do not discuss any RDF missions, equipment, ships, routes, or personnel with anyone."

Basil sat staring at the flexcom and his empty cup. *Back to Karaghia,* he thought. Basil used the flexcom to put his thank-you note from the RDF and the Talus message in his own records, then attempted to find out more about *Ecliptor* through the Talus network, but the flex would not allow it.

"How do I log on to my company's network?" Basil asked the trooper who had returned to clear the teacups.

The crewman showed him.

In his slot of a bunk in the crowded bunkroom, noisy with horseplay, Basil opened his virtual display to study his new assignment. He had been appointed first officer on Talus ship *Ecliptor*, now at Karaghia orbit. “Report to Captain Mersing, Royal Tiran Naval Reserve.”

He called up *Ecliptor*—an old C-200, one of the oldest in the Talus fleet. The voyage record was lengthy. “Current assignment, haul ora from Karaghia to Sourav.” Then the notation: “Identification number discontinued.”

Ecliptor would be making her last voyage—to a salvage yard at Sourav.

Chapter 23

Before the RDF ship made a hyperbolic swing around Karaghia's star, it slowed enough to allow Basil to transship to a K2 cutter returning to base on Kara from a one-month patrol at the gate.

Basil pushed himself through the white tube between ships; a young trooper in a light-blue K2 field uniform greeted him. "I'll show you your bunkspace." Basil was led down a corridor littered with plastic glassware and bottles. "Party last shift," the young man said over his shoulder. "And every night until we get to port." He laughed. "We're on R&R." The young man slid open the starboard crew's quarters. Only emergency lights glowed inside. Snoring issued from several bunks. "Take any empty bunk—we're only half strength on these patrols, plenty of room. And we'll be in port in one more day."

He slid the door closed, and Basil picked his way through scattered clothing and unidentifiable litter to a bunk, pushed a pile of papers off it, and lay down. He managed to get bits of sleep despite the carousing going on up and down the passageways. When the shift tone sounded, he went to the exit hatch, where a trooper in a wrinkled blue uniform was prepping the entry for a tube connection.

"Is there an inter-orbit transfer I can make?"

The kid looked up, exasperated. “Here’s the situation. No interorbital connections unless you’re on orders, and you aren’t. The air freighter’s going straight to surface. At the freight base, you can catch a ride up to the orbital. Or you can ride with us to Main Base and try to find ground transport back. Your choice. You want off here, get through this tube to the freighter.”

Basil clambered into the lock, then through the tube into the freighter. In zero gee he pivoted, touched the lock seal, and pulled himself to one of the half-dozen empty seats. The air smelled of cold plastic. His inner ear spun as the pilot reoriented the craft in zero gee. The freighter decelerated hard, then went back to zero gee as reentry started. The ride to the surface was an eternity of short, sharp decelerations, some lateral maneuvers, and zero gee. When the aircraft rolled to a halt, Basil hurried out into air smelling of approaching rain. A row of automated cargo haulers were lined up on the empty runway. The first one quickly attached to the freighter and boxes began rolling out.

The freighter pilot joined Basil, staring at the stump of the elevator.

“When the pieces of the top started coming down, it really changed the weather,” the pilot told him. “ That’s why we’re flying them manual these days.”

Basil looked around the empty field. “Where’s the dispatch office?”

The pilot pointed. “That building over there.”

The storm was fast approaching, but the pilot seemed unconcerned.

“Guess I’d better get started then,” Basil said. It looked to be about a half-kilometer walk.

“Wait a few minutes and you can ride one of these cargo haulers. They’ve got a couple of seats up top. I’ll show you.”

“Thanks. You going to be able to take off ahead of this storm?”

"Sure. Doesn't take long to load and unload."

The automated loaders were efficiently moving boxes in and out. "Ora, I suppose," Basil said to make conversation.

"You know Karaghia?"

"I've been here before."

"Probably a lot better back then, before Kaleege's takeover," the pilot snorted. "Don't let the troops hear me say that. From what I hear, ora production is way down. Local workforce has deserted the plantations because of looting and harassment by K2 troops. Martial law just made it worse. And the weather. Heavy rains. Harvest equipment can't operate in the mud, and the crop itself is…well, anyway. I get paid to run stuff up to orbit and down. What happens on the plantations is none of my concern."

The automated loaders had apparently finished their job and were waiting authorization from the pilot to clear the field. The pilot showed Basil the ladder up to the empty cab of one. "Just sit there until the loader stops at the loading station. Then get out and go around to the front door. You'll see the dispatch office."

Basil made it around to the front door of the cargo handling facility just as the storm front hit, rain rattling and booming the sheet metal. Inside, a part of the tall warehouse had been partitioned off into open-topped offices.

Basil approached two young K2 troops at the first desk.

"I'm Basil Ajami, a Talus Shipping Company employee." Basil laid his flexcom on the bare wood counter. One of the troops glanced at it.

"I need to get to the orbital…"

"I got some anti-personnel rockets," the troop said sarcastically. "Strap one on and go. 'Cept I need them to quiet down some unruly locals, so can't give you any of them."

The other troop grinned. "Don't you kill anybody in my villages.

They belong to me. I got a good thing going there—women, food, drink—lots of drink."

The first troop took his feet off his desk. "We can't help you," he said flatly, sliding Basil's flexcom back to him. "No orders." His gaze dropped down to the RDF utility suit Basil was wearing. "If you're RDF, you can try the liaison people." He pointed to a doorway.

Wind drummed the sheet metal, then a burst of hail like machine gun fire hit the roof.

Fuming, Basil went down the corridor indicated. *Kaleege's troops aren't an occupation force, just a mob in blue uniforms.*

The next bay held another maze of open-topped office cubicles.

"Yes, sir. Can I help you?" A young trooper in RDF utility uniform with a gaudy Kaleege crest armband approached.

Basil explained and was led back to a sub-commander's cubicle deep in the maze.

The man stood as Basil approached. "We've not been advised of your coming," he checked his screen, "but that's no surprise here. Com here is crap, like most everything." He consulted a screen. "*Ecliptor* is in orbit. Scheduled to depart orbit in ten hours. Next air freighter to the orbital is in four hours. Plenty of room. I'll put you on the roster." He closed his virtual display. "There's a waiting area—I wouldn't quite call it a lounge—over by the exterior doors."

Basil stretched out on a battered couch and tried to doze. The storm outside rattled and rumbled the sheet metal. He drifted into a troubled dream of Yonna Ble walking down a dark corridor of wide black wood. The plantation night was raucous with the sounds of insects. A tepid night wind moved the sheers inside the electronic inset screen. Ble, the languid secret-keeper, opened a silver box, and a crimson glow filled the darkened room. "Red onyx," Ble said slowly, mesmerized by the glow.

Basil shifted on the couch. There was a steady waterfall of rain on the metal roof. The door banged open, bringing a gust of wind and a slim figure dressed in field armor. She slammed the door, switched off her electromagnetic torso shield. Basil caught the glint of short silver hair as she pulled her helmet off and glanced his way. They stared at each other in the dim light.

"I know you," they said in unison.

Chapter 24

"Come with me," Ria said. "I've got to sign in." He followed her into the next section of the building. "Hold your nose," Ria told him. They moved quickly down a narrow aisle between two walls of steel mesh. The stench of fear and unwashed bodies was intense. In the dimness of the cages, Basil made out dark figures everywhere, lying, squatting, and standing. A cacophony rose. A pale face in the crowd pushed its way forward to the steel mesh. "Get me out. I can pay you, pay you well, just get me out!"

Ria and Basil hurried on.

"Wait!" screamed the off-worlder. "I know you! You're from Talus Company. You know me!" He was jostled and shoved by the mob in the cell.

The voice seemed vaguely familiar, but Ria pulled Basil along, through the next door. An RDF sergeant behind a wooden counter took Ria's weapons and armor, made a notation on a com, and locked the gear in a steel cage behind the counter.

Basil pulled Ria to the far side of the room. "Who are those people in those cells?" He hooked a thumb at the cage room.

"Anybody Kaleege's troops suspect of being anti-royalists. Hundreds of them all over…even off-worlders. You saw that guy, probably one of the plantation operators. No wonder the ora export business is in a shambles, but K2's troops don't care." She shook her head. "How did you get here?" She sat down with Basil on the worn couch.

"It's a long story," Basil said. "Tell you later. I want to hear about you. Last time I saw you, you'd conned me into helping you get Piaro off Tiran. I thought Tiranian security had you. I got away on *Deokar*..."

She grinned a pixie grin. "I have my ways. Your buddy pulled his ship out fast—Cereclo, wasn't he? Talus ship *Rafale*?"

"You remember. So, how long have you been assigned here?"

"Too long!" Gray-green eyes snapped at him. "It's a bad assignment. One RDF Special Ops company assigned as advisors to Kaleege's army of riffraff." She stood. "But my assignment is finished. Papers are approved. I'm ready to rotate out, just waiting for transport off this hellhole."

Basil stood, listening to the rain's diminishing sigh above them. "To where?"

She looked around the gloom. "I don't know. Maybe leave the RDF..."

Basil wanted to touch her but didn't. "First time I've heard you sound unsure," he said finally.

She started to move away.

"There's a Talus ship in orbit, leaving soon for Sourav," Basil said. "I'm going to be on it. You could go too."

She looked at him for a long moment. "I'll go," she whispered fiercely. "Anything to get out of here." She pulled him into a quick hug then pushed him away, craning to see the chronometer above the sergeant's head. "Air freighter to orbit leaves every day at 0700."

"That's what I'm waiting for," Basil said.

"I'll get my gear." She hurried off.

Basil leaned back on the worn couch. He tried to analyze his feelings, but they slipped away, elusive as silvery fish. He found himself grinning.

Delayed fatigue settled over him. He pulled his jacket around him and laid his head back against the hard couch, watching fans turning overhead. He dozed, dreaming of plantation fans, Ble's low, open house where the ora fields met the jungle. Ria returned with a small duffel bag.

"That royalist air freighter to orbit going to depart on time, sergeant?" Ria asked briskly.

He glanced at a screen. "Yes, two hours from now. Weather looks passable. This gentleman is on the manifest."

"Put me on the manifest too," Ria told him. She showed him her orders. "Available transport."

The sergeant made a notation. "Be on board by 0630, departure at 0700."

Ria came over to the couch and stood awkwardly in front of Basil.

"Having second thoughts about leaving?" Basil asked.

She shook her head and slid onto the couch beside him. "No. I need out of here." Silence fell between them.

"What are those prisoners being detained for?" Basil asked to fill the silence.

An expression of disgust came onto Ria's face. "Nothing, really; K2 troops just round up anybody who resists their looting. Poor bastards."

"Could you get one released?"

She shook her head. "You don't want to get mixed up in…"

"I know him, one of the off-worlders. Slightly. Used to work for Ambai Company, running one of the plantations upcountry. I can't imagine he's any danger to the occupation."

"Why so solicitous all of a sudden?"

Basil leaned close and whispered, "He would pay us to let him go."

"Pay us how?"

"He told me when I was here before that he's got some illegal red onyx stashed somewhere near the elevator base. I believed him then and I believe him now. We take him there, get some of the red onyx, then let him go."

"And where would he go then?"

Basil shrugged. "Anywhere. If we leave him at the elevator, he won't be able to get back here before we leave. And anyway, he'd be crazy to return and get thrown back in the cages. He'll go the opposite direction. Check out a vehicle. We can get to the elevator and back before the air freighter leaves."

Ria stared at the chronometer on the wall. "You believe he'll give us red onyx?"

"To get out of there, yes."

Ria shook her head. "He'll say anything to get out of there, but who knows if his story is true."

"We can always put him back in the cage. The base of the elevator is only five kilometers from here. You get a vehicle and we can be there in a few minutes."

Ria leaned close to Basil and whispered, "So why risk our ticket out by taking a chance on some lunatic from the cages? Let's just get on the air freighter, ride up to orbit, and get aboard your ship."

"Why not leave with enough cash for a good start somewhere away from all this?"

After a minute she took a deep breath and went to the sergeant behind the desk. "I need to interrogate one of the detainees. He's a tall, yellow-haired off-worlder, easy to identify. Haul him out and bring him to interrogation room five. And check my weapon back out to me."

"Yes, ma'am." The sergeant saluted, made notations on his com, and slid a heavy RDF-issue Saris pistol across to her. He spoke into a hush box then said, "Detainee will be in room five."

In the interrogation room a haggard Yonna Ble huddled on a wooden chair. "We're going to take you to your stash of red onyx," Basil told him.

Ble looked up, a lizard-like expression on his face. "And then kill me."

"We can put you back in the cages now, if you want," Ria said.

Ble rose on shaky legs. "Take me to the elevator, take some of the red onyx. But leave me enough to buy my way off Kara."

The sergeant at the desk said nothing when Ria and Basil marched Ble out at gunpoint. "We're taking one of the all-terrains," she announced.

Inside the armored vehicle, Ria got into the bare box that was the back half. "You can drive one of these things, can't you?" she said to Basil. "Two levers. Pull the left one back to turn left, same with the right. The farther you push them forward, the faster you go. No brakes, just back pressure."

They moved quickly across wet sand toward the base of the elevator silhouetted in predawn gray and purple.

At the stump of the ruined tower, Ble directed Basil to a doorway. "We go inside here."

Basil parked the machine and started to climb out, but Ria waved him back. "Stay here, ready to go. I'll herd this guy to his cache."

They disappeared into a doorway.

Basil flipped open the heavy glass side window and breathed air sweet and cool. The gray light and the delicate scent of wet sand was dreamlike. Nothing moved. He checked his chronometer—still an hour until the air freighter lifted. Five minutes went by with agonizing slowness. It would be easy enough for Ria and Ble to take all the red onyx, go out the other side of the building. Or just hide in the ruin. He'd never find them.

How well do I really know Ria? thought Basil. *A couple of nights on Tiran, nothing more. She's kind of a hot-head, brave, but impulsive.*

He thought about driving around the complex of buildings at the foot of the elevator, but it was a huge complex. Instead he sat watching the doorway.

Ria walked out and pulled herself up into the transport passenger seat. "Let's go."

"Did you get some onyx?"

"Yeah."

Basil drove fast along his tracks toward the airfield. The eastern horizon had turned gold. "Where's Ble?" The transport jounced as Basil turned too fast.

Ria didn't face him. "I let him go."

Is she telling the truth?

"Did you say something?" Ria asked without taking her attention away from the sand dunes ahead.

"No," Basil said. They topped the last dune and came fast down the sand road to the RDF end of the complex. The air freighter was there, parked near the terminal building on the RDF side of the airfield.

"Stop here," Ria said. "You go aboard, I'll check this thing back in and meet you in a minute."

Basil slid out and trudged past the terminal building on the cracked pavement toward the air freighter.

The Oranie pilot was sitting in the cockpit with the window slid open. "Waiting on you two," he snorted and slid the flexglass closed. Ria trotted out to the vehicle, and they ducked in the aluminum hatch and into the smelly cargo bay. "Close her up," the pilot shouted down from the cockpit. Basil checked the seal and turned the big locking handle until a green indicator lit.

Basil and Ria strapped into seats. The ground thrusters were already rumbling as they taxied over cracked pavement, turned sharply, and accelerated hard. There were no windows, and the space was lit only by a row of dim utility lights in the ceiling panel. A short takeoff run, four minutes of three gees, then zero gee as they drifted toward rendezvous with the Talus ship.

"You still have the red onyx I gave you?" Basil asked.

"No," Ria said.

In the dim light he was surprised at the suspicion on her face. A twinge of anger touched Basil. "It was a gift, that's all. I thought you might like it."

Her expression softened. "I did like it. So did the guard I gave it to as a bribe when things went bad at Tiran Station." She squeezed his arm and gave him her pixie smile. "It saved my life. You saved my life."

The freighter drifted toward docking at the Talus ship. "I'm glad we let Ble go. Poor bastards down there," Basil whispered. "Hope he is able to make his way off-world."

"The K2 occupying forces are like wild dogs," Ria said without looking at Basil, "killing and smashing just for the pleasure of it."

"Power without responsibility…" Basil said.

"And without purpose," Ria added. "I never saw an op order the whole time I was there. They're not occupying Karaghia, they're destroying it. At least the ora production capability."

"Maybe that's Kaleege's plan."

"I don't want any part of that…" she said.

"What about Ble?"

"He's not our concern."

Through a corner of the pilot's windshield they could see a slice of the ochre and pale-green planet. The ship creaked and popped with thermal changes.

The personnel connector tube self-extended, and the green bar over the lock door lit. Basil and Ria made their way to the hatch.

"Thanks for the ride," Ria told the pilot.

Basil and Ria slid through the white tube that connected the two ships.

Ria snorted, "Not sad to leave that place. It didn't take me a week on Kara to realize these royals know nothing—about running a colony, about military organization, tactics, anything. They're morons, all of them. All the K2 officer corps' training is outsourced to a contractor on Epsilon, Ildara Company, who I'm sure is paid well to see that none of these idiots fail a course. They come here with no military knowledge whatsoever, much less any meaningful experience. All they've got is blue blood and a royal commission."

Basil took her hand. "Relax, you don't have to deal with them anymore."

The maneuvering thrusters of the shuttle glowed and pulled away toward the next orbital rendezvous.

Basil and Ria went onto the cargo deck and up the companionway to the crew deck.

"What cabin are you assigned to?" Ria asked.

"I haven't talked to the captain—half the com on Kara doesn't work—so I don't know. But I'm supposed to be first officer, which is generally the first cabin on the right side as you go up the companionway. Captain's cabin will be across the corridor from it. You'll see the Talus logo and the nameplate on his door. Take the cabin opposite and put your own lock on it. Then come up to control. I'm going up there now to meet the captain and see what needs to be done."

Basil came up the companionway into the control room. The big board was lit, departure course data on the screen. But there was no one there. On the visual segment of the screen, Karaghia lay huge below them, its normal ochre and avocado colors pockmarked with a band of impact craters from fallen elevator pieces.

Ria soon joined him in control. "No captain?"

"No. I guess he's in his cabin."

"What the hell," Basil muttered as he glanced at several indicators. "Lot of mass for a small box." He scrolled through a few more screens. "Everything we need for departure is working. No departure approval, but Karaghia orbit control probably has other things on their mind than traffic management."

"Yeah, like survival." Ria had come up close behind him. "This ship smells," she whispered, "and our cabin is filthy, litter all over, dirt everywhere. I'd hate to think what the air regen unit looks like."

Basil shrugged. "Ship's been leased to K2. That's the way they live, I guess." He queued a different set of views. "Ship maintenance… all these yellow indicators. Guess it doesn't matter; she's going from here to salvage." He turned to Ria. "Better get into buffers. Take the weapons station. I'll stay at nav until the captain shows up and tells us what he has in mind." A minute went by. "I hate to call him on the com."

"If it's time to go, let's go," Ria said. "The sooner I'm away from Kara the better."

"Yeah," Basil said. "Nothing to be gained by waiting." He enabled the AI's autonomous departure. "From here to Sourav via Tiran Gate," Basil mused. "Hate to go near Tiran, but no choice I guess. It's already logged by Captain Mersing."

"If you don't need any help, I'm going to go rest for a while," Ria said.

Basil nodded. "Good idea. Rest while you can." He waved at a constellation of red and yellow maintenance lights. "Even if Mersing stays in his cabin all the way to Sourav, it won't matter," he said, still trying to comprehend the array of ship's systems needing maintenance. Most environmental indicators were yellow, two were red. "Water, food regen, crew health," Basil read aloud. "Well, we can make it. There's no problem we can't live with until we transition to lightspace. Then we need to clean the regen system…" He studied screens and clicked through figures.

"I'm going below now," Ria said. She gracefully made her way down the companionway.

Basil and the AI made a variety of adjustments. Basil checked that the departure course and speed was right, then rose, and found himself facing a thin Oranie with a black beard and a bitter twist to his mouth. The man wore an immaculate Kaleege royal guard dress tunic with red and blue shoulder boards and a modest row of citations. There was a polished silver symbol of The Way at his throat, centered under his perfectly trimmed black beard.

Chapter 25

"Captain Mersing?" Basil stuttered, saluting awkwardly. "I initiated departure…"

"Very well." Mersing went to the command chair and seated himself. He ignored the departure checklist the AI had displayed on the board. *Ecliptor* exited Karaghia orbit, her unmaintained thrusters imparting a slow wobble to the ship that the internal gravity could not quite compensate for.

Basil keyed his com. "Ria, better get up to control now. We're departing."

"Be there in a minute." Her voice was groggy.

Mersing hit his com override. "Get up here immediately. That's an order," he snapped.

"Recommend buffers," the AI stated calmly. They were departing at max acceleration, Basil noted. Several indicators were already yellow. Basil said nothing. Ria dragged herself to the com station. Mersing was silent.

Ecliptor pulled out of orbit hard and aligned for the first waypoint. Basil and Ria kept their heads down and busied themselves with their control panels. Basil noted nearly all the movement controls were out of calibration, and both engine indicators showed problems. He set to work adjusting things to improve efficiency.

"Captain Mersing," Basil said, "request permission to familiarize myself with course and cargo. You have me locked out of both at the moment…"

But when Basil turned, the command chair was empty.

Basil went back to making adjustments to improve the efficiency of their very inefficient high-speed track toward the waypoint. The displays the AI put up for him showed Mersing intended to maintain max speed through the first waypoint and on to the transition point.

"Who is this guy?" Ria said low.

Basil finally figured a way around the cargomaster lock-out and put the cargo on his console screen. "See if you can access the K2 royal data site; his officer profile might tell us something."

Basil spent a few moments trying to find the trip plan *Ecliptor* should have filed for the trip to Sourav but could locate nothing. After a while he told Ria, "Either he's better at hiding data than I think he is, or we haven't filed a flight plan with anyone. I guess the military governor on Karaghia likes to keep it informal…"

"Or secret," Ria volunteered. "And there is nothing on our esteemed captain. In the official record of the Oranie court and Five Family military senior staff, he doesn't exist."

AI spoke. "Accelerating to threshold, recommend buffers."

Basil and Ria activated theirs.

"He's in a hell of a hurry," Basil said. "Which is fine with me, although I hate to see this old ship pushed so hard just to get to the salvage yard."

"And our commander doesn't even bother to stay in the control room. No com, no attention to other shipping or any defensive measures we might…"

"And no attention to profitability," Basil added. "This course and fuel burn rate will cost twice what Talus should pay to move this ship to salvage." He paused. "I'll try to get some time with Mersing, try to figure out what he's doing…"

Basil checked the display on his console. Something strange in cargo, mass very high, emissions, but the spectrum looked like they were being suppressed. It didn't make sense. He'd check it out himself after they transitioned to lightspace. Better to stay at nav with the ship's power so far out of sync.

"Transition in forty minutes," AI announced.

"We're still in the Kara system comet cloud ecliptic," Basil said to AI. "Is it wise to proceed so fast? And with engine status as bad as it is?"

"Probability of problems due to ecliptic objects, dust concentrations, or engine performance is less than 50 percent," AI informed him.

Basil shook his head. No Talus project he'd ever been on had less than 75 percent safety, and with well-maintained engines.

"Leave it alone, Basil," Ria said, her voice tight with anger. "Who cares what Mersing's doing or about Talus's profits? Let's just get to Sourav fast."

They transitioned on time. "Cinar builds them right," Basil whispered as the board shifted to lightspace display. He sat silently, brooding at the controls. *A year ago I would have felt pretty good—ship handling, nav.* He brought up a diagrammatic star chart showing Tiran, Kara, Sourav, Sigma, distant Orane. He tried to regain the feeling of wonder about distance and far places he needed to explore, but the emotion eluded him.

He turned control over to AI and leaned back to the limits of the buffers. "I need some answers from Mersing." He disengaged buffers and staggered toward the exit against surging inertial forces. "It won't affect us getting to Sourav fast. He's got that locked already. We couldn't change it if we tried."

"Then let AI drive," Ria replied.

They stumbled down the short corridor directly behind the control room to the captain's suite and activated the screen by the door.

"Request permission to discuss our course, captain," Basil said. The screen lit with a flashing message: "Do Not Disturb."

"This is absolute nonsense!" Basil whispered. "I'm going down to cargo and restow."

"Meet me in the wardroom when you're done," Ria said. "I'll buy you a beer." As they walked away she caught Basil's sleeve and whispered, "He's in there praying. The door was open earlier and I saw his altar. Now I smell incense." They went down the companionway to crew level. "I didn't think the Five Families were very serious about that stuff. Quite the opposite, in fact."

"A fanatic," Basil said, "perverting the teachings of The Way to something…else."

Two hours later, a dirt-covered Basil clomped up the stairs in the woozy gravity and into the wardroom. Ria was lying on the deck, only her legs protruding from under the food generator console. Basil's heart leapt into his throat. He knelt down beside her and touched her leg. "Are you alright?"

She jerked. "Damn! Don't scare me like that." She slid out from under the console, a dirty plastic screen in her hands. She washed the screen and quickly reinstalled it while Basil dialed two beers and took a seat at the table.

She cleaned her hands and joined him at the table. The wardroom, the whole ship, had a swaying motion, like sailing a small boat in a sea with long calm waves.

"On Sigma there is still one Aquaria, left over from two hundred years ago," Basil mused. "I loved going there. A miniature ocean. You could sail, or dive, or rent tiny submarines…"

Ria eyed his filthy utility uniform. "You been scrubbing the deck for our honored captain?"

"Checking cargo stowage, which was way out of alignment. Then I had to get out and assemble the hydraulic pallet shifter since none of the automatics were working. I've never seen a ship in such bad shape. One box, and we're running as fast as we can to deliver it. This trip will certainly lose money." Basil downed the last of his beer and poured himself another. "That box is surprisingly high-mass for ora. But royal seal on the locks."

"Meaningless," Ria said. "There's so much corruption…"

"Hey," Basil snapped, covering his mouth with his beer glass, "isn't there something more pleasant we can talk about? You seem so bitter…"

Ria looked at bubbles rising in amber liquid.

Basil took a big slug of beer. "How bad is the food machine?"

"Bad. I've got it mostly cleaned now."

Basil stood, swaying gently in the grav motion. "I tried to engage Mersing in a conversation about our cargo transfer plan, and he wouldn't even talk to me. I couldn't log on to the Talus network to discuss our project plan—he's got the link disabled."

"Might just need maintenance," Ria ventured.

Basil realized he had drained his beer, poured himself another one, and began pacing six steps each way—the length of the wardroom.

Ria caught his arm. "Relax, would you? You're making me nervous."

"I need to work this frustration off. The fitness booth and the sim sleep box have been stripped out of this thing…"

"She's going to salvage, Basil," Ria sniped. "Anyway, medbox is still installed." She rose and made her way over to it. "How many complaints do you have?" She bent over the medbox.

"Lots. Here's the next one: I know enough continuum physics to realize that even though the ship's physical properties don't exist in lightspace, there are certain properties of a ship's entry that will affect exit properties. We're going to come out of the gate at Tiran like a bullet."

Ria straightened up. "Tiranian approach control won't like that.

I want to get through Tiranian space fast, but if we go too fast, the patrol will intercept…"

"What are you doing at the medbox?" Basil asked Ria.

"Quit hovering over me!" she snapped back. She returned to her seat on the bench. "I scraped my hand, back on Kara." She waved her left hand, covered in clear sealer, then put it in her lap, out of his sight.

Basil sat down, dark thoughts growing in his imagination. He stared across the green wood table at her. "Did you kill him? Ble."

She returned his stare.

Basil shrugged. "How much red onyx did he give you?"

She studied her glass for a time. "I may not be going with you to Sigma, Basil. After we get to Sourav, we go our own ways, alright?"

Basil sipped his beer. "So I'm just your free ride off Kara? And along the way you pick up a little cash by killing Ble. You are not the person I thought I knew." Basil rose, anger clouding his face. He slammed his beer glass down on the table.

Ria studied the bubbles rising in her glass of ale.

Basil controlled himself, sat back down, and took Ria's hand. "You know, the last time we sat by ourselves and talked was that night in that little bar in Delphine, on Tiran, remember?"

Ria smiled and lifted her beer. "Yeah, I remember."

"I've missed you. And I'm sure glad I ran across you on Kara." Basil looked at his beer thoughtfully. "You sure you're doing the right thing leaving the RDF? Once a soldier, always a soldier, you used to say."

She shrugged. "Maybe." She took a small sip of beer, rubbed her finger over a crack in the tabletop. "They'd take me back if I asked. My career is a mess already. Special Ops is always a dead end—career wise." She laughed her quick laugh that Basil liked so well.

"Here's a thought," Basil said. "And don't blame it on the alcohol, although this has got to be my last beer. I need sleep."

She grinned at him. "What's your thought?"

"You go back into RDF, assigned to Sigma. I work at the Talus home office on Sigma."

She snorted. "Sigma's a logistics center. I'm not going to sit counting cargo boxes with the rest of the fat-assed RDF bureaucrats on Sigma."

Basil covered his hurt feelings by drinking more than he meant to.

Ria, self-absorbed, continued, "Back in the RDF, I'm just one more sub-commander, low on the list for promotion. I'm five years older than everyone else in my rank cohort. I should have spent the last five years back on Sigma kissing the ass of the RDF brass, but I won't spend the next five years doing it."

Basil finished his beer and made motions to leave.

"Sorry, Basil, I'm just fed up with the RDF, that's all." She took his hands in hers and changed the subject. "You also need to keep your head down until we get out of Tiran space. You have direct knowledge of Naru's secret weapon."

"It's a drive unit, not a weapon," Basil corrected.

"Not to Naru. And he may think you can help him find it and convert it."

"I'm no continuum physicist," Basil replied. "Besides, I told you the RDF backed away when they ran across Xbalc patrols. It's in Xbalc hands by now. With the Tiranian economy in ruins, and the royalists sniping at him from all sides, I suspect Naru will have no time for his mysterious artifact. Especially with Kapil Sheer dead."

Basil stood up, wavering in the uncertain gee field. "We're both tired. Let's get some sleep."

They moved into the companionway, holding onto the walls. "I've got to get some sleep. My damned AT20 woke me at least five times when I was trying to rest. Beeps for a while, then quits—something wrong with it." Ria yawned.

"What's an AT20?" asked Basil.

"Weapons detector I was using on Kara. It thinks it's sensing transuranic explosives. Probably just emissions from a leaking system on this old boat."

• • •

Ria was beside him in the darkness whispering something. Basil rolled over. A hand-light came on. Ria was kneeling beside his bunk.

"Get up, Basil," she hissed. "We've got a big problem!"

The chronometer said it was still half an hour until he needed to be in the control room to prepare for emergence.

"This is a suicide run. Those K2 bastards have loaded a bomb in that cargo box. That's what my AT20 was detecting."

Basil got up and dressed quickly. "We might be able to dump it out into space once we emerge…"

"No time," Ria said. "That crazy bastard Mersing moved up our emergence time. We'll break out of lightspace in ten minutes. He's up in control now, controls on manual."

Basil took a step toward the door, paused. "Let's take Mersing out now," Basil said. "Maybe we still have time to divert. You contact Tiranian approach and try to explain what's happening…"

"They're not likely to listen to explanations. They'll intercept and blow us apart once they understand what this course and velocity means. And that won't take them long."

They crept up the companionway to control and peered around the end of a console. No one was there. The big board was flashing, and AI said, "Emergence in two minutes. At this velocity, recommend buffers. Would you like to assume manual control? Course and velocity violate Tiranian approach control regulations."

"He may be down in cargo setting the bomb controls," Basil said.

"Don't go down there," Ria snapped. "He'll kill you. He carries a sidearm and he's got nothing to lose. You need to stay here, get this emergence done, then see if you can start slowing us down, and convince approach that we are diverting. I'll go down to cargo…"

"You'll go to your nav station and stay there," Mersing said from the top of the stair, his pistol aimed at Ria.

She hesitated, then took her place.

"Emergence at 200 percent of recommended velocity. Buffers required," AI said.

Basil activated buffers. Mersing seated himself at the master's station and Basil saw him activate his buffers.

Ecliptor made one of the worst emergences Basil had ever seen. They were in the Tiran approach lane, but just barely. Basil tried to synchronize the sublight engines whose howl and thumping were driving him crazy, but his tinkering with the collimators only made it worse. He felt sick to his stomach, his sinuses hurt.

"This is pleasant," Ria said from her nav station. "Expect we'll be hearing from approach control soon."

As if on cue, Tiran control began screaming at them to decelerate and regain their spacing and trajectory within the high-speed section of the inbound traffic lanes.

"We will miss the bracket at the inbound beacon," AI said. "Recommend an alternate. Probability 75 percent that…"

"Denied!" Mersing snapped.

"We have to reduce speed," Basil shouted over the thump and whine of the drives.

Tiranian approach control override crashed through the annunciator. "Reduce speed immediately and divert to emergency reroute!"

"Two interceptors launched and converging on our projected course," AI said calmly. Red fans of light ahead of the streaking red points indicated the estimated range of their gravitic nets.

"Damn!" Basil shouted. "Decelerate!"

The drives were screaming. Basil staggered up in the thumping gee field and struggled to the command console, where the gun in Mersing's hand sagged down to the console top.

"Ria, get down to cargo and see if you can disable that bomb!"

Mersing chopped Basil's hands away with an upthrust. A gee surge threw them both to the floor. Basil sprang forward on top of Mersing, grabbed the pistol he had drawn. They rolled painfully down the four steps to the control main floor, thrashing and kicking for the gun.

As the number two engine began a banshee scream, Basil got hold of the pistol and bent Mersing's hand back. A fortuitous grav shift slammed them both into a console. Something gave in Mersing's wrist, and the gun clattered free. Basil dove on it, but a gee surge lifted him away from it, and Mersing scrabbled across the floor, clawing with his good hand. Basil stamped a boot down on Mersing's hand and grabbed the gun. Another gee swing slung him off his feet, and he rolled between consoles.

"This is control! We will fire on you in one minute unless you begin deceleration and course change!"

Mersing was behind a console somewhere. Basil staggered forward and was pitched off his feet and into the com station chair. Red warning lights and alarms lit up. "Emergency deceleration," AI said calmly.

A giant hand pushed Basil back into the com station chair. The engine scream escalated into the supersonic. Another giant grav swing pushed Basil sideways. The buffers buzzed like saws cutting steel.

Suddenly, Mersing hauled himself up and flung himself down the companionway.

On the big board tracks appeared to converge. "Higher res," Basil shouted to AI. "Will we make it through before those missiles…?"

"Probability 40 percent."

"Emergency power override," Basil said. The red bar above the big board began flashing. Basil moved the virtual power controllers forward. Engine condition lights overlaid the screen. "Get them out of my way."

"You have two minutes' power at this level," said AI.

Basil got hold of the corner of the command console and pulled himself to it. "Full override power, both engines!"

Basil noticed the interceptor tracks flashing past on the big board. Systems display showed all red indicators on the number two engine. "Number two collimator failing!" the annunciator blared. "Containment marginal but acceptable," the AI said, unperturbed. "Interceptors converging. Will be in missile range in twenty seconds."

A com screen popped open in the big board, displaying the face of a glaring Tiranian in black uniform. "You are ordered to divert and decelerate immediately, or you will be fired on!"

Basil desperately tried to comprehend *Ecliptor*'s course and velocity numbers on the big board. "We have been hijacked by royalist troops," Basil said. "I've just now resumed control. I am a neutral citizen of Sigma, an employee of Talus Company…"

"We know who you are," the officer snapped. "Decelerate now!"

"One engine has failed," Basil said. He flexed in access to engine output numbers so the Tiranian AI could read them. "Velocity is such that we have only one course—leave through the Tiranian exit gate." Basil glanced at the course lines and numbers on the big screen. "In two minutes."

The Tiranian stared at Basil, and Basil knew he was being given information from the course plots in the approach corridor. Basil flexed for a recheck of numbers. *This might work.*

"Interceptors will escort you to the exit gate," the Tiranian security officer told Basil. On the big board, the interceptors' projected course lines shifted.

Basil shifted to intercom. “Ria, have you got the bomb disabled? Ria?” There was no answer.

The com screen inset changed to an older Tiranian in gray general staff uniform. “I am Todros, Tiran security. You are being allowed to exit Tiranian space; however, you are guilty of attempted terrorism and will be apprehended at Sourav…”

“We are innocent. This ship is…was…leased to the government of Tiran in exile on Orane…”

“We recognize no such government,” Todros interjected. “Due to your terrorist activity, your ship is confiscated and is now a Varil Company asset.” Todros’s image skittered in scintillation radiation as *Ecliptor* raced toward the Tiran exit gate.

“Ria!” Basil shouted into the intercom. “Is the bomb defused?”

“Transition in one minute,” AI announced. “Recommend maximum deceleration prior to transition.”

“No!” Basil said. He held the manual override down. He activated the emergency override annunciator and blasted a message throughout the ship “Ria! Answer!”

The interceptors were slowing and maneuvering to bypass the gate.

“Transition now,” AI announced.

Basil felt a wave of nausea. His vision dimmed, partially buffered inertial stresses racked his body. He could see the big board was a pattern of red and yellow indicators. “AI…”

“Automated systems…” Basil heard the AI say, then he lost consciousness for a second. “Lightspace realign to exit at waypoint 214,” he heard AI announce. He saw course lines on the board. His vision was clearing, but his inner ear and stomach churned as the out-of-sync inertial gee field wavered and pulsed.

“Yes,” Basil managed to gasp out. “Figure a velocity-reducing maneuver at the waypoint. How long until exit?”

"Four hours at our estimated virtual velocity," AI said. The bar over the big board went from red to yellow—they'd made the transition intact, but *Ecliptor* was moving at a dangerously high rate of virtual speed inside the miniverse.

Basil released his buffer and was immediately slung out of the chair, crashing painfully into the nav console. Basil got to his knees and clawed his way down to the command console.

"Remain in buffers!" the safety annunciator blared. "High and unbalanced gee forces probable."

But Basil knew he had to get down to cargo level. Ria might be injured. At the command console, Basil paused and shouted once again into the intercom, "Ria!"

There was no answer.

Chapter 26

Basil rattled down the companionway stair. Ria lay crumpled against one of the cargo boxes, the control panel cover off.

"The bomb, Basil. It is going to go off; nothing can stop it," she said.

"How soon?"

"Twenty minutes."

Basil ran to the innocuous-looking cargo container and unlatched it from the stowage tracks. Then he set the cargo door controls and helped Ria up the companionway stairs. "Close the cargo deck, AI, and open the cargo door!"

Ria was groaning with every step.

"I've got to get you to the medbox, then I'm going to eject that box…"

"At this velocity, they'll get pulled back by the gravity of the singularity," Ria said through clenched teeth. "No one knows the effects…"

"Don't talk." He half carried her to the medbox and laid her on the fold-down panel. The automated diagnostics took over.

"I can't stay," Basil said urgently. "I've got to eject that box." He looked into her gray-green eyes for a long second. "I love you."

"I love you too, Basil. Hurry."

Basil sprinted to control and slammed himself into the command seat. "Activate rollaway one." On screen he saw the tongue of a rollaway extending out of the open hold into the gray nothingness of lightspace. He touched the eject button and watched the cargo box move down the rollaway, then stop at the safety lip at the end. It had sensed there was nothing there to receive the box. Basil raced down to cargo level, pulled on his gloves, cinched his boots, closed his helmex, and cycled through the emergency hatch into vacuum.

He went out on the rollaway on hands and knees. In lightspace the conventional laws of physics diminished by the inverse square of his distance from the Istan engine's lightspace generators on the skin of the ship. The rollaways were fully extended—ten meters. He crawled out, braced his boots against the lattice of the rollaway, and tilted the box up and off the rails. He snaked under it and pried up for all he was worth. It began to tip up and over the safety lip.

Basil slithered back down the rollaway and into the cargo hold. At the control panel he retracted the rollaway as the box tumbled slowly into emptiness. Once the rollaway was fully retracted, he touched the controls to close the cargo door.

Then he bolted up the companionway to control.

"Activate emergence now!" he directed the AI.

"Significant stress to emerge this far from the gate at this velocity. And I remind you this ship has one engine dead, and the other…"

"This is an emergency. Transition us out of lightspace, regardless of distance to the edge."

The board changed as Basil activated his buffers. He checked the med station readout—Ria was being treated, the med buffers were engaged. Mersing was still somewhere aboard, but he didn't have time to worry about that now.

With a mind-numbing surge, the *Ecliptor* exited lightspace a half lightyear short of the exit point at Sourav Gate. They were dangerously close to the event horizon of the black hole that drove the gate. Radiation warnings flashed, but anti-radiation fields seemed to be sufficient.

"We're within limits on radiation exposure," Basil said, trying to convince himself. He saw several internal environment indicators deep in the yellow zone.

Emergency klaxons blared all over the ship. "All personnel stay in buffers," the automated warning system shouted. The ship battered and buffeted its way down the exit lane toward open space, the AI keeping it balanced on its high-speed trajectory.

If the ship held together, if they exited and weren't blown to atoms by Tiranian interceptors, he still had a killer on board. Once they decelerated, he'd have to confront Mersing. Basil checked engine systems and saw that engine two's internal controls had shut it down due to multiple circuit overloads.

On the big board a spark fell away from *Ecliptor*.

"What was that?" Basil asked AI.

"Something went out the emergency hatch on crew level," AI said. "It is accelerating back toward the approach lane. It appears to be a life raft, transponder not lit."

Mersing.

AI put course projection lines on the screen, and Basil could see that Mersing was trying for one of the remote unmanned auxiliary beacon stations of the Sourav approach control network. There'd be emergency supplies and some kind of escape vehicle.

"It is illegal to dump cargo in an approach zone," the AI said unhelpfully.

"AI, plot the trajectory of that box." Curved lines appeared on the board.

In four minutes, even if the bomb detonated, the energy waves would be deformed by the edge of the gravity cone leading down to the singularity.

Basil sat watching the engine indicator lights. One more minute.

The minute ticked away, the spark that was the cargo box disappeared behind the invisible edge of the singularity. There was nothing.

"Engine one is now only 70 percent functional, and we are in a high-energy hyperbola around the emergence gate," the AI said.

Basil beamed at the screen. "The best place to be. See if you can start slowing us and bringing us back to some semblance of an approach course."

"Very small probability," AI said, unperturbed.

"I'm sure we've got enough people mad at us that they'll come and get us. Try to improve controllability, and shut down or decouple some of these subsystems running on overload." A dozen red indicator lights went to yellow.

The emergency communication system alarm went off. The face of a scowling man in Sourav Republic uniform filled the screen inset into the big board. "What the hell are you doing?"

"Jettisoning a bomb planted aboard this ship by Oranie rebels."

The man's eyes shifted as he looked at something off-screen. "Two Tiran Defense Command interceptors have emerged at the Sourav outer gate claiming jurisdiction over your ship," the man said. "They have requested we surrender you and your ship to their authority. We intend to do just that."

An older man in Sourav Republic uniform crowded into the screen. "We have transmitted your new course to your AI. Hold to it!" he roared. "We are tracking the device you jettisoned. You will be held responsible for a terrorist act in Sourav space and will be charged accordingly if that is an explosive device that detonates."

"It won't," Basil said.

The Sourav officer glared at Basil then clicked off.

Basil noted the AI had an approach to the Sourav safety zone plotted and deceleration was underway. "Can we stay on the course they gave us?" Basil asked the AI.

"I will maintain direct steering control, and if the number one engine does not deteriorate, we can assume an elliptical orbit around Sourav Station, within the deceleration capability of their tugs."

"How soon?"

"About one hour."

Another emergency com override blared into the control room—Talus Operations Center. Thelis's face appeared on the big board. "What the hell are you doing?"

Basil grinned at Thelis's lined face on the screen. "You're the second person who's asked me that."

"We got a directive from Commander Todros himself," Thelis told Basil, "telling us to surrender that ship to his interceptors upon emergence at Sourav." Thelis leaned toward his screen, his pale-blue eyes boring into Basil's. "They will destroy you if you do not comply."

Basil said, "A K2 commander was attempting a suicide bombing…"

"Where is he now?"

"Escaped," Basil said.

"That complicates our dealings with the Orane court," Thelis said, "who are also demanding surrender of *Ecliptor*. Othman has resigned, under pressure…"

"What?" Basil gasped.

"*Ecliptor* is about to become the incident that will trigger a full-scale conflict between Tiran and Orane." Thelis scowled, shaking his head. "You surrender that ship to Tiranian security as soon as they arrive in Sourav space, Basil. No more of your hijinks. This episode has caused more trouble than you know."

Basil leaned toward the screen. "Othman is gone?"

"It's a long story, and you don't have time for it now. The interim director's instructions are for you to surrender yourself and that ship to Tiran authorities. Talus still has the offer from Arixa to salvage *Ecliptor*…" he eyed Basil, "…if there's anything left to salvage."

Basil tilted his head. "I had to run her pretty hot; the engines both took a beating." He looked steadily at Thelis. "Thelis, do me one more favor. We'll surrender *Ecliptor* to whichever authority boards us first, but get us out of Tiran's jurisdiction. This whole bomb attempt on Tiran was the work of a royalist named Mersing, possibly under orders from K2, but also possibly working alone. K2 will no doubt deny any involvement either way."

"Already has," Thelis said. "The Orane court denies any knowledge of an attack on Tiran."

"Mersing exited *Ecliptor* on a life raft. He's probably hiding out on one of the Sourav approach system unmanned beacons until he can slip into Sourav somehow. Thelis, call Sourav and Arixa, confirm that Talus wants to proceed with the salvage, then notify Tiran authorities that the bomb on this ship has been ejected back into lightspace—this ship is no threat. But the man responsible for the attempted bombing of Tiran is at large here in the Sourav system. That's who Tiran and Sourav authorities ought to be searching for. *Ecliptor* is no threat to anyone."

Thelis bowed his head then shrugged. "Alright, I'll do that. But surrender *Ecliptor* to Sourav authorities immediately, do you understand? This is still just business. If Tiran extradites the ship, Talus loses the price of the salvage, so you make sure you contact the Sourav forces immediately. Show them the Talus salvage agreement with Arixa. It's in their records and in the data on *Ecliptor*."

"I will," Basil said.

Basil contacted the Sourav authorities and repeated what he'd told Thelis. "The terrorist Oranie is likely hiding on one of your unmanned beacons, waiting for a chance to get aboard Sourav Station. You find him, and you've got the person responsible for the bomb that was aboard this ship."

"We'll investigate. And," the bearded officer glanced off screen, "you are fortunate. We have evidence of an energy burst past the

Sourav Gate event horizon. The weapon you had aboard your ship?"

"Yes!" Basil snapped. "But it was not my weapon. I was as eager to get rid of it as anyone. Did you track a life raft exiting this ship as we emerged?"

The man glanced off screen again, then nodded. "As a matter of fact, we did track something exiting your ship. Not enough mass to be a large weapon…"

"It's a man on a life raft. He's your terrorist, not me. I would suggest you capture that man and surrender him to Tiran authority."

Basil and the Sourav officer traded glares. "Do not tell us what to do! You follow the track we have given you. We will board your ship as soon as you dock. After we have investigated, we will address the salvage contract on your ship."

No love lost between Sourav and Tiran, Basil noted. Basil turned control of the ship over to AI and went down to the crew deck.

"I've got to get out of this medbox," Ria said.

"You are far from being well enough to move around…"

"Then carry me to our cabin. I can rest better in a real bunk, not this thing."

In the cabin, settled in her bunk, she said, "Go open my locker and bring me a box you'll find there, in my duffel bag."

Basil brought a gray plastic box to her.

She smiled. "Open it."

He tilted the lid back and a miraculous red glow suffused the cabin.

"Ble's bloodstones." Ria grinned.

Basil turned a sour look on her.

"I left him enough to buy his way off Karaghia," Ria said, "but he owed us something, don't you think?"

"There's a small fortune here," Basil said, stunned.

"I checked red onyx market price. With what it would cost us to buy the ship from Arixa and have them install two rebuilt engines, we've got enough—barely."

Basil closed the box and set it aside and kissed her.

Much later, just prior to docking, Thelis called. "Todros has agreed that if you and Ria stay out of Tiran space, he will not chase you for sentencing." Thelis shook his head. "I can arrange an administrative assignment on Delta Station…"

"Actually, we have other plans," Basil said.

Chapter 27

In the senior executive conference room at the top of Government Tower, Naru sat at the head of a large table made of black Tai wood. His five senior directors sat waiting. All around them, viewscreens showed the lights of Tiran City stretching to the horizon under a hazy night sky.

Without preamble, Naru began speaking quietly. "If Kaleege thought Piaro valuable enough to kidnap, he is a man we need."

"Piaro is an idealist," the director of culture said. "Brilliant theorist, a believer that populist government, despite all its inefficiencies, is more effective than autocracy, and it is morally right. I am not sure he is the man we need."

"I don't disagree with either of your points," Naru said, "but I want you to find him and bring him here." Naru turned to the military director. "With Kaleege senior gone, the royalists have become vulnerable."

The director, a large man with jet-black hair, leaned forward a bit as he spoke. "Lord Kaleege II is a weak leader, no strategist, and no tactician. His forces are led by political appointees, his military training has been outsourced. To exploit these weaknesses, the general staff has developed several options..."

"Not now," Naru interrupted softly. "I want us to think collectively of the larger picture. I want all of you to leave this room with a single, integrated vision of where Tiran is going." Naru turned to the director of industry. "Cinar and Varil are central to our industrial strength. And all conflict is ultimately won with economic, not military, power."

The director nodded deferentially to Naru, then said, "We are rebuilding Varil the fast and cheap way by leasing ships. Letters of marque are being issued to all Varil ships, leased or owned. It is an inefficient way to rebuild our shipping capacity, but it is fast. We have had the Istan plants running continuously for three months; we have enough assets to reverse the balance of trade." The big man glanced at Naru. "The cost to our workforce has been high. I must reduce the pressure on our young engineers; we sacrifice original thought and engineering efficiency when we manage with threats."

Naru nodded. "I agree. Change your management regime to a more reasonable style."

The man nodded, clearly relieved.

"And speaking of Cinar, Istan, and the labs," Naru continued, "Kapil Sheer is gone, but we have a prototype sunkiller that works. However, I don't want them manufactured, not yet. For the present, let privateers fight our war. We want to appear non-belligerent until the RDF has pulled further back. At the same time I want our special weapons division to continue work. You have heard rumors of a superdrive. Those rumors are true. The single existing prototype has been lost in Xbalc space." Naru turned to his minister of external affairs, ser Vhon, and waited expectantly.

"I have recently returned from a meeting with the Xbalc border zone leader," ser Vhon said, his cultured accent emphasizing his understatement. He was a small man of aristocratic bearing and a long royalist heritage. As the Imperium formed under the Ziani dynasty and the Kaleege family formed a coalition to oppose it, the

Vhons declared themselves neutral and stayed on Tiran when the government in exile was formed on Orane. Both he and Naru knew that Naru hoped to use the Vhon family to negotiate with Kaleege, but to negotiate from a position of strength.

"Xbalc will accept a Tiran trade mission," Vhon went on. "They are irritated by RDF incursions into their space. They have been in search of the artifact that Kapil Sheer…lost. I believe they need reminding of RDF arrogance and the errors of the Orane government. We should give no sign we want the artifact. I recommend we build trade with them, build their confidence in us. I do not think we should ask to enter their space and search for the artifact. Not yet. In any case it may not be there."

"What do you envision we trade with them?"

"Istan C-7 engines," Vhon answered quickly.

"Agreed. Establish a trade mission with one of the Xbalc worlds," Naru said. He glanced at his security chief. "Include your operatives in the trade mission, but do not overwhelm it with spies."

Naru fell silent, staring at the thousands of points of light beyond the windows—of the city, of the stars.

"Leader Devir remains cloistered, seeking enlightenment," Naru said. The men at the table remained expressionless. "But the principles of his revolution remain very much alive. Power is accomplished through industrial strength and trade. Warfare is a short-term solution only." Naru touched an economic report in front of him. "Our economy appears to be strong." His pause communicated to the assembled men that he did not believe the numbers in the report. "The RDF will continue their slow but inevitable withdrawal. Pirates, privateers, rapacious companies, and rapacious governments like Orane will fill the Curve with confusion for a time, and since warfare is dependent on resources, soon there will be only a few strong players. The new Tiran will be among those few. We need to rebuild our trading links and capacity before the next-generation ship drive becomes available. Research indicates there are, theoretically, at least three ways to drive ships faster than light. We must reestablish the domination of transportation that Tiran once had. To do that, we must be the first to achieve the next-generation drive technology. Tiran has two objectives: a web of trade partners including the Xbalc, and a practical engine technology allowing for 5X speeds."

He gave them a moment to consider this, then nodded in dismissal. They filed out silently, leaving Naru centered in a constellation of city lights and stars.

• • •

On Sigma, Director Othman left Talus Headquarters at his usual time, pondering how to repay Etir Leasing for the two C-800s Talus had leased from them, and Shuard had stolen. The lease was old enough to have a clause exempting liability due to acts of war. But Shuard had stolen the ships as an act of piracy, not war, and Othman valued his professional relations with Etir so intended to negotiate a settlement reasonable for both of them.

His com signaled with his private code. The message was recorded with no visuals. Unusual. *Please meet a representative of Tiran Imperial government at Orep restaurant. As soon as possible.*

Othman transferred slideways and made his way to the restaurant which had always been one of his favorites.

Inside the door, Othman stood puzzled. The restaurant appeared to be empty, the virtuals turned off. Four men in suits so conservatively cut they could have been uniforms stood nearby.

"This way," one said and led Othman to a booth where a slim man in a dark-blue tunic sat alone.

"Thank you for coming," the man said.

Othman, who remembered faces very well, could not recall who this young man was. Then it came to him. "Ser Kaleege."

The young man nodded, making the light sparkle for an instant on the tiny silver crest on his otherwise unadorned tunic.

Othman sat down.

The young man said, "We have made arrangements which I wanted to personally inform you of." His slim face was impassive, his eyes colorless in the subdued light. "My father had great respect for you."

"And I for him."

"He was particularly proud of what you built Talus Company into."

Othman sat silent, understanding the unspoken point Kaleege was making, that his father had provided the money and the influence in Sigma administration that allowed Talus to succeed in its early vulnerable years.

"Now it is time for the next step." Kaleege's eyes were steady on Othman's. "Tomorrow your chief of Planning will succeed you as director of Talus. He is being notified of his new responsibilities and of the revised strategic plan for the company."

Othman's expression tightened.

"Your personal items and electronic files will be delivered to your home. It is our hope, our expectation, that you will cooperate in this change of direction."

"You might have contacted me in advance," Othman said.

"That was not possible. The illegal administration of Tiran would have taken steps to divert Talus to themselves. However, the RDF representative here on Sigma has been notified."

"Why are you doing this?"

"Talus is a well-respected company. Demonstrating its allegiance to the rightful government of Tiran will cause other companies to join our cause."

There was silence in the empty restaurant.

• • •

Othman took the escalators down to dock level and walked along the wide thoroughfare in front of the wall of buildings. Sixty years ago he had started Talus Company out of a two-room office right here at the docks. But he could not identify exactly which one. The buildings had changed over the years, remodeled and remodeled again.

He made his way through a narrow alley. There was a tiny flower shop in the alley; the delicious aroma of flowers filled the narrow space. For the first time in longer than he could remember, the image of his wife, dead twenty years, rose up in his mind. He let the sadness come this time, not pushing it away as he had so often since her death. While she had lived, there had always been flowers in the house.

"Very beautiful, aren't they? Can I wrap some for you?" came a woman's voice at his elbow.

He picked up a white bouquet and inhaled its delicious aroma. "Yes. Just one. One of these."

"Beautiful." She efficiently extracted one and wrapped it in red paper and put it in a transparent tube.

He paid her. "I'm sure they have a name, this species…?"

"Yes, it's a very old species, very resilient." She thought for a moment.

"Ketera," the woman called into the back room. "Could you come here for a moment?"

A tawny-haired woman with calm features emerged, drying her hands. "That species is Alba, very old lineage," Ketera said.

Othman started to greet her, to inquire where they had met, but stopped himself. She gave no sign of recognition, though her eyes told him she knew him.

He thanked the women for the flowers and departed.

• • •

At home, Othman sat in the living room of his spacious house in one of the best neighborhoods on Sigma. The silence was oppressive. He activated a virtual of people on a wide terrace having dinner under a night sky filled with stars.

"Kaleege," Othman said softly, "your father helped me make Talus successful. Now your son is confiscating it."

After a time, he stood and prowled around the room, then all the rooms of his house. He tried to remember which of the objects of art had been chosen by his wife and found he could not remember. He paused in one of the guest rooms. The virtual view was of waves sliding smoothly up a black sand beach under two yellow moons. He tried to let the sound and scent of the waves settle his mind.

He breathed deeply, then hurried out of his house and made his way back to the flower shop. The scent inside the air barrier was fresh and wet.

"I wonder if I might speak to…Ketera, I think her name is?"

"Is anything wrong? You were in earlier today."

"Nothing wrong, I just want to learn more about the Alba I bought. She seemed knowledgeable."

The woman smiled, and indicated the back of the shop.

Othman found Ketera trimming the stems of a shipment of tall yellow flowers.

Othman bowed slightly. "I was wondering if you could tell me more about the Alba flower I bought here."

But before she could speak, he held up his hand and looked away from her. "No…I…this is very improper, but I must ask you about reconstruction. How long does it take and…"

"Is it painful?" he said.

He bowed slightly.

"I will tell you what I know. Have you talked with the recon center?"

"I don't want to. Not yet."

"You are thinking of a voluntary reconstruction."

He said nothing.

"It is not painful," Ketera told him evenly. "And I believe it took about six weeks of orientation after the initial treatment. Part of that, the last couple of weeks, is job training. There may have been some voluntaries in my class, but no one discussed the past." Ketera shrugged. "Part of the time we spent studying the precepts of The Way. Other time was spent in practical exercises, like learning to remember to smile when expressing certain things." Ketera smiled.

Othman nodded, still avoiding her eyes. "And probably how to avoid over-inquisitive people like me."

"Yes, that too."

He took a long breath then bowed again. "Thank you for... speaking with me. I won't bother you any longer." He stared at some hybrid scarlet flowers.

"Part of our training was learning to make decisions without certain emotional content," Ketera said.

He looked into her eyes. "I apologize for asking you all this. I should not have imposed..."

"I am not offended. We also learned to be candid about who we are now. And to avoid thinking about the past."

He nodded. "I envy your clarity."

Then he hurried away.

• • •

Ecliptor lay docked at Arixa Yard Station. Basil and Ria lay together in a makeshift double bunk he'd assembled in the control room. "I've never seen such a fast and cursory condition inspection," he said. "Talus must have really been pressing Arixa to get *Ecliptor* off their books fast. We just paid 2.5 million eris for this old ship. And we have another 2 million on account with Arixa for re-engineering. They say it will take about two months. We could get a little house in the mountains on Sourav."

Ria was frowning.

"No?" Basil kissed her gently. "What's the problem?"

"I was just thinking. You are the only person outside the Tiran labs who's ever seen Kapil Sheer's artifact, this superdrive. You've ridden it. That makes you valuable to the RDF and a potential info leak for Tiranian security. One or both of them may come after you."

"I know virtually nothing about it," Basil said. "And I suspect the people in Tiran labs know that. Kapil Sheer told me which button to push, when to get out at the other end, that's all. The artifact disappeared on a planet near Xbalc space; the RDF couldn't find it. That's where they'll look."

"Doesn't mean they won't keep looking for you."

"Don't worry about it. Let's just rent a house somewhere on Sourav." Basil put his arms around her. "When *Ecliptor* is ready to go, we leave Tiran, Orane, and RDF jurisdiction far behind."

The com chimed.

"Don't tell me anything about where you got the money," Thelis said, holding his hand up, his familiar gesture. "I don't want to know anything."

Basil grinned.

"And if I were you, when you take *Ecliptor* out," Thelis said, "I would avoid both Tiran and Orane space."

Basil sobered. "Understood." The two men sat looking at each other for a moment. "I want to thank you for all your help over the years," Basil said. "I appreciate all you've done for me, and for others. You've helped many people, Thelis."

Thelis shook his head again. "Talus is changing, Basil. With Othman gone…well, there's no knowing what the future will bring."

He grinned across the lightyears. “I always said you were a smart young man, Basil. You’ll get what you want, it will just take a little time.” He nodded. “Good luck, to both of you. Let me hear from you sometime.”

“You will,” Basil and Ria said together.

But neither of them ever spoke with him again.

www.ingramcontent.com/pod-product-compliance
Lightning Source LLC
Chambersburg PA
CBHW021623030826
48979CB00036B/1911/J

* 9 7 8 1 9 5 1 9 6 0 7 0 4 *